SCAR

SCAR

DEVIL'S NIGHTMARE MC
BOOK FOUR

LENA BOURNE

Copyright © 2018 by Lena Bourne

All rights reserved.

No part of this book may be reproduced in any form or by any electronic or mechanical means, including information storage and retrieval systems, without written permission from the author, except for the use of brief quotations in a book review.

ISBN: 9798884931022

PROLOGUE

About 12 Years Ago

LYNN

I'M a waitress at the Starburst Diner in the town of Fairview, Illinois.

I'm a beauty queen, Miss Teen Illinois, Miss Earth United Illinois, hoping to become Miss Illinois next year.

I love working with animals.

I *was* a waitress.

I *was* a beauty queen.

I *loved* working with animals.

I *am* a prisoner.

My mind wants to live in the past, wants to remember only the good times. But my reason still won't always let it. Even though I've been locked up in this dark, windowless room for a long time. Years it feels like, although if it were years, then I'd already be dead.

I've been beaten and raped and choked until I almost died. Blindfolded and threatened and tied up for so long my arms went numb. It feels like this torture has lasted a lifetime. But it can't have, or I'd be dead by now. I'll be dead soon. A part of my mind already is.

Day and night have no meaning for me anymore. Hours and minutes have no meaning anymore. My past—who I used to be—has no meaning anymore. I'm not even inside my body anymore.

My body is just a shell, a thing to be used by the cruel, vicious, ruthless men who locked me up in here, tore my clothes off and tied me to this bed. The man who abducted me visits. Many others visit too. Often. Sometimes one at a time, sometimes in groups. I don't see their faces anymore. They're not real. I'm not real anymore. This is just a nightmare.

Some are worse than others. The man who tied me up is the worst. I imagine a snake slithering across my body when he rapes me. Maybe it's because he told me his name is Lizard. He's a coldblooded snake, he doesn't need the name to announce him. I'd know it even if I never knew his name. He's not the same man who grabbed me in the dark parking lot behind the diner I worked at. I don't know that man's name and I don't want to know it. I hardly know my own name anymore.

Lynn! It's Lynn!

But maybe it's better to forget. Because I'm never getting my life back. All that I was is already gone, and I will die in this room. I'm still holding on, but barely, and it grows harder and harder to do. I no longer feel anything when they grope me, rape me, hit me and choke me. Hear nothing when they speak to me.

Just nothing.

Maybe it's time I forgot my own name too. There's nothing left to hold onto anyway.

I can hear yelling and crashing through the door of the room I'm in. They're coming to me and they're loud. In the beginning, I used to cry and scream when they came. Now I don't make a sound. Because I feel nothing at all. Even the pins and needles in my arms from being tied to the bed for hours and hours and days are gone.

Sometimes they untie me. It's not mercy, just a practicality. If you keep a person in the same position for days and weeks on end they get bedsores and other problems. I know, because my great-grandmother spent most of my childhood lying in bed. She had to be turned. Had to be talked to. But she never spoke. Just like I don't. She was ninety-four when she died, I'm twenty-one. But what does it matter? Years have no meaning when you can't count the hours. I'm ready to die. But I don't even wish for that anymore. I don't wish for anything.

Thudding footsteps are growing louder in the hall. I can hear the sound of boots kicking against doors, wood crashing against concrete walls.

"Lynn! Lynn, are you here?" It's been a long time since I heard my name.

The man who took me doesn't use it. He calls me Lollipop. I don't answer to that name. I don't answer to anything.

There's more crashing in the hall. It's getting louder, closer, more urgent.

"Lynn! Where are you?"

I recognize this man's voice. Barely. It belongs to the guy

who always hung around the diner during my shifts. Except on that night when I was taken. He wasn't there then. For awhile I feared he was one of the men raping me while I was blindfolded.

But, no. None of them were him.

Sure, he was a rough and rugged biker, but he was different. He almost asked me out a few times, but couldn't quite get the words together. But I would've said yes. Despite the scar that covered half his face and was the ugliest thing I'd ever seen when he first walked in. I would've said yes, because he had kind eyes and a soft voice, and he made me feel safe and wanted and seen the way no other guy who came into the diner to gawk at me and flirt with me ever had. The way no other man ever had. I liked spending time with him and I wanted to spend a whole lot more time with him. But he never asked me out, so I never could say yes.

"Lynn!" he yells again. "Are you here?"

"Yes," I croak out, my voice too soft to be heard through the door, my throat pulsing in pain because I haven't spoken in so long. Or maybe it's because the last guy who was here choked me. Or maybe it's because I screamed.

"In here!" I yell louder, because this could be my last chance to get the hours back. To get my life back. Although I'm not even hoping for that anymore. I just want to see the sun again, feel the fresh air on my face.

Two kicks and the door to my room crashes open, thuds against the wall, the bright light in the hallway blinding me as it does every time they come to visit.

I can't see his face, can only see his black outline against the light. So I don't know if it's him. Not until he comes closer and moves so the light hits his face as he kneels beside my bed.

1

LYNN

I DREAMT OF LOVE, of being loved, of making love, of feeling love. But the soft, pleasant feeling brought by the dream only lasted until I opened my eyes. Now the bed feels cold beneath me, and I'm fighting the onslaught of half-remembered images, of memories I don't truly have anymore, because they're buried so deep in the back of my mind, I can't even call them out consciously, let alone deal with them.

But they come out on their own at times like this, times when I manage to forget the nightmare and think that maybe I have my life and my body back.

I don't.

Memories of being tied to a bed and raped by brutal men are very vivid before my eyes right now, because I dared to dream of giving my body to someone I loved. After I was rescued, they told me I was a prisoner for just over two weeks.

It doesn't sound like much time at all. But I lost myself in that time, forgot how to count time, forgot what it meant, forgot myself. Gave myself up for dead.

I'm back. I'm safe. I'm well.

I repeat the mantra over and over in my head, until I remember that I'm not in that dark room anymore, but in my comfy bedroom at home. A psychologist taught me to use the mantra years ago to try and stop my mind's flight back into the empty, black nothingness where my mind and my soul hid to protect me from the terror I went through during those two weeks. I don't know if my soul ever truly returned. It was ripped from my body on one of those horrible, painful, scary nights, and the scar where it was once attached to my body is thick and still hurts.

I'm back, my soul is back, but it just sort of bounces inside my body with no real anchor to hold it in place. It could slip out again at any time if I'm not careful.

"That's idiotic thinking, Lynn," I tell myself out loud, as I throw my covers off and get out of bed. My voice sounds stern and inpatient like my mom's, only she'd never call me an idiot, she'd use some euphemism that means the same thing. Or just let me know what she means via the tone of her voice.

I'm back. I'm safe. I'm well. I'm back. I'm safe. I'm well. I'm back. I'm safe. I'm well.

I repeat the mantra all through my shower, until those words are the only thing left in my brain, and I can start filling it again with normal, everyday things. I'm all about routine. Routine keeps me going. Routine suffocates me. But it keeps me safe. Keeps me well. Keeps me in the present.

Mom already has breakfast ready when I come downstairs. A shiny porcelain plate is waiting for me on one side of the table, two slices of perfectly browned toast on it. Next to it is a hardboiled egg in a porcelain holder that's shaped like a hand and just as shiny as the plate. Mom even put a fresh red rose from our garden into a small crystal vase at the center of the table.

Everything in my mom's kitchen sparkles and is just perfect. Everything in her home is clean and in its place. Everything except me.

I used to be perfect. Used to be a beauty queen, as pretty as a doll. I'm still pretty, but I'm not perfect anymore, and I never will be again.

"Good morning, Lynn. Did you sleep well?" she asks as I enter the kitchen, her proper greeting perpetuating the facade of perfectness some more.

I smile at her and take my seat. "Sure did, you?"

She tells me she did, then starts spreading butter on her toast, getting not a single crumb on it in the process, or on her plate for that matter. I have no idea how she manages that, and maybe I should ask her to show me her trick one of these days.

My guilt over thinking all these critical things is probably making me blush right now. No one—absolutely no one—has done more for me than my mother. She's the reason I'm able to function at all after what I went through, and the reason I'm alive. Her and the man who saved me from the nightmare. Scar. I never saw him again after that night. And I never got to thank him.

"I thought I'd try that new recipe tonight, you know, the vegetable and tofu lasagna. I think it'll be perfect for watching the Rockaway Sisters marathon to," Mom says with a smile, showing her perfectly straight gleaming teeth which are almost as white as the porcelain plates we're eating off.

My mom is always so perfect in everything she does, from her perfect cooking to her perfectly curled hair and perfectly manicured hands. Growing up, I wanted to be just like her—in fact, I was just like her—but now I don't make myself pretty anymore.

We look almost exactly alike. I have her auburn-brown hair and the same big blue eyes. We also have the same nose, mouth and chin. The only difference is that I haven't cut my auburn-brown hair in almost a year, my nails are short and I never wear makeup. I don't like drawing attention to myself. I already get too much of it, because I'll never be a plain Jane, no matter how hard I try to be. I'm tall and slender and have an hourglass figure, but that can be hidden by baggy clothes. It's attention from men that I don't like.

I wish I still could. I used to like talking to men, and I liked flirting with them. I also liked the way most of them looked at me as though they could fall in love with me in a heartbeat. Maybe I was too vain and this is my punishment. No! I was never vain, and no one deserves what happened to me. No one deserves to have memories of it. Which is why I try very hard to forget. Having a routine and a calm life helps most of the time.

I nod and crack open the shell of my egg.

"Sure, Mom, that lasagna sounds great," I tell her. "But I might be late tonight, with the fire changing direction and all. I probably won't be back before eight, but I'll make the start of the Rockaway Sisters marathon, don't you worry."

That's one of our favorite TV shows, and I've been looking forward to this marathon for weeks.

I stop cutting up my egg and grin at her, but her lips are pursed and there's disapproving shock in her eyes.

"Just once, I'd prefer it if you just stayed as far away from the fire as possible," she says. "They're saying this is the worst wildfire in the last fifty years."

"They say something like that for every fire," I say and shrug as I take a bite of my egg, ignoring the other part of what she said.

It's wildfire season in California. When we first moved here from Illinois eleven years ago that used to be a set period of time each year, but for the last couple of years, fires are popping up all the time. It's because of the drought, they say. But whatever the reason, someone has to make sure as many of the animals living in the path of the fire are herded to safety as possible, at least the domesticated ones from the many ranches and farmsteads in the hills in this area. I've volunteered for that job for years, much to my mother's displeasure.

"I worry about you so much," she sighs and her words feel like a fist is crushing and twisting something soft in my chest. It's been twelve years, I'm recovered! Or as recovered as I'm ever gonna be. There's no need for her to baby me anymore.

"I wish you'd just stay away from that ranch during fire season," she continues.

I feel very foolish over that internal tantrum I just had. Good thing I didn't blurt any of that out.

"But I know you won't," she concludes.

"The animals need me," I say.

She's shaking her head as she lays her piece of toast back down on her plate untouched. "No, this is your father in you."

My dad was a cop. He was shot and killed by a fugitive during a routine traffic stop when I was four years old. I hardly remember him, but my mom's told me so many stories about him over the years that I kinda feel like I know him very well. He was a brave man, a man who knew what had to be done and did it, even if he did put himself in harm's way more than was necessary, as Mom puts it. But that kind of selfless bravery is not why I'm the first in line when it comes to saving animals from the fires.

The animals need me and I don't have a lot to lose. I'm grateful to have my life back, but it's not exactly worth living, not with all my fears and bad memories and the way I can't always control my mind from taking me back and making me relive all of them. So if I can use my life to save someone whose life is worth living, I'll do it gladly. And I always loved animals. These days, I like them more than people.

I hurry up and eat the rest of my breakfast without saying anything more, while Mom nibbles at hers. I have to stay safe for her. She wouldn't survive losing me. She'd drink herself to an early grave if anything happened to me again. But she has no reason to worry. I always stay safe, and I will return home tonight.

"I'll see you later, Mom," I say after I finish my breakfast, get up and kiss her cheek. "Don't worry about me. I'll be fine, you know I will."

She smiles, but it's a faint and sour kind of smile. Then she points at a small lunchbox on the counter. "I packed your lunch. It's rice salad and a piece of corn bread."

"Thank you, Mom," I say and grab it on my way out the door.

If I stayed in there with her any longer, the terrifying shadows that live very deep inside my brain would come out again. I love my mother, the last thing in the world I want to do is hurt her any more than she's already been hurt, but her constant worrying about me, and her taking care of me like I was still in middle school is suffocating. It's also a constant reminder of what happened to me and that I'm still not well.

I want a normal adult life. But even as I think it, I know that's not for me. I need the routine, I need Mom's companionship and being taken care of. And I need to know my life matters to someone. Else I'll just get lost in the black nothingness that was my life for months after I was rescued, as I struggled to make sense of what was real and what just a dream.

SCAR

Our MC tracked down and finished off the last remaining member of Satan's Spawn MC that we could get to a couple of days ago. And now we're officially out of the mercenary line of business and in the safer, less violent area of weapons trafficking. I don't know what to do with myself, and I have no idea how I'll fit into this new MC I'm suddenly a part of. There won't be a whole lot of people to scare and torture into submission anymore now, and that's all I've done for almost my entire adult life. It's all I'm good at doing.

Not even Tank is opposing the shift of operations anymore, and he was my last hope for things staying as they were. I wish he didn't chew so loudly as he eats his breakfast across from me. That and his exaggerated rustling with the newspaper as he turns the pages is driving me insane.

"Man, I hope this fire doesn't change direction and come by Sanctuary," he says with his mouth full, turning the paper towards me so I can read the headline.

Sanctuary, our HQ, is an old stone building deep in the

forested hills of California. In all the years that I've been a member of Devil's Nightmare MC, and it's going on twenty, only two fires ever threatened us here, and even those were more or less false alarms.

"We'll be fine," I say and focus on my own breakfast.

But Tank's still looking at me with that annoying-as-fuck sarcastic gleam in his eyes.

"What?" I ask when it becomes clear he's trying to communicate something to me, and I'm just not getting it.

"We'll probably be fine from the fire, you're right about that," he says. "But you're worried about yourself not being fine, since you're pretty much out of a job now that the Spawns are history. But don't worry, I'm sure we'll still have need of a torturer."

Tank is our VP and my old and close personal friend besides, but he has this tendency to say exactly the wrong thing at exactly the wrong time just to be sarcastically annoying. Anything I say back right now will be the wrong thing too, so I don't say anything, just get up and leave the room.

"Was it something I said, Scar?" he yells after me, but I ignore that too.

He's not wrong, which is another reason I don't want to talk to him anymore. I guess the cause of my sour mood lately has been figured out by the brothers and Tank is just the first one confronting me about it.

I'm at a total crossroads in my life right now, suffering a total loss of identity, as new-age bullshitters would put it. I suppose it's as good a name as any to put on it, but I never had any kind of need to name it before. I used to be good at drinking, brawling and fucking my way past anything, but this...this feels like a life-altering situation, and I don't appreciate getting laughed at and made fun of over it.

I joined Devil's Nightmare MC when I was seventeen years old and had enough of my father's and brother's bullshit to last a lifetime. The Devils rode through our small Illinois town, stopped just long enough to be noticed, and I rode out West with them when they left. They were based in California, far enough from my hometown to suit me perfectly. I was a member before the guys who run the club now were even a blip on the horizon. This includes Tank, but also Cross, our president, and Rook, our Sarge. So, yeah, it makes sense I'd have a harder time letting go of what we were.

I wander into the garage in search of my bike. I've been toying with the idea of just taking off for a couple of days to get my head back on straight, and Tank's crap just now made me decide it's time to do it.

Ice has the same idea, it seems. He's in the garage tinkering with his brand new bike, which probably doesn't need it. His saddlebags are already packed, judging by the way they're bulging.

He's been talking about leaving for awhile now, and I guess the time is finally here. He's also probably the only one who can come close to understanding me right now. Not that I need understanding, I just need some peace and quiet.

"So, you're not joining the MC and staying, after all?" I say as I walk up to him and get a cold, kinda murderous look in return. That kinda look always heats up my blood and has my fists itching for a fight, but that's a distant reaction right now. Maybe I'm going soft in my old age.

Maybe it's for the best that we're switching away from being guns for hire. In that line of work, you go soft and you die. I've seen it happen to a couple of guys who got old before me. Not that being thirty-six is old.

"Yeah, joining up's not the plan right now," Ice says and starts polishing the handlebars of his bike, which don't need it. "I'm going home to see what's left of my father's house and his legacy there. And to pay my respects and such."

Our MC took on Satan's Spawn MC to avenge what they did to Ice's MC and to Ice himself. For six years, they kept him locked up and made him fight in cage tournaments like he was no better than a fighter dog. He was the champion for those six years, so there's that. He also got his revenge now, but he doesn't seem as happy about it as I expected him to be.

I still fantasize about taking revenge on my brother for the lovely scar on my face that makes people flinch and back away from me on a good day. I'd be way happier if I got that revenge, but my brother's been locked up for the past ten years and has at least another ten to go. I should've gotten my revenge before he was sent down, then I'd sleep easier at night. But I'm a patient man, and I'll be waiting for him when he gets out.

"Yeah, I get it," I mutter.

"You do?" Ice asks. "'Cause no one else seems to."

I suppose the "no one" he's referring to is Roxie, Cross' old lady and Ice's sister. Cross has been hounding him to stay and join the MC on her behalf almost everyday. Although, to be fair, Ice would be a good addition to our MC.

"Never felt much need to revisit the past myself, but I kinda see your point. Some chapters have to be closed, or something. But do you ever worry about what you'll do now?" I ask.

I'm referring to the fact that Ice liked getting his revenge on the Spawns a little too well and now that's all over. That reference is not lost on him going by the killer look he's flashing me.

It looks like he means to start shit over me mentioning it, but he just shrugs and goes back to polishing his bike.

"I got shit planned for about the next month or so, and after that who the fuck cares?" he says.

From his tone it's clear that *he* certainly doesn't. I suppose his sister cares, but that's their business and none of mine, so I don't say it.

I have some unfinished business in Illinois too. Maybe I'll join him. Lynn, the woman Lizard abducted and turned into a sex slave before I saved her, is from the same town as Ice. She was in the back of my mind during all the Spawns killings, and avenging *her* was my biggest reason for taking part in almost every one of them. I didn't necessarily think I'd ever look her up to tell her about that, but maybe I could. I haven't seen her since the night I dropped her off at the ER after rescuing her from the Spawns. I could find her and tell her she got her revenge now, since Lizard and all the motherfuckers who raped and beat her are almost all dead. All except one, but he's still on my list and I'll get him as soon as he gets out of prison.

Maybe telling her that will scare her, but I think it'll also make her happy. Getting revenge is one of those things that makes everyone happy.

"When you leaving?" I ask Ice. "I might ride with you."

He shoots me a look that tells me he's not too thrilled with the idea. "Did Cross and Roxie put you up to this? Tell them I'll be perfectly fine out there in the big bad world on my own."

"No, they didn't put me up to this. There's another person who deserved to get her revenge on the Spawns, and it's time to tell her she finally got it," I say and get a blank stare from Ice.

"The waitress Lizard abducted in your town when we were there," I explain. "Remember her?"

"Oh, yeah, I remember Lynn, who wouldn't? She went to my school. Gorgeous piece of ass and not too stuck up over it either," he says, a slight smile playing across his face as he remembers her.

This sour taste of jealousy his words caused in my mouth isn't something I expected. Sure I liked her, sure I wanted to take her out and fuck her, and I even had vague ideas of being the only man who does that with her, but I didn't think those feelings were still so strong after all this time. I thought about her some over the years, but not too often. She was broken by the time I rescued her. Beyond repair, I figured. And there was no way to go back and check, because her hospital room was guarded by at least two cops at all times, until one day she just vanished.

"It's fucked up what Lizard did to her. Good thing I killed him," Ice says, still speaking in that happily reminiscing sort of voice. Right now, I wish I'd gotten to Lizard first.

"You're welcome to ride with me if it's to tell Lynn that piece of shit is dead," Ice adds.

"Good, glad we're on the same page," I say.

The jealousy over Ice telling Lynn *he* dispatched Lizard, and them taking a nice little trip down memory lane afterwards, reminiscing about their high school years, tastes very bitter, but I push it back. She's probably married by now, so Ice is the least of my problems in that area.

"But first I have to find out if she's still there," I add. "It could take a couple of days."

He frowns, but finally shrugs and nods. "Fine, I'll wait."

Hawk will do some of his internet juju and find her for me. And by the time me and Ice visit her, I'll have this jealousy under control. I'm not sure where it's coming from, because even before she was abducted, I'd decided she was way too gorgeous to waste her time on an ugly, scarred and soulless killer like me.

I saved her because I knew where she was held, and because I wouldn't be able to live with myself if I just left her there. It was also because she didn't make me feel like an ugly, scarred monster, while we chatted at her diner. She made me feel like a regular young guy the way no woman before or after her ever has.

But saving her was the last good and kind thing I did. Maybe going back to that point now that I'm at this crossroads is exactly what I need. It sure seems that way the more I think about it.

2

LYNN

THE SHELTER I work at is a tiny operation, but with massive amounts of barn space that is largely unusable, because there's been no money to keep up with repairs. It's a ranch up in the hills and could once house up to two-hundred head of cattle and other livestock. But these days all that space houses five abandoned dogs, four cats, one donkey and a goat named Milly.

The ranch belongs to Bethany - a middle-aged widow. I work there with her, her daughter Tammy, and Raul the handy man. Most of the small amount of funds we get from the state go for the upkeep and pay, and we augment that by renting out the space to other ranchers and farmers in the area when they need it. They count on us to house their livestock when the fires roll through and they have to evacuate. They pay well, but even with that income I barely get enough to cover lunch and gas, and on some months I don't even take that.

I should get another, paying job, but Mom keeps telling me not to worry about the money. She runs a successful home-based business making custom, hand-drawn greeting cards, calendars and such, and keeps telling me she makes more money than she can spend alone whenever I bring it up. She was always telling me that before too, while we still lived in Illinois and was seriously against me taking that job at the diner to pay my own way with the pageants. She doesn't begrudge me the money she spends on me, I know that she's happy I found work that fulfills me. But I also know she used to dream about traveling the world and the money doesn't stretch that far while she has me to take care of. I wish I could go with her, but that would involve too much peopling, and I'm no good at that.

I told her she should go on her own or with some of her friends, but she just purses her lips and shakes her head when I suggest it. Bethany, Tammy and Raul live at the ranch full-time. I could move here too, if Mom went on a trip, and I've mentioned that to her, but the answer was just more silence. She doesn't even say no. Just doesn't do it. Because she's too worried I'd fall apart if she wasn't near to hold me up and take care of me. I don't think that would happen, but her constant worrying still makes me think it might. It's something else I try not to think about.

But this morning's dream and the memories it dredged up, stirred these other things too, and they're taking a long time to settle back down into the depths of my sub-consciousness.

I'm having trouble concentrating on the road as I drive, since all these things are buzzing inside my brain, but I've ridden up here so many times, I know every bump in the road by heart.

As I near the ranch, another thing starts buzzing in my head.

Bethany is very close to pulling the plug and selling it all.

No more! I tell myself, and just concentrate on those two words for the rest of the ride. And it works. By the time I reach the ranch, my head is as clear as the world at dawn.

"They're saying this fire's gonna be huge," Tammy says just as I join them in the kitchen, which also serves as our main office and the place where we have our morning meetings to discuss all that needs to be done that day.

"I know," I say as I deposit the holder with four coffees and the box of donuts I got for us on my way here. "It was all over the radio this morning. But you know how they always hype it up."

Just like pretty much everything else on this ranch, the kitchen is in desperate need of repair. The appliances are all from the 1970s, if that new, and even the huge, hardwood table, which Bethany says has been in the family for a hundred years at least, is showing signs of old age. But as long as the animals are safe and fed, we're all happy. Tammy is a vet, Bethany has worked on the ranch all her life, and Raul is a very conscientious and hard working man, despite his badly damaged knee. He's also the only man that doesn't make me feel too uncomfortable to be around, although I avoid being alone with him. He reminds me of my uncle, and I think that helps.

They each take a coffee and a donut, and I take my latte and sit on one of the rickety chairs that groans and creaks under my weight. One of these mornings, it'll send me crashing to the floor, but for today it's still holding.

Tammy nods solemnly. "Yes, I know a lot of what they're saying on the news is just doom-calling hype, but it's working. We've already gotten requests to take the animals from the Millers, Hartmans, Blacksmiths and Venturas."

She just recited the names of the five biggest ranch owners in the area, each with fifty head of cattle easily.

"What about the McDonnells?" I ask. They're new in town, hailing from Australia, and they've opened a horse riding school near here just six months ago. They have twenty horses and a couple of goats.

Tammy shakes her head. "I called them last night, but they said they'll be fine. I got the feeling the owner thought I was just fishing to get paid. She spoke to me like I was some insurance saleswoman trying to scam her."

"Good thing she said no," Bethany says, rather crossly. She's not much of a morning person, but today it sounds like her annoyance is over more than just that.

"We have neither the space nor manpower to take even the ones that already signed up," she elaborates after Tammy gives her a sharp look. "If we didn't need the money desperately, I'd turn half of them away."

Tammy's eyes soften as she looks at her mother. "I know, Ma. But who else is gonna do this if we don't? I never want to see another animal die in flames for as long as I live."

When Tammy was a teenager, a fire swept over this ranch. The house and buildings nearest to it survived, but the stables were mostly destroyed. With the animals in them. They never recovered from that blow, neither financially or psychologically. Her father took his own life a couple of years later and Bethany and Tammy have been trying to make it work on their own ever since.

"The condo people called again," Bethany says. "They still want to buy this land, and they're offering a lot."

Drops of water hitting the metal basin from the leaky faucet behind me suddenly start to sound louder than drums warning of some imminent disaster. I've successfully ignored thinking about this in the car earlier, but now my heart is racing so hard that my vision is turning black at the edges. *Where will I go, if Bethany sells this place? What will I do?*

The fact that I know perfectly well—and understand perfectly too— that she can't afford to keep this place afloat, and that she's getting old and might want to retire, isn't preventing my panic attack. But I do know all those things, and I won't stand in her way. Nor will I say anything right now, because then they'll know something's wrong with me. They don't know about my past, I never tell anyone about that. But they do suspect that something bad happened to me before I came here, because I'm no good at hiding it completely.

Tammy is telling her mother something, but I don't hear the words. She keeps glancing at me like she wants me to back her up, and I can see both of them are getting agitated. But my hearing isn't back yet, and my heart is still racing, although not as violently as before.

"We can discuss this after the fire has come and gone," Raul says in his steady, booming voice, which has the power to cut even through the black fog in my brain.

It has a similar effect on Tammy and Bethany. They both nod and take a sip of their coffees at the same time, blushing the exact same shade of soft pink as they do.

"Raul's right, we'll discuss it after the fire," Tammy says. "But for now, I've managed to secure us a couple of volunteers, and they won't cost us a thing. A friend of mine from university, Josh, if you remember him, Ma, just started teaching at the San Fernando community college and he's more than happy to bring his class and maybe even some of the faculty up here to help us prepare everything for the animals, and to take care of them once they're here. None of it will cost a thing," Tammy explains and smiles at her mother. "Well, I did say you were an excellent cook, Ma and would feed them your signature chili and corn bread."

Bethany smiles at her too. They always smooth every argument over quickly and hold no grudges.

"So we're all set," Tammy concludes and smiles at me too.

I try to smile back, but I'm not sure I succeeded, because my heart is beating too fast in an entirely different kind of panic right now. I don't people well, and I don't deal with the presence of men well at all. Yet I've dealt with this fear before, and with this nausea it always brings that's washing over me right now, dealt with it over and over again.

We've had volunteers here in the past and I was just fine then. Well, I was distant and quiet and came off as a weird woman each of those times, but I was fine. I'm even fine with all the ranch hands and cowboys that come up here when they bring the livestock to be housed. They're always the same guys, and I think Raul's spoken to each of them and told them to leave me alone, although I'm not positive about that.

So why won't my heart stop racing and why is my mind threatening me with reruns of the most terrifying two weeks of my life again.

"I'll go walk the dogs," I say and get up.

They all look at me sharply, probably because of my toneless voice. But I'll be fine once I get to work. Taking care of animals always calms me. Sometimes it's the only thing that can. I don't know what will happen to me if I can't work at this ranch anymore.

SCAR

I made the decision to find Lynn and tell her about Lizard and his MC being gone, but I've been dragging my feet on actually doing it for the last couple of days. Now Ice is itching to leave and getting impatient that I haven't made up my mind yet.

But the thing is, I haven't made up my mind. I'm the kind of guy who needs a reason for everything I do, and I don't know if my reason for this is any good. Lynn could've forgotten all about that, and I'd just be dragging it back up for her if I visit.

I also think I was a little in love with her back then. Hard to be sure, I've never been in love before.

When my brother told me about where and why she was taken, I nearly lost it, and being a little in love with her was the reason. I should've dealt with him long before he got the chance to boast about how sweet she was to fuck. But I didn't, and Lynn paid the price. When he called to tell me about her, I could've tracked him down and killed him, but I decided to help her instead. By the time that was done, he was long gone again.

"Careful, Scar!" Cross's daughter, Lily, screeches at me. "You're trampling my garden."

I stop and look down, but there's nothing but dark brown soil beneath my feet, so I have no idea what she's yelling about.

"Just back up the way you came," she instructs. "Step in the footsteps you already made."

She knows how to give an order, just like her old man, I'll give her that. I don't even consider doing anything other than what she wants.

"I didn't see no flowers," I tell her once I join her on the gravel path I veered off of when I stepped into her flowers.

I've just been walking around the garden in front of Sanctuary for hours. It calms me usually, but not today. I have to make this decision.

"I only just planted them a couple of days ago, they haven't had time to germinate yet," she says, peering at the patch I trampled over, her face so close to the ground that her long, jet-black hair is trailing along it.

She straightens up and stares me down with the exact same black gaze I'm used to seeing from Cross. "You should be more careful where you're stepping. Now the flowers might never come out."

"Sorry," I mutter, since I have nothing else to tell her.

She shrugs and joins me on the path. "It's too late for sorry now. What's done is done."

She's the reason the MC's no longer in the killing for hire business, because Cross wants her to grow up in a less dangerous environment. But I'm pretty sure she can handle any environment, because Lily is one tough kid. She's also the most down-to-earth child I've ever met. Not that I've met many children, and the ones I had mostly just cried at the sight of my face. Even back when it happened. I was younger than Lily is now. Twelve years old. A fucking lifetime ago.

Lily barely flinched when Cross introduced me to her, and since she was all attitude at the time, all she said was, "Good, at least I'll remember his name since it's all over his face."

In the beginning, two years ago, when her mother dropped her off with Cross to take care of from now on, she didn't want to stay here, and Cross wasn't too thrilled at the idea either. Now she's part of the family, and me and her get along surprisingly well. She keeps coming to me for advice for some reason.

"Sorry, I yelled at you," she says. "I'm just nervous, because I have a brother on the way, my uncle is leaving, and now I heard you might be leaving too. But it's mostly because of my brother. What if he doesn't like me?"

She starts walking down the path, deeper into the garden and I fall in step with her. I could tell her all about what it's like when brothers hate each other. Me and mine hated each other all our lives. Or more precisely, my older brother hated me all his life, and I hated him for most of mine. But even with my limited knowledge about children, I know that's not a story Lily should hear.

"I'm sure he'll love you," I tell her instead.

She gives me a sidelong glance and rolls her eyes for good measure. "You can't possibly know that."

She's right. I can't know that for a fact. But her father's been keeping the peace in this MC very well for the past eight years since he took over, and I'm sure he'll keep the peace between his children too.

"Why wouldn't he?" I say instead. "You're a great little girl and you only yelled at me a little for trampling your garden. If you show the same restraint with him, you two should get along just fine."

I laugh at my own funny wisdom, but she's not amused, doesn't even crack a smile although the look in her eyes isn't quite as black and pointy as she's trying to make it.

"So, when are you leaving?" she asks. "Ice says tomorrow at the latest."

"I might not be going with him," I say and shrug.

"Why?" Lily asks, probably picking up on the undertone in my voice, which sounds bitter even to my own ears, and I'm the one saying it. "Because I said what I said? I just have a problem with people leaving, but I'm handling it. You should go if you want to."

"It's because I don't know if I should," I tell her because nothing else better to say is springing to mind.

She doesn't say anything to that. How could she? She's a child and can't handle abstract questions yet. And the thing is, I can't handle them either. Yet this one just keeps floating around in my head.

To me, it makes perfect sense to tell Lynn she's been avenged. But it also makes perfect sense to leave the past where it is. Done with and forgotten. My inability to decide whether to find her or not, could also be because I don't want to find out she never recovered, and that I never really saved her. I've never seen a person as out of their mind as she was that night. Not before or since. She couldn't even speak. I didn't do a lot of good things in my life, but I saved her, and I don't want to find out I didn't. Abstract shit. I'm no good at figuring out that kinda thing.

"Well, you thought it was a good idea when you told Ice you were going with him. Maybe you should just go with that," Lily says and she sounds like she's really trying to give me good advice, but isn't sure she's doing it right. She is.

I'll find out where Lynn is and then I'll still have time to decide whether I should visit her or not. Although, I'd prefer to just stop thinking about it and either do it or not.

"That's some good advice, Lily," I tell her. "I should come to you with my questions more often."

"Are you making fun of me?" she asks, her eyes pointy and flashing again.

I shake my head and tussle her hair. "Not even a little."

It's time to find Hawk and get things moving. Enough thinking. I was never good at that sorta thing.

3

SCAR

HAWK, the guy whose job it is to find information about the work we take on—from getting us plans to buildings, to finding people we're tracking down — said he could find Lynn for sure, especially after Ice was able to supply her last name, which I never knew. He also couldn't help crack a few jokes to the tune of *Beauty and the Beast*, even though the whole saving Lynn event happened well before he joined the MC, back when he was just a hacker living in his momma's basement. I replied with something to that effect and that shut him up quick. Not so with Tank, who somehow found out I was looking for Lynn, and had some choice jokes of his own to share with me. He's harder to silence, so I've just been avoiding him for the past day or so, since I asked for Hawk's help.

"How's it looking for our departure today?" Ice asks, walking into the garage where I've been fixing the muffler on my bike

...ce dawn. I've put the task off for a long time, but it needs to get done, if we're gonna ride.

"I'll finish this up and go ask Hawk," I say evasively.

I know Ice wants to leave as soon as possible, but I also know Roxie's happy he's staying for a couple more days, so I don't feel like a complete asshole over making him wait for me.

He glares at me the whole time I'm tightening the last screw, then as I clean off my hands and put the tools away. Ice has calmed down a bit since we've killed the last of the Spawns, but he's still far from being the cool-headed guy I'd prefer to ride with. A part of me is glad he's not joining the MC and I know I'm not the only one thinking it. Not that he hasn't proved his worth a hundred times over, or that we gossip about him with the other brothers like a bunch of women. But he's unpredictable, to put it mildly, and we need to *know* who has our back in our line of work. Yet I know Rook appreciates very much what Ice helped him with down in Mexico. As for me, I just think Ice needs some more time to get his head back on straight, and then I'll be happy to call him brother.

"Alright, alright, I'm going," I say even though he hasn't actually said anything to hurry me along. Just grunted a bunch and glared at me.

"Try not to take another two days about it," he says to my back as I exit the garage. I don't bother replying, since I have no fucking idea how long it'll take and the whole thing is nerve-wrecking enough as it is. I still haven't decided if I'm actually gonna go see Lynn once I find out where she is.

Maybe Hawk'll also know more about her life now and that will help me decide. Like where she works, is she married, how many kids she's got, that kinda shit, which I'd rather not know. Although it'd be better for her if she did have all those things.

"You got something for me?" I ask, startling Hawk as I barge into his basement room that looks like an electronics store with all the gadgets he has set up in here.

"Ever heard about knocking?" he barks at me. "What if I was watching porn or something?"

"Then I'd still want to know what you got for me?" I say, pulling up a chair.

He mutters something under his breath then types a bit on the keyboard in front of him, making what looks like a bunch of official police records and correspondence disappear from the screen. I don't know what he's working on right now, or if this is even for the club, but it looks like it is. Maybe Cross isn't out of jobs for me to take on just yet. Good, then I can stop thinking about all this abstract bullshit and get back to work.

He presses a few more buttons on the keyboard, and I stop thinking about all that like someone switched off my brain like a TV. A picture of Lynn in a bathing suit with a glittering tiara on her head, and a huge bouquet of flowers obscuring her curves is filling the screen. In a flash, I remember exactly how I felt about her, and know the reason why I don't want her to be married with kids. Hell, I don't even much like that Hawk's grinning as he checks out the picture.

"This is her, right?" he asks.

"Yeah, that's her," I grunt more than say.

"Well, she changed her last name and this was the last beauty pageant she ever won. It's also one of the last pictures of her anywhere online," he says. "She's using her mother's maiden name these days — Carlyle— and she went to school to become some kind of veterinary technician. It looks like it's brains and beauty with this one. But she's not a full-on vet, just a—"

"I don't need her schooling and employment history," I

interrupt, and I don't know if it's because I don't want him to get to the part about the husband, or because I just want to see her again as soon as possible. "Do you have her address?"

Hawk chuckles and types some more on his keyboard. This time he brings up an official looking document with Lynn's headshot and a bunch of info I can't read from this distance, but I assume is her DOB, her address, and such.

"She lives right here in California, right here in the county for that matter. Has been for the last decade or so, as near as I can tell," Hawk says, cementing my breath right in my chest. "200 Hyacinth Drive, San Fernando Falls. Do you need a phone number?"

I nod, because I can't actually speak. She's been right here all this time? Living in a town not even an hour away from me, and I never knew anything about it?

"And she works at some weird-ass shelter for livestock and horses called, Second Chance Ranch up in the San Fernando hills," Hawk says. "You want that address too?"

"Yeah, give me all you got," I say, my voice hoarse and higher pitched than normal, but at least it's working again. "It's probably best if I visit her at work. Don't wanna explain why I'm there to her husband."

Hawk nods and presses something that starts the printer behind us. "No husband. She lives with her mom, as far as I can tell."

Now that just made my decision to go see her a no-brainer.

"You really came through for me, man," I say, take the printouts, tap Hawk on the back and leave. I won't think any more. I'll just go see her and let this fall how it will.

LYNN

It's Saturday and ten volunteers are helping us house the animals that belong to three different ranchers in our stables. This is the first day since I started working here eight years ago that I want to not be here. Tammy had the idea to have them all bring their animals today, since we had help coming and we might not after the student volunteers see how much work it actually is getting everything prepared, and all the animals housed.

But the twenty-year old students or their middle aged professor—who definitely still has some sort of strong feelings for Tammy—aren't the problem. My problem is the additional ranch hands the Millers sent to help us out when it became obvious we bit off more than we can chew. Only three are guys we've worked with before, the rest are new and they've all been leering at me all day. One of them is especially insistent and has been eyeing me flirtatiously since he spotted me. He makes sure he's near me at all times, smiles at me every chance he gets and rolls his eyes when I just stare at him blankly and don't smile back. Raul is helping some of the other ranch hands fortify one of the older stables, or else I'd be working somewhere near him, but there's nothing for me to do there.

I want to leave, curl up on the sofa, watch TV, and ignore the fact that I'm a total failure at having a normal life. And that's all I'm thinking about as I try to lead one of the goats into the pen we set up for them this morning on the other side of the house, so they won't be bothered by all the comings and goings.

Goats are very gentle and sensitive animals. Almost as sensitive as horses. I never knew that until I started working here, but it's proven true on more than one occasion. Like right now, as I'm coaxing the last one of them to follow me to the pen, where I'm planning to stay too until I can get this panicky nausea that's starting in my stomach back under control.

All the excitement plus the very interested cowboy has frayed my nerves to the point that my hands are threatening to start shaking uncontrollably, and I'm having trouble thinking about anything but my need to be away from all these people, and from that guy who keeps smiling at me. I still get stuck in these loopy thoughts sometimes, where I'm just thinking about one thing over and over again, but I don't remember the last time it was this bad. I hate the reminder of just how not normal I am, and just how not normal I'll always be, because it's been more than ten years since I was saved and I'm still not well.

And this damn goat has now dug its hooves in and won't move at all. Who can blame her? She doesn't want to be stuck with a nervous, pathetic wreck like me. Who does?

"You have to talk to them softly, and then they'll do whatever you want them to do," a man says behind me and I freeze, my stomach a hard ball that's gonna make me throw up any second.

I manage to turn towards the voice, but then I'm face to face with the guy who's been smiling at me all morning and from the look in his eyes there's no doubt that *he* wants *me*. That's probably why he's talking so softly.

"Here, let me try," he says and makes sure that his fingers brush my hand as he attempts to take the goat's lead from me.

"No need, thanks," I mumble and pull my hand away so hard the goat actually screeches in shock as I yank too hard on the leash.

"Let me help you out," he insists. "I know a thing or two about a thing or two when it comes to goats and such."

"No, please, I got it," I say, my voice feeble, because I am actually pleading and because I totally do not *have* this.

A normal woman would be happy to have this rugged cowboy come to her rescue. I'm so petrified my bones are shivering and the nausea makes it hard to speak. My heart racing in panic and feeling sick to my stomach is my involuntary reaction to men when they show interest in me. I've tried therapy, I've done meditation, I even tried hypnosis, but I can't shake that reaction. Nothing helps, except staying away from men. I don't want it to be like that, but it's the only solution that works. It makes me angry at myself, but it is what it is.

"You can go help the others," I tell him in a stronger voice, hoping he'll get the hint that I want him to leave me alone, and that my decision on it is final.

The noise behind us is growing louder by the second, at least to my ears, with cows mooing, horses neighing and stomping, people yelling at the animals and each other, agitating everyone even more. I think I can hear the rumble of a helicopter flying overhead, or maybe it's a Harley approaching. I know the sound very well, it still plays a big part in my nightmares, because I could hear bikes ride up to the house where I was held prisoner and then moments later, I'd get raped. The sound of a motorcycle and the memory of getting raped will always go hand in hand in my mind, and I really hate my mind for mistaking the helicopter for a bike right now. As if I needed any more fuel on this slow burning panic attack I've been struggling with for the past couple of hours. And now my hands are shaking for real, the goat is baying like crazy and the guy is grinning at me like I didn't just send him away two seconds ago —like he's never gonna take no for an answer.

He reaches for the goat's lead again and doesn't let go this time. "I'll put the goat into the pen for you, and then you and me can have a nice cool glass of lemonade together in the shade, what do you say?"

That is literally the last thing in the world I want to do and that's all I know. But if I tell him that, he'll be offended and I'll have a completely different problem on my hands if he doesn't take rejection well. We're alone behind the house, far away from everyone else, and even if I scream it's very likely that no one will hear me over all the noise they're making. Somewhere I find the strength to yank the leash from him, and this time, by some miracle, the goat moves with me when I start walking.

"Hey! Why don't you want me to help you? I was trying to be nice," he yells after me and his voice is no longer playful. It's laced with a very hard and angry tone now. I keep walking, praying in my mind that he won't follow me.

"Why didn't you answer me?" he yells again.

I think he's following me, and the terror of what he might be planning next is making the edges of my vision turn black.

"She don't wanna talk to you, that's why," another guy says harshly. His voice sounds so very familiar, but I don't dare turn. It could be one of the cowboy's friends. The only guy whose voice sounds familiar to me is Raul's, so I could just be imagining things. I need to get as far away from them both as fast as I can.

"And what, you think she's gonna talk to you, buddy?" the cowboy asks after barking a harsh laugh. "One look at your face and she's gonna run away, let alone not talk to you."

"Get outta here before you get hurt," the familiar sounding guy says.

I stop and turn because I have to find out where I know him from.

My whole body goes soft when I see him, the goat's lead slipping from my limp fingers as I stand there staring at him, not sure what I'm feeling. But it isn't fear. And I'm no longer nauseous, nor wishing to run away like I did a second ago. My hands aren't shaking anymore either, and my racing heart is no longer making me feel like I'll pass out at any moment. The only clear thought in my mind is how glad I am that I fought my panic and stayed here today, so he could find me.

He's looking at me like maybe he's not sure what's going on either.

"Hello, Lynn," Scar says.

I open and close my mouth, because I don't know where to start saying all the things I wish I had said to him when I had the chance. Like, "Thank you for saving me", "Thank you for giving me my life back", and "You should've asked me out, why didn't you?". That last one is something I haven't even thought of consciously for a long time, but somehow it's right up there with the important stuff I need him to know right now, and maybe that's why I can't find any words.

"See? Never mind that she'll never talk to you, but you just gave her a heart attack is what you did," the cowboy says.

"No, he didn't," I say and start walking towards him before I blow yet another chance at telling this man just how grateful I am for all he has done for me.

"He's the only man I want to talk to," I add and that's a weird thing to say, but the words came straight from somewhere very deep inside me and not from my rational mind. It's the complete truth, and I don't regret saying it.

"So, you're happy to see me, Lynn?" Scar says, grinning at me, which makes the scar covering half his face shift. But he has a very beautiful face beneath that scar. I always thought so after

I got over the shock of seeing him for the first time. And after awhile, I didn't even notice his scar anymore. And his eyes are the nicest shade of deep green I've ever seen. They remind me of the forest, of the peace being alone among the trees brings. They always reminded me of that, I now remember. I also haven't wanted a man to take off his shirt so I could get a closer look at his naked skin and bulging biceps in a very long time, but a part of me wants Scar to do just that right now. That's how I felt about him before I was abducted. I wanted him to take me out then take me and make me his, and it's all coming back to me now from a usually silent part of my mind, but it's insistent.

I stop just short of grabbing both his hands in mine. "I wanted to thank you for so long, but I didn't know how to find you. I don't even know your real name, but what you did for me all those years ago…you gave me my life back after I was sure I lost it, and I never even thanked you properly. It's given me some sleepless nights, I'll tell you that. I'm so glad you're here right now."

He's got a rather sheepish look on his face as he listens to me, like he's not used to getting thanked. But then he clears his throat and his eyes are very steady as he looks into mine. "You're welcome, Lynn. I only wish I could've come sooner, or prevented it altogether."

You and me both.

But I don't say that. He nods anyway like he's thinking the same thing.

"I came to tell you something," he says, and glances at the cowboy still standing a few feet away from us and gawking. "But it best be done in private."

"Sure, come this way," I say and start walking towards the main house.

"What about the goat?" the cowboy asks.

I freeze and look back at the goat that's now leisurely looking for tufts of grass to chew on right were I left her when Scar appeared. She's no longer nervous and fidgety, she's content, as though all is right in the world.

"How about you help her out and take care of it, buddy?" Scar suggests, putting it better than I would've.

Then he motions for me to lead the way, which I do. Although a kernel of the fear he chased away from my chest when he showed up is growing again. I haven't seen a biker for twelve years. Scar is the last one I saw. Now he's here with *news*. And that can't be good.

4

LYNN

By the time we enter the kitchen, which is empty like I expected it to be since everyone is outside working, I don't even remember wanting to leave, or how uncomfortable I was with that cowboy, or how scared I got that he's here with some terrible news that might uproot my mom and me. Scar always made me feel very secure and safe whenever he was around and it's happening now too, especially once we're alone.

I told the cops who abducted me, but I never gave my official statement before we left town. One afternoon, a younger detective working on my case came to the hospital on his day off to warn my mom and me that going against an outlaw motorcycle club was very dangerous, and that if I want to have a normal life, I should consider just disappearing. I still wasn't thinking very clearly at the time, but my mom took his words to heart. We left three days later, cutting ties with everyone back home. Mom asked me where I wanted to move to and I said California, because I knew Scar was from here. But my mom and me both changed our names, so it's amazing Scar was even able to find me. But can Lizard find me just as easily?

"Would you like something to drink?" I ask, my own throat very dry.

"Just like old times, huh?" he says and chuckles. It takes me a second to realize he's referring to the old days when he'd visit me at the diner.

"Not really," I say and smile at him. "This time the drink would be free."

It was so easy to joke around with him back then and it still is.

He grins but shakes his head and takes a seat at the table, tapping the chair next to him. "I'm good for now. I'd rather just get this over with first. Sit."

I don't know if I should be offended that he considers this visit—the visit I hoped would come for a long time—an errand, or glad because it sounds like he doesn't have any kind of world destroying news for me.

I push both of those thoughts to the side and sit down next to him. He smells almost exactly like he did on the night he held me in his arms after rescuing me. Of petrol and asphalt, leather and denim, and something else, something faint but powerful that even in my delirious state reminded me of long summer afternoons in some wild field, of freedom, laughter and happiness. It still reminds me of those things.

"I'm no good with words, so I'm just gonna say it." He pauses just long enough to take a breath, but not long enough for me to get scared. "Lizard is dead and the rest of his MC are all dead too. Satan's Spawn MC doesn't exist anymore."

I'm frozen again, paralyzed, unsure what to think. My mind is a vast plain of white nothing right now. A chorus of very joyous voices is celebrating on one side and the dark clouds of my memories are gathering on the other. In between, I don't know what to think.

Scar is looking at me very intently, and it takes me awhile to notice.

"Was I wrong coming to tell you that?" he asks when I finally manage to focus my eyes on him.

I can understand my thoughts a little more clearly when I look into his eyes. The dark clouds aren't as threatening anymore either, but I still can't speak.

"I thought you'd want to know he's not a threat to you anymore," he says. "And that he paid for what he did to you."

"Did you do it?" I blurt out without thinking about what I'm actually asking him— namely, whether he killed a man.

He shakes his head. "Wasn't me. I just made it possible for someone else to do it. Someone who had a score to settle with him too, maybe even a bigger one than you, but what do I know? Bottom line, he had a knife and the opportunity to use it and he did. But you don't need to know all that."

Don't I? I have no idea. I've always been a soft person, a sensitive soul, a gentle flower, as my mom puts it, right from the start. And what happened to me didn't toughen me up. It just made me even softer.

"I didn't think much about getting revenge for what they did to me," I answer him truthfully. "I mostly just thought about escaping and forgetting."

I only achieved one of those things, but he doesn't need to know that.

He nods his head thoughtfully, but I have no idea what he's

actually thinking. "You don't have to worry about escaping anymore, you've done it. And you seem to have a good life here. I'm sorry if I unsettled you with this news and made you remember. I'll go now."

He stood up while he was talking and is now just holding onto the backrest of his chair. In a moment he's going to walk out of this kitchen and then I'll never see him again all over again. I don't know or understand much right now, but I do know I don't want *that* to happen.

"I'm sorry, you just really shocked me with this news. I haven't forgotten, so you didn't bring anything up that wasn't already up," I say and stand too with a vague notion of getting closer to him. His grin is very wide and I don't know what he's thinking, but it's definitely making me feel better about admitting I'm not over what they did to me.

"I'd like to buy you dinner tonight to properly thank you," I add more confidently. "I've been so quiet around you, but there's so much I want to say to you."

So much is an exaggeration. There's really just thank you. But I want to say it right very much. There's also the fact that I liked him, I could tell him that, but if I just blurt that out now he'll think I'm crazy.

"I get that it's hard for you to talk about it, so don't think you owe me anything," he says and I know he means it. But he couldn't be more wrong.

"I owe you my life," I tell him. "And now I owe you my peace of mind."

Truthfully, I stopped worrying that Lizard would find me years ago. There just wasn't any indication that he was looking for me at all.

"You don't owe me anything. As for dinner, I'll just say, hell yeah to that." His grin grows wider, and I'm no longer unsure about what he's thinking. The surprising part is that the idea of a date with him doesn't make me want to throw up, not even a little bit. It's starting to, as I begin to think about it, but it's pretty easy to ignore.

I tell him where to meet me and when, refuse his suggestion that he come pick me up at my house, since seeing a Harley drive up would probably give my mom a heart attack. She's not soft like me. She craves revenge, and she never stopped worrying that bad men were gonna find me and drag me back to hell. It's another reason she stays so close to me, to protect me, because she knows how soft I am. She bought a gun after I was rescued and had it with her at all times for the first few years afterwards. I think she still keeps it in her nightstand.

Scar seems disappointed when I refuse the ride, but grins at me again as he agrees to my plan, and again right before he leaves the kitchen. I smiled at him both times, just like I used to smile at him all the time when he came to the diner. I smiled at everyone back then, all the time, but it doesn't come naturally anymore. Right now it did. He grinned at me a lot back then too, I suddenly remember very clearly. I remember it even after he's gone and I'm starting to panic about being alone with a man in a restaurant—with a man who clearly expects more than dinner. That much was evident from all the grinning.

I haven't been on a date in twelve years. I hardly went outside after dark in all that time either. And I'm about to change both of those things in one fell swoop tonight.

But I know I'm safest with him, and I want to see him again tonight. So I just won't listen to that screaming voice inside my head telling me I can't go through with it, so I might as well not even try. I've been hiding for long enough. And I've waited for my first date with Scar for a very long time.

He saved me from Lizard once, now maybe he can save me from the memories of that nightmare. It's a vague notion, a hatchling of an idea that frightens me, but not enough to run away from it.

Mom gawked at me with her mouth wide open for a full couple of minutes after I told her I'm going out for dinner tonight. I said it was with Tammy, since she might not even let me go, if I told her who I was really going out with. She's just as thankful to Scar for saving me as I am, perhaps even more so, but she's a sensible, down-to-earth woman who has no illusions about who he really is. At least that's how she put it.

I didn't wait for her to start asking questions after I told her of my plans, just rushed upstairs to shower and get the smell of goat and horses off me. And dog too, since I took them for a long walk after Scar left and the cowboy started showing interest in me again until I absolutely couldn't handle his attention anymore.

Once upon a time, my life used to be all pretty dresses and evening gowns, makeup, hair styling and beauty pageants. Now I only own one dress, which still has the tag on it, since I've never worn it. But I'm wearing it tonight. I have no high heels to go with it, or I'd wear those too. I threw out all my feminine clothes after I was finally recovered enough to start planning for the future again. Mom's forever convincing me to buy and wear more dresses and pretty outfits, but buying this dress was the only time I caved to her pressure.

It's a pretty summer dress, with a wide skirt, a button up bodice and three-quarter sleeves. The dress itself is white, but it's covered with slashes of bright colors in shapes that look like abstract flowers. The skirt hits at mid-calf and has three-quarter sleeves, while the bodice buttons up all the way up to my throat, and no part of it is too tight. It's really just like wearing jeans, a t-shirt and a sweatshirt, which is what I wear every day. It's a huge step I'm taking going on this date, and I don't know how far I'll get, but I want to look the part.

And I won't think too hard about it, because otherwise I'll just change my mind and stay home, eat the dinner I know my mom is already halfway done making and watch some mindless TV show until I can't keep my eyes open. Then I'd get up tomorrow morning and live the same exact day I've lived every day for the last twelve years.

No.

I can go back to doing that tomorrow.

But tonight, I'm going to do what has been long overdo.

"You look gorgeous," Mom says, looking in through the open door of my bedroom as I'm checking my reflection in the mirror. "I keep telling you to wear dresses more often. Would you like to borrow my pearls to go with it? I'll go get them."

She rushes to her own bedroom before I can say anything, but my answer would've been yes anyway, so it's OK. I follow her, because I have to borrow some of her makeup too. I don't own anything except mascara and even that's all dry and flaky.

She gives me a very surprised look as I ask for her makeup, so I don't stop, just go find it in her bathroom by myself.

"You and Tammy must be going to a very nice place." It's her way of asking why I'm getting so dressed up for dinner with a co-worker.

She's asking a lot more than that. Such as, "How come you're going to dinner out at all?" I almost never go out in the evenings, and when I do it's with her. This dinner date of mine came as a complete shock to her, that much is clear in the undertone of her voice.

"We're going to some nice Italian place that just opened." It's not a complete lie, since that's where I'm meeting Scar, but it's still a lie and I don't like lying, especially not to my mom. "It's been so long since I dressed up, so I thought I would tonight."

"You should dress up more often," she says, brushing my hair back from my face. "You're a stunning woman and there's no sense in hiding away."

None at all, except that…No, I won't think of that tonight!

"I wish you'd called and told me you had plans for tonight," Mom adds when I don't say anything. "But I'm happy you're going out with friends."

"I'm sorry," I say pick up the eyeliner. "It was a very short notice thing and the battery on my phone died."

For someone who doesn't like to lie, I'm sure doing a lot of it today. And smoothly too.

Something in my mom's eyes tells me she's not buying my story for a second, that she knows I'm lying, and that she's very sad about it. But that could just be paranoia borne of my guilt over lying to her. But I have to know what's what before I tell her about Scar.

Back when we first met, I never told her about him either, since I didn't think she'd approve of him. I don't know if she ever believed me that we were very close friends by the time I did tell her everything after he rescued me and disappeared.

I look away and pull my eyelid to the side to apply the eyeliner. And proceed to poke myself in the eye with it.

"Let me help you with that," she says and plucks the eyeliner from my hand before I even offer it.

I did my own makeup for pageants, since I turned sixteen. But before then, Mom used to do it for me, and she's still as deft at it as she was back then. She started entering me into pageant soon after my dad died, and had huge dreams for me, believed I could be Miss Illinois, maybe even Miss America. She envisaged this successful supermodel career for me, which was something she wanted for herself but never pursued, because she got married young and started a family. I used to want all those things too. As a little girl and later as a teenager. But by the time I was abducted, I'd begun to dream of other things too, of a career that didn't involve people gawking at me on stage.

But right now, as her deft fingers apply my makeup—not just the eyeliner, but everything else too—I'm back in those happier times, when me and my mom shared big dreams of my future which seemed bright, and everything was exactly as it should be.

But it's over as soon as she's done, and I'm looking at my face in the mirror. I'm all made up and pretty, my big blue eyes accentuated by black eyeliner, my eyelashes thick, long and curved, my cheeks rosy and my lips shiny and plump. I want to grab the tissues and wipe it all off. My hand's in a cramp, because a part of my mind is already doing just that.

Being pretty ruined my life. Not just ruined, it destroyed my life and all my dreams. It destroyed my mom's life too and all her dreams.

"What's wrong, Lynn?" Mom asks in a soothing voice, which never fails to collide with my heart and make me feel loved. Even when I was in that dark place where no light shone, where everything was just fear and pain and numb nothingness, her voice never failed to make me feel loved and wanted. I know she regrets nothing. She often tells me so, often tells me I should regret nothing either. We only get one life. I almost lost mine, but I got it back. And I've done the best I could to make the most of it. But my best isn't very good at all.

"Nothing, Mom, I'm fine, it's just been so long since I've seen myself with makeup on. It's a shock," I say and smile as best I can.

It's a far cry from the radiant smiles I used to give to the audience and the jury as they handed me bouquets and placed tiaras on my head.

"I should go, I don't want to be late," I say and squeeze her arm.

She stops me on my way out of her bedroom to clasp the pearls around my neck, then walks me to the door and watches me leave from the porch. Tomorrow I'll tell her who I went to meet tonight.

She'd stop me from going, or she'd want to come with me if I told her now. But I need to do this for me. And by myself.

It's the first step towards something new, something that deep down I've craved for a long time, but haven't been able to go after because of what happened to me. I don't know how far I'll get tonight, or if Scar is even interested in me that way. But I know I need to try, and that I have to do it without my mom holding my hand.

5

SCAR

I'M NOT that guy who takes women out to nice restaurants, and I'm certainly not the guy who gets invited to such restaurants *by* women. My scar took care of my desire to be out in public with normal people a long time ago, and my lifestyle since took care of the rest. But if a gorgeous woman asks you out, you say yes. And that's pretty much all I've been focusing on. Namely, just how gorgeous she still is. Even though she nearly folded in on herself while that cowboy was making his move on her before I chased him away.

She was flirty when I first met her, not in a forward way as most women I meet are, but in a good-girl-next-door kinda way. At the diner, I watched her fend off guys who went too far with smiles and gentle rejections. Today, she couldn't even speak when that guy put his moves on her. She's still as gorgeous as ever—even more so because she's all woman now—

but she's clearly damaged. While I was rescuing her, the fantasy of her wrapping her arms around my neck once I got her out, and telling me I'm the only one for her right before we rode off into the sunset together, kept playing in my mind.

But the reality was a completely different story. She could hardly speak, hardly even focus her eyes on me, and I knew I was too late, knew Lizard and the rest of that scum broke her. There's no coming back from that. I've seen women broken like that, more such women than I like to think about. I fucked more of them than I care to admit too, but that's because they're easy, and I like things easy in general, and especially when it comes to women. That's more or less the kinda women I can get with this face of mine—easy ones. And they're the most fun to be with besides, so it works out.

Lynn was out of my league then. Now she's still out of my league and broken besides. But she did say she's been waiting for me to visit for a long time and she did invite me on a date, so I'm gonna forget all that and take it all the way tonight.

The restaurant Lynn wanted to meet at is a family sort of place. I checked it out on my way back to Sanctuary and promptly realized I have nothing suitable to wear to it. But I never fitted in anywhere except with the MC, so I'm used to being out of place.

We're meeting at seven-thirty, and I got here early, which earned me fifteen minutes of getting gawked at in fright and disgust by passersby. But I'm used to that too.

That's not how Lynn looks at me as she parks her car aways from my bike and walks up to me. She's looking at me like she's very happy to see me. Almost as happy as she looked when I showed up at her work this afternoon. She dressed up too. Damn, but she should be on the cover of some magazine not getting an early dinner with an ugly motherfucker like me. In a perfect world, that would be a fact. In this world, we're both fucked up and it makes perfect sense that we're here together.

The dress she's wearing covers her up completely, but is still sexy as hell. The women I usually meet wear tight, skimpy outfits that hide nothing, but this is better. The wind is blowing her skirt here and there, and my dick swells a little more each time it blows hard enough to give me a glimpse of her ankles and calves.

Cool it, bud. The sun hasn't even set yet.

"Hello, Scar," she says when she reaches me, her voice faint and strangled like she's scared. But she's smiling. "Am I late?"

"No, I'm early," I say reassuringly, since she seemed genuinely worried. "Let's go in."

The urge to place my arm around her shoulders is strong, but I fight it. It's too early for that. We gotta talk some first, see if we're on the same page about this date.

She's so elegant and so gorgeous, and she always seemed more like a dream than a real person to me. Back then, she was saying my name with a smile on her face, and talking to me with a smile on her face. That never made much sense to me. A woman like her and a guy like me? That has to be just a dream. I wanted to fuck her from the moment I saw her—what warm-blooded guy wouldn't? —but it was more than that with her. I was happy just spending time with her, listening to her stories and telling her some of my own. But I was younger and more naive then. That guy is gone.

"This place, huh?" I ask and offer her my arm so we can start walking.

"Yes," she says and almost takes it, then flinches and folds her arms over her chest.

I pull my arm away and pretend I never offered it in the first place. The gesture was part of that dream I was remembering before. Because in reality she was broken by a bad man, and the only reason she's smiling at me is because I rescued her and saved her from more torture.

Probably the only reason she smiled at me before then was because she's a nice and kind woman who felt sorry for me. This ain't no fairytale, it never was. I could probably fuck her once or twice because even good girls like to go slumming with bad men sometimes, but anything more than that is just a fucking fantasy.

We walk in step to the door, where I do remember my manners again, and open it for her.

The place is crowded and the interior is all done up in dark wood, which gives the light a reddish tone, and that's something I'm used to at the other establishments I frequent. It's also kinda dark, which suits me perfectly. They direct us to a booth, which is so small our legs would be touching if she didn't keep hers tucked well away under the bench.

A frazzled looking waitress with bleached hair that looks yellow in this light comes to take our order and Lynn looks after her with a knowing look in her eyes when she leaves to bring our order.

"She must be dead on her feet," she says. "I remember what it was like during busy times at the diner. We called it "rush hour" and it was especially bad, if you got stuck working it alone."

"I should've been there to walk you to your car that night," I say since that regret's been floating in my mind a lot today.

She blinks in surprise, then looks at me like a doe caught in the headlights. A very graceful and pretty doe. "I would've told you I was fine and said, "No, thanks". I was all about being independent and making my own way back then."

She tries to smile, but can't quite do it.

"And you'd figure I wanted something more besides walking you to your car, which is another reason you'd say no, right?" I ask and grin at her.

She shrugs and her smile is a little more pronounced now, but still faint as hell. "Maybe. Probably. But with you it was different."

Our drinks arrive just then, snatching away the moment for me to ask, "Different like how?", and breaking this tension that I remember existing between us back then. Maybe she remembers it too, maybe she felt it too, maybe she's trying to get back to it too.

But her face grows very serious, almost stone-like after the waitress leaves, so it was probably just me living in that fantasy again.

"You couldn't have done more for me than you did," she says.

We both know that's an exaggeration.

And the way she stopped my attempt at flirting in it's tracks with another "thank you", just told me this really is just a thank you dinner and nothing more, as far as she's concerned. Maybe it's for the best.

She's worth more than a fuck and a, "See you later" afterwards, but there's not much more I can give her. She has her life and I have mine, which is no place for her. Besides, what woman in her right mind would want to hang on the arm of a scarred monster like me?

That thought is always in the back of my mind. Most of the time I don't even hear it anymore, but it's there. It was plenty loud when I was getting ready to ask her out that first time, before Lizard took her. And it's plenty loud right now.

"You're welcome, Lynn," I say. "Any decent guy would do as much for you if he could. Rescuing you is its own reward."

The waitress brings our food before she can explain the thoughts that are bringing that cringing, skeptical expression to her face.

She thanks the waitress the way a colleague might, showing that same warmth I saw in her back then, the one that made me think she could see past my scar. But it's just her spiel, just an act. She's Miss Congeniality, for sure. I wonder if she ever won that title. She must have, the way she just flipped from frowning to smiling. I'm the one she's frowning at and that should tell me everything I need to know.

She ordered something called risotto and I got the same thing, since I had no idea what else to order here. I should've gone for spaghetti, that's Italian, I realize as I'm staring at the rice on my plate. I hate rice.

That, the people turning in their seats to stare at us, and the fact that I don't know what I'm supposed to make of this thankfulness of hers is making me wish dinner was over, so I can either find out what's what or go home. I could just hear the waitress thinking, look it's Beauty and the Beast over here, while Lynn was being all nice to her, and that pissed me off too, not so much for my sake.

I know what I am. I don't hide from it and I don't deny it. I'm a beast through and through, a very bad man. And I'm also at a crossroads, because my brand of badness is no longer required.

But this pretty, delicate lady sitting across from me is not someone I can take with me down any road. She deserves more than I can give her. I knew that then and I know it now and I should've just left things alone instead of looking her up. Now this dinner is just adding to the pile of shit I'm already wading through.

I thought we'd smile at each other and then go somewhere private to have some fun afterwards, but the longer I look at her, the more I realize this is all just part of that fantasy that can't be.

I start eating, since I can't very well leave a full plate when I leave.

"I'm glad you looked me up to tell me about…about…" She can't say Lizard's name, and she once again reminds me of a frightened doe as she struggles to compose herself.

"If it were me, I'd want to know a thing like that," I say to help her along.

"I did want him punished," she says and smiles kinda apologetically, holding her fork up but not touching her food.

"Only by the cops, right?" I ask, swallowing a mouthful of the crunchy rice without chewing it, because I hate uncooked rice worst of all.

She shrugs and nods, again very apologetically.

"He got punished the only way he was ever gonna get punished. Cops couldn't touch him," I say and try to eat more of the rice, but give up on the idea before I bring it to my mouth. It's too disgusting.

She nods and finally starts eating, not saying anything more. Though I think plenty more is going on in her mind, judging by the shifting in her gorgeous stormy sky blue eyes. Most people find storms depressing, but I always liked the wind and the rain.

She comes out of her trance by shaking her shoulders a

little, then looks first at her plate and then at mine.

"You don't like it?" she asks.

"Let's just say that if I'd known it was rice, I wouldn't have ordered it."

"We can go somewhere else if you want," she says, and maybe she's just saying it, because she's Miss Congeniality through and through, but I'm gonna seize it. It's time to get out of my head and find out what's what.

So I grin at her. "Like to your house?"

She freezes, even the storm in her eyes does. She's not a doe caught in the headlights anymore. She's a doe that's already been hit. And killed. I missed my chance to be here twelve years ago, and this dinner is just a very annoying reminder of that fact.

Never mind my scar, never mind the fact that I torture and kill people for a living. That's not the problem. She wasn't in a fit state to ride off into the sunset with me when I rescued her, and she never will be again. And it's pissing me off so bad, I can't sit here and be reminded of it anymore.

I didn't save her. I just freed her.

"So that's a no on your house?" I say to break her weird silence, which reminds me too much of that night I dropped her off at the hospital when she just stared at me with her gorgeous, thankful big blue eyes, but didn't speak at all. I can deal out pain and death all day long, but I could never stand witnessing delicate, fragile things suffering. And that's what she was that night. A trampled little flower. A dead doe. Not much has changed.

She doesn't say anything, doesn't even look at me, just stares down at her hands. But things are happening in her mind, I can see it in the storm raging in her eyes.

Maybe I'm blowing this way out of proportion and she just doesn't want to fuck me, but doesn't know how to say it. Either way, I'm ending this shit now.

She's not eating, I'm not eating, and now we're not even talking anymore. I wave the waitress over so I can pay and get out of here. Lynn still isn't saying anything while I take care of all that.

But I'd prefer to end this night on a friendly note. "I had to try, Lynn. You're too beautiful not to try, and you did ask me out. But I won't bother you anymore. I'll just go now."

She clutches my arm as I move to get up, and looks so deep in my eyes I can feel the wind and the rain in them hitting my face.

"You should've asked me out back then. I would've said yes. But now I'm just too messed up. You're the first guy I've been to dinner with, since it happened, can you believe it?"

I just shake my head, since I have a hard time believing that, a very hard time, but my mind is too stuck on what she said before that to answer her.

Yet all she's telling me is in the past, so far in the past I barely even remembered it until my life got turned upside down by Cross' decision to make the MC only about running guns from now on.

It all came back to me the second I saw her, but that doesn't change much.

"Well, it's true," she says and smiles faintly. "And I hoped this dinner would go better than this, but I can't. Just thinking about having sex gives me a panic attack. If I had to do it, I'd probably have a heart attack. I think I just already had all the sex I was meant to have."

She chuckles darkly at her own joke, the sound the exact opposite of her giggles, which I loved listening to back then.

"I'm not gonna lie, Lynn. That's not exactly what I hoped to hear tonight," I say. "But I guess it's my fault for being a big pussy and not asking you out when I had the chance. I figured you finally fixed that by asking me out earlier, but…"

I should've stopped talking long before now, and I finally do when I notice the sad expression on her face.

"I can't," she says in such a soft voice, I barely hear it, and I'm not sure I was meant to either.

"It's alright, Lynn, don't worry about it, " I say and toss a couple of dollars for the tip on the table.

"We're not the people we were back then," I add and get up.

She nods and clutches her purse to her chest as she stands up too. I follow her outside where the gusts of wind are strong enough to seriously shift her skirt to and fro, giving me glimpses of her thighs, not just her calves, and I wish I could just enjoy the sight of her bare legs without all the extras.

I like to keep my life simple. Lynn is a complication. She was a complication from the moment I saw her. I never had any idea what to do with her, just as I don't right now.

She turns to me suddenly as we reach her car and I almost run right into her. I like being close to her. The closer, the better. That part of things was always easy and simple to figure out. The rest, not so much.

"We could use some help at the ranch for the next couple of days," she says breathlessly, her eyes very wide, but not in that scared way. More in an excited, I can't believe I just said that way. "I realize this dinner didn't go so well, but I'd still like to see more of you now that we reconnected."

I grin a little, can't help it. "Or you just need someone to scare off all those cowboys up there at the ranch?"

She blushes a soft pink, but then smiles slyly, the way she always would before saying something funny. "There's that too, if you wouldn't mind."

"I wouldn't mind at all," I say and grin even wider.

It's scaring off other guys I'm agreeing to, not so much the actual ranch work. I don't know the first thing about working on a ranch, but I'm sure she'll teach me, and I'd love to learn from her.

I over-complicated things in my brain with all that thinking before. Lynn and me, we're probably never gonna fuck, but I like spending time with her so that's all good too.

Between her saying I'm the one guy she's been longing to see again, the way she keeps smiling at me, her saying I'm like her goddam prince savior over and over again, and how dressed up she got for this dinner, I let my dick get ahead of my brain. And it wouldn't hear reason even after she told me it was impossible. But I got it back in check now.

"OK, I'll see you tomorrow morning at eight," she says and unlocks her car, then lets me hold the door open as she slips inside as gracefully as any doe I've ever seen.

"Yes, you will," I say and she smiles and I grin back and then close the car door, because she's already got the keys in the ignition.

That was simple. A simple request that was simple to say yes to. I want to see her again. And what could be simpler than that?

All those other things, they're not gonna go away by thinking or talking about them, so why bother?

LYNN

That dinner was a disaster! I went in there thinking I'd let him take me home, or at least let him kiss me goodnight, but the problem was, I kept thinking about it. So by the time he suggested we go somewhere private, I was on the verge of a full blown panic attack. I froze when he mentioned going to my house, just like I always do, and he couldn't wait to get out of the restaurant after that. Forget Miss Illinois, I was Miss Mixed Signals tonight. No wonder he got pissed.

But I can't be with him. Not that way. Not yet.

No, not ever.

I can't stand being touched by a man. I'd just go right back into that black hole in my mind where I hid so I could forget and recover. I won't risk that.

Trying to explain that to him didn't go very well either. Few people understand what it's like, and I guess a huge, muscled, scarred biker is probably very low on the list. But I never saw him as just that.

By the time we were walking to my car, I wasn't even thinking about any of that anymore. I was just hoping for a do-over to the whole thing. I messed up and he was leaving, and I didn't want to never see him again, but we were heading down that road fast.

I still can't believe that after all that, I just asked him to come help at the ranch, just like that. And that he said yes, just like that. Simple and natural. Better than I hoped for. I wish everything between us was that simple all the time. I wish there was no need for hard conversations. But the rest—other than joking and laughing and talking and spending platonic time together—is impossible for us.

Thank God, he said yes to my request or my heart would probably hammer right out of my chest in that parking lot.

The living room light in my house is on. I'm sure Mom is waiting for me to get home and will wait until I do. I drive past the house, because my face is hot, I'm breathing fast, and I know Mom would know in a second that I'm not returning from a quick dinner with Tammy. I'm not yet ready to talk to her about Scar.

My mind is whirling in a thousand different directions right now and none of them make much sense. I was always so unsure about my feelings for him, but at the same time, deep down, I was always very sure. I haven't forgotten him, and it's all coming back to me now. Along with every second of the failed dinner we just had.

Maybe I shouldn't have told him the truth about me and men. Maybe that was too much. But he's coming to the ranch tomorrow, so maybe it wasn't too much?

I told him, because he's easy to talk to and I could always tell him anything. But also, because he's the only person who knows. Knows exactly what I went through, because he saw me at the bottom, saw the room I was locked up in, saw the bruises and the blood and my filthy naked body. I was just a thing when he found me, a well-used thing nearing the end of her usefulness. Like a sofa that needs to be replaced.

Even my mom didn't see that, because the ER nurses cleaned me up before she was notified that I was rescued. Scar also knows, because that's his world and I'm sure he's seen it all before and probably since.

My mom can't talk about it, and I'm sick of explaining it to psychiatrists, because I can't stand their pity. I also don't want to take the pills they keep prescribing. We all know that the only cure for me would be amnesia, or something else that would make me forget it all. I need to just wake up one day not knowing who I am. I mentioned that to my last shrink and she almost had me committed, because she was afraid I was suicidal. I'm not. I appreciate this gift of life that was restored to me. But if I could give the memories back, I would.

I'm driving too fast, but I'm on an empty road going up into the hills that I know very well. I'll stop once I get to the top. Then I'll sit there and look down at the valley where I live, watch the lights twinkling below me and the stars sparkling above me, until I once again remember that the world is full of beauty that's worth living for, and that appreciating it is enough.

After half an hour of sitting in the grass by my car on top of the hill, the sparkling, peaceful world all around me works its magic. My thoughts are no longer a runaway train in my brain.

Scar is the only person apart from my mom who knows me from before, who remembers me as I was. My mom doesn't remember that girl anymore, and I hardly do either. But I think Scar remembers her very well, and maybe, just maybe he can bring her back, so I'll see her again too.

There's such a tiny chance of that!

Besides, it's a whimsical, poetic and naive wish of the kind my head was full of once upon a time, back when I still sorta believed that I could actually help save the world, if I was crowned Miss Illinois.

These days I can't even save myself, and I've stopped trying. But I want to try again. And somehow, under this blanket of stars, on this night, with the promise of seeing the only man I ever fell in love with tomorrow, I kind of feel like I'll succeed this time.

6

SCAR

Lynn's a gorgeous woman and I'm happy just looking at her. It was the same back then, when the MC was stuck in her town on a job for over a month. I visited her diner at least once a day after I saw her working there. My favorite times were when it was empty so we were alone. We watched TV together, but mostly I just watched her. Should've watched her more closely. But maybe I can make up for that now. After I figured that out, I could fall asleep easily, but before that I kept tossing and turning and cursing my luck for only getting her after she'd already been used up and spent.

Only thing is, I don't know the first thing about ranch work. I had a couple of dogs growing up, and I know a lot about hunting animals—tracking them in the wild for days and then killing them, even skinning them afterwards—but taking care of them, not so much.

I don't want to make a complete fool of myself today. So I've been waiting for Doc in his office since dawn. I know he likes to come in here and prepare everything right after breakfast, which he eats early. I could go find him in the dining room, but I'd prefer to keep this meeting private because my patience for the brothers' jokes at my expense is thin at the best of times.

Doc was a farm boy from Texas before he went to war as an army doctor, which was all long before he joined the MC. I hope he can give me some pointers about cows and horses and such.

"Scar? I didn't know you were waiting for me," he says as he finally walks into the infirmary, as he wants us to call the huge ass room on the ground floor that he transformed into a futuristic doctor's office over the years. Good thing he did, since the MC's been throwing a lot of work his way, and he's good at patching us up. We're lucky to have him.

"Your arm been bothering you?" he asks, while I'm still deciding how to ask what I need to know.

I cleared it with Cross that I might be away for a couple of days last night. He didn't ask for my reasons, so I didn't give them. But he's the only brother I can trust not to poke fun at me when they find out what those reasons are. Good natured poking fun, but still annoying as hell. Especially since that whole beauty queen and monster fairytale ain't happening anytime soon, going by the beauty queen's belief that she's had all the sex she was meant to have. It's good she can find humor in it, even if it's a very dark kind. I can't find much humor in anything, let alone that.

But ranch work is sweaty, hands-on business, so who knows, maybe she'll change her beliefs. A guy can hope...

I flex the arm I got stabbed in while we were rescuing Ice

and taking Lizard with us. "Nah, it's pretty much healed. Just throbs sometimes when the weather's bad."

"That was a million dollar wound," Doc says as he goes about tidying up the already very tidy counter by one of the walls. "A centimeter to the left and you'd have lost the use of your arm for good. If the nerve had been severed and not just nicked—"

I don't exactly know how big a centimeter is, but judging by the way he uses the word, I assume it's very small.

"Let's be thankful it happened how it did and stop talking about it," I say more harshly than I wanted to, mainly because knives and cuts are like my kryptonite, have been my whole life, and I still get nightmares of choking on my own blood as I die from a knife wound. Besides, saying I'm lucky when it comes to wounds is too stupid an exaggeration to even grace with a comeback.

"Alright, then why are you here?" Doc asks, equally harshly since my tone clearly didn't sit well with him. He's got a temper, our good doctor does, and I sometimes forget that. I'm also going about this all wrong, since I wanted him in a good mood, but that ship has now sailed.

"I'm helping a friend on a ranch today," I say. "And seeing as I know nothing about livestock and you grew up on a farm, I was hoping you'd give me some pointers."

"A friend, huh?" he says and grins. And he doesn't have to say anything more to make it clear the beauty queen story has reached him too.

"Do I know him?" he adds, but I know full well he knows it's a she.

He was still patching up soldiers in some war when we rescued Lynn, else I might have brought her to him to fix. Tank's been pretty excited over the prospect of me reuniting with her, and he's been telling the whole MC about it. I guess even that pretty red-headed girlfriend of his can't rein him in completely.

"Yeah, OK, it's my beauty queen friend, what of it?"

"Nothing, I'm just asking," he says, throwing his hands up as though in surrender. "Ranch work, you say? Makes perfect sense that you volunteered for it. I'd wrestle a bull for a beauty queen any day, though I don't recommend it."

His eyes glaze over like he's remembering doing just that.

"No bulls, I hope," I tell him. "Just a bunch of goats and some horses and such. I think I saw some cows too."

"And I take it you've never worked with any of those before?" he asks, grinning at me.

I shake my head.

"In that case, I'd suggest you don't start now," he says and laughs, but stops when he glances at my face and sees what must be a very murderous look on there.

"Fine, fine, my serious advice would be to let her take the lead and show you the ropes," he says, just a shadow of a grin still on his face. "It'll bring you closer, if nothing else. But in general, just do easy shit like digging holes and general shoveling stuff. You won't make too much of a fool of yourself doing that."

I nod because he's right and it's sound advice. Doc can always be counted on to give sound advice.

"It would take years for me to explain to you how to handle livestock like a born cowboy," he goes on. "But as a general rule of thumb, you gotta let the animals know who's boss. That means you show no fear, and no pussyfooting around them either. Knowing you, that shouldn't be much of an issue. Just treat them as you do anyone you're trying to get something out of. No causing extreme pain, but a little goes a long way, which you, of course, already know."

He's right. I might be the club's torturer, but I avoid going to extremes. Nine times out of ten, the fear of extreme pain is the better way of getting info than actual pain. Once you hurt them bad, their info turns more useless too. The guy who taught me all I know told me that too, and he was right. My face and the stories people tell of me are enough to have guys shaking. I don't have to do much to get them talking once they're alone in the room with me. And it's not exactly that I'll miss the work now that we won't be having so much need for it, it's just that I'm good at it, and I'm not good at much else.

"Show 'em who's boss and no fear. Sounds like good advice," I say and hop off the examination table where I've been lounging.

"And let her teach you," he adds. "That should be enough to get things rolling."

"There's also that hope," I say then leave.

It's almost seven thirty. I need to hit the road if I'm gonna be on time to meet Lynn. Doc didn't have a whole lotta advice for me, but what little he gave me, I plan on following. Because I'd like to spend a whole lot of time with Lynn, and if it's sweaty, hands-on time, so much the better.

LYNN

I've been at the ranch since seven fifteen, waiting for Scar to arrive. I only went into the house to say good morning to everyone and tell them a friend of mine will be helping out today. Then I came right back out to wait for him before they could ask any questions. Now it's almost eight, and he's not here yet.

I'm starting to worry he won't show, which I'd like to believe wouldn't be like him, but I really don't know him that well. Back when I still worked at that diner, he showed up like clockwork at three PM or ten PM, when it was slowest. Sometimes it was just the two of us in there for hours, since most of the afternoon shift was so dead, even the cook went home to nap on most days. We'd sit at the bar, watch TV and he'd listen to me talk about myself, my next pageant, and later also about how I didn't really want to be a supermodel anymore, how I wanted to work with animals, how I sometimes felt like I was just doing the beauty queen stuff to make my mom happy.

I'd just found out there was a vet technician program at the local community college when we met, and I told him about wanting to attend that too, even before I told my mom about it. A huge part of the reason why I took the job at the diner was so I'd have some funds of my own when I decided to tell her that I wanted out of the beauty pageant sphere. I think I was too hard on her at the time, she would've supported me in that decision just like she's always supported me in everything else. Scar listened like he cared, so I kept talking even after I realized he wasn't quite so open about his own life.

The rumbling of a Harley approaching brings me back to the present, and my fear of the sound is mixing with the giddy excitement that he didn't go back out on his word after all. *Or is that because I'll see him again in a minute?*

I can't answer that question so I ignore it.

"I'm not late, am I?" he asks in answer to my greeting as he parks the bike next to me and gets off.

He's wearing an old denim shirt which has seen better days, the sleeves rolled up to his elbows, showing off his forearms. I always liked looking at guys' forearms, and their hands, but that was so long ago, I'm remembering it as though through a sheet of fog.

"You still half asleep or what?" he asks, grinning at me as he takes off his leather sleeveless jacket — his cut, is what it's called — and puts it into one of the saddlebags on his bike.

"Sorry," I say and shake my head like that'll help dispel the fog in my brain, which is now parting and showing me glimpses of other things I used to like too, besides guys' arms. "You're right on time. I'll introduce you to the others and then we can get started."

He nods, but walks closer to me and not in the direction of the house. It's a rush, this way he looks at me, like me and him are the only two people in the world and he likes it just fine that way. I used to feel that way around him back then too. And I liked it. I like it now too. Although the thick dark clouds that are my fear of that kind of thing are roiling angrily just behind the fog showing me these things.

"About that..." he says and pauses for effect, or maybe it's to wait for my eyes to focus on his. I manage it by ignoring the rest.

"I don't want people knowing who I really am," he adds.

"That should be easy, you never told me much about yourself," I say, because kidding with him comes easy too. But his face tightens into a very hard expression, telling me this is a subject he's serious about.

"Don't worry, no one here knows anything about my past either. No one except me, you and my mom do," I say growing more serious too the longer I speak. "I was going to ask you not to tell them anything about me either, or about how we know each other. I just told them you're my friend from way back."

He grins, the tightness gone from his face.

"I didn't mean to get harsh with you over it," he says, and I know he means it, but kinda not, too. He always got this way when I tried to ask him about his life and never told me anything. "I won't tell anyone anything. But that's not all I wanted to ask you…"

He pauses again, and this time it's purely for effect because I'm looking at him as intently as I rarely do at people. I nod to encourage him to keep talking.

"I don't actually know jack shit about helping out on a ranch," he says and chuckles. "I said yes because it was you asking, but honestly, I don't know if I'm gonna be a whole lotta help. Except if you just need help shifting some heavy objects. I'm pretty good at that."

I don't doubt it, and my gaze shifts from his forearms up to his bulky upper arms, the muscles of which aren't hidden by the shirt he's wearing at all. His back is wide and his chest is wide too. I bet he's as strong as an ox.

There's a very soft, questioning look in his meadow green eyes when mine finally meet them again, but that softness is hiding something sharp, dark and dangerous. His eyes are like a cat's, a big predatory cat's. Warm and inviting, but so very dangerous underneath that.

"You guys coming in or what?" Tammy yells from the doorway to the house. I shake from being startled, he just chuckles.

"Yes!" I yell back, grab his forearm and start leading him to the house.

Only I freeze before I even take the first step, and he's kinda rigid too. I release his arm like it burned me. I used to be very feely with my hands, and used to touch people when I spoke to them all the time. But I haven't been doing that anymore for the last twelve years, and I certainly haven't touched a guy like that in all that time. In fact, he might have been the last guy I touched like this. And here I am doing it like it's no thing. Like it's perfectly natural for me to do it. That deserves a pause.

But I have no idea if it means anything, because I'm still petrified of getting touched in return.

7

LYNN

Scar wasn't exaggerating about having no skills whatsoever in working with animals. He tried his best though and didn't complain at all. I liked having him by my side as I exercised the horses that were brought in yesterday and fed the goats. Thankfully, we got no new animals today, because we're still trying to properly house the ones we do have.

Only half of the volunteers that were here yesterday showed up, but the cowboy with the hots for me was one of them. He told me he came in on his day off to help me, but left quickly enough when he spotted Scar already doing that. In the end, I tasked Scar with distributing hay to all the barns that needed extra and that job he excelled at.

It's late afternoon now and most of the volunteers have already left. Scar's leaning on the fence of the goat pen, watching me replace the water, his shirt dirty and unbuttoned and hay sticking out of his hair. It's sticking to his chest too and his abs, which look like someone took chisel to stone to create them. I wonder if they're as hard to the touch as they look.

At the same time, I'm trying not to wonder that, because it's bringing in the black memories of being held down by men that seemed heavier than a slab of marble at the time. Most of them looked like Scar too. But they weren't him, and those memories aren't so very black right now, they're just kinda grey, and my hands aren't even shaking from having them.

He doesn't know I've seen him come up to the fence, but I did, and I kinda wish he was closer still, as in, right by my side.

"Got any more pressing tasks for me?" he asks suddenly, and something in his voice tells me he knows I've been watching him this whole time.

But I still pretend he surprised me as I turn to him. "We're pretty much done for the day. I'm just finishing up here, then I'll take the dogs for a walk and that's it."

"Cool, I'll come with you," he says. "I know dogs."

The way he says it suggests he knows nothing about any other animal.

"You'll learn," I say and pet the goat that's closest to me. It's the same one I was trying to house when he came here yesterday. "Animals are easy to work with."

"Yeah, for you they are. You're calm and patient, and just really pleasant all around. Animals sense that kinda thing," he says and sounds completely sincere, not like he's laying it on thick to flatter me. But it is very flattering to hear him say it. He moves to open the fence for me so I can come out to meet him. "Me, I'm just rough all the way and the animals know that too. I'd need a lot more practice."

"Good, you'll get it," I say and smile at him. "You're coming again tomorrow, right?"

He winces in an exaggerated way, but doesn't stop smiling at me with his eyes.

"Right?" I repeat myself, since he's not answering.

"If you ask me to real nice, I will," he finally says. He means ask as in with more than just words. And that scares me, it bothers me, makes my heart race, my breath get stuck in my throat and my palms cold and clammy. But it doesn't bother me as much as it did last night, and not as much as it has with every other man for the last twelve years.

I clear my throat because I froze up a little again. Maybe he didn't mean it like that, maybe I just heard that because my mind isn't healed and thinks every man just wants to use me for sex. I don't want him to run away from me again like he tried to last night.

"Pretty please, will you come help out tomorrow?" I say and give him a smile to match my words—sweet and warm, and just a little flirty—and he doesn't have to say anything for me to know how much he likes that smile, it's written all over his face, he even groaned a little.

"When you put it that way, how can I say no?" he says and grins. "Now, let's go walk those dogs. Then I'll need to be fed too, because I'm fucking starving."

Last night's dinner was a disaster, and I think tonight's would be too if we tried again. But I ignore that thought just like I would any other bad one, smile at him and finally walk out of the pen so he can replace the latch. I just nod and don't say anything, because I'll just make an excuse if I do, and I don't want to do that.

He doesn't say anything either, but follows so close behind I can smell him, and it's making me wish it'd be easy for me to give in to his advances. But it's not easy. It will never be easy for me. They broke something inside me, those men who held me captive and raped me, something that can't be fixed, something I can't ignore.

"Those are some vicious looking beasts," Scar says as we reach the kennel and he sees the three German shepherds, one Rottweiler and one mix between the two — Scrap, which I raised up from a pup— that constitute our dog family. "Do you walk them one at a time?"

There's concern in his voice, and he's eying the dogs warily. I don't know why he's panicking, since the dogs are all wagging their tails and squealing happily.

"No, all at the same time," I say and grin over my shoulder. "They're the sweetest creatures."

"If you say so," he says and keeps a good distance from the door as I unlock it.

"I'll introduce you to them," I say. "Come closer."

"This is Lucy," I say, letting out the Rottweiler first, since she's the boss. "She's their leader when I'm not around."

"Leader of the pack, is that what you are?" Scar asks me and laughs like it's the most surprising thing in the world.

"That's me," I say and giggle, as he lets Lucy get a good whiff of his fingers before petting her.

He's wary of the dogs, but not scared of them. I can see that plain in his stance. He'd take them all on and he's sure he'd win, but he'd rather avoid it. I admire that kind of confidence. I wish I had more of it. And I suppose that also makes him a smart guy, but there's no need to be wary with this bunch. They may look scary, but they're pretty much just lap dogs.

I let out the other ones—Fido, Butch, Scrap and Dolly—and

he repeats the getting acquainted process with each. Lucy took to him, so the rest do too, although Scrap and Dolly keep their distance, as we start walking towards the trees. They're wary of people they don't know, especially Scrap who I suspect someone just released into the wild near the ranch before he was anywhere near ready to be out on his own. He was skin and bones when I found him.

"How does this place work?" Scar asks once we exit through the wooden fence that surrounds the property. "Do you just rent the stables out or what?"

I shake my head. "No, we're a shelter. We take in unwanted animals, although we just haven't had the funds to keep more than the dogs, Milly the Goat and Ricky the Donkey for a long time. Apart from the odd injured fox or bird or hedgehog and such, that is."

"But now you have a full house. How come?" he asks.

"Because of the wildfires," I say. "Their projected path will pass us by miles, but most of the bigger ranches in the area are in its direct path. Most fires miss us, since there's such a huge gap between the houses and the trees here and we're in a bit of a valley. We have plenty of room, so we rent the place out to those threatened by the fires."

He's nodding along while I talk like he's genuinely interested, but I'm growing more and more aware of the fact that I'm alone with a man and going deeper into the woods. The dogs all bounded off into the trees as soon as we reached them. Maybe they'll come if I call them and maybe they won't. They usually do. But either way, I doubt they'll protect me from him. They're neither guard dogs nor attack dogs. They're pretty much just pets because that's how I raised them.

I don't know why I'm suddenly so afraid. This is the man

who saved me from the bad men who broke me. I don't want to fear him, I want to enjoy myself with him like I used to—like I know we could—but the dark stormy clouds of my fear aren't just in my head right now. They're all around us, making the world bleak and frightful, even though the setting sun is still filtering through the branches overhead. My heart's beating so fast I can feel it in my throat, I'm growing nauseous, and I see the world as though twilight has already fallen.

"Why'd we stop?" Scar asks, his voice sounding very distant. But it's loud enough to make me realize I did in fact stop, and that I have no idea why.

"Do you wanna head back?" he adds, and as I finally focus my eyes on his, I know he's asking me a lot more than that. They're predatory right now, belying the casual way he asked the question. He knows I'm scared. And he knows I'm scared of him. I don't want him to know that!

"I—" my, "I don't know" is interrupted by a blood freezing whine from one of the dogs.

"What the hell?" he asks and turns to the sound that originated from just beyond a ridge ahead of us. My heart is thumping faster than ever. Now whimpering is coming from there, joined by the barking of the other dogs.

"We gotta go see what happened," he says and his clear instruction finally breaks through my black-shrouded trance of fear.

"Yeah, we should," I say in a shaky voice and follow him to the ridge.

As soon as I see poor Scrap caught in something, blood spraying from his leg as he thrashes around all my other fears disappear, replaced by only a heart-wrenching need to stop the dog's suffering.

Scar reaches the dogs before I do, which wasn't good because all the uninjured ones are there now, standing around Scrap and guarding him. They may be pets but they are a pack. Lucy, their leader, is growling at Scar who luckily saw the danger in time and stopped in his approach.

"Down, Lucy!" I say and thankfully my voice has the command necessary for her to heed it.

She stops growling and allows us to pass her to reach Scrap.

"He's caught in an old bear trap, look," Scar points out, but I already saw it. Over the years, we cleared a lot of these traps—the remnants of a crueler time in these woods — but clearly we haven't gotten all of them.

"We need to get him out," I say and Scar reacts immediately, getting too close to Scrap who's clearly in a lot of pain and very scared.

"Motherfucker!" Scar hisses and lunges back as the dog's teeth graze his arm.

"Careful!" I screech quite needlessly and rush to check Scar's wound. "How bad is it?"

Dark red blood is oozing from the gash on his left forearm.

"It's just a scratch. Let's get the dog out," he says, and I know he must be in pain and is hiding it. The fact that I have to be reminded to save the dog before I take care of Scar's wound says something too. Normally, I'd see nothing and no one but the injured animal that needs my help, and here I am, needing to be told to do it.

"OK, yes," I say, my hands shaking, which never happens when there's an animal to be helped. "I'll get his head and calm him, and you try to open the trap to free him.

Scrap is whimpering again, Lucy whining at me to help him, the other three dogs following her lead.

"Yes, let's try it that way," Scar says and grins at me. "My way obviously didn't work."

I can't believe he can joke as though the dog didn't just rip his arm open, but his calmness calms me too, so I'm able to hold Scrap and soothe him while Scar struggles to open the trap.

"Damn rusted thing," he complains, his injured arm shaking, so I know he's in pain. But I also know he'll work through it and get the job done. There's no doubt in my mind that he'll help me fix this no matter what, that he'll stay by my side helping me until the problem is solved. I have no idea how I know this, but the knowledge comes from somewhere deep inside.

"We're almost there," he says through gritted teeth. "Hold him well now, he might jerk and bite again."

I keep speaking soothingly to Scrap, locking eyes with him as I grip his head. He screams again, his eyes begging me to make the pain go away, as Scar finally manages to get the rusty trap open, a part of it breaking off from the force of his pull.

Once he's freed, Scrap tries to stand amid more whimpers and screams and I let go of him. Scar pulls me to my feet and out of the way of the thrashing Scrap, who wants to but can't regain his feet. Scared, injured animals are the most dangerous and I do know that, but sometimes I forget, especially with my little pack here, since I've been taking care of them for so long. And especially with Scrap, who's like my baby.

Scar keeps his uninjured arm locked around my waist, and I like the pressure, like the safety of his body behind me to shield me, like the fact that he's here so I can lean on him and let him support me. Like it right up until the second I fully realize it's happening.

Then the fear of being trapped explodes in my mind. I rip

myself from his embrace, my fear so clear and strong that Lucy starts growling and baring her teeth at him.

"Easy, dog," Scar says and kinda sounds like he's growling too.

"Down, Lucy," I say and she heeds *me*. Scar's eyes are very angry as I finally meet them.

In front of us, Scrap is still trying and failing to stand and blood is gushing from the wound on his hind leg.

"Get the other dogs away from here, and I'll carry this one back to the ranch," Scar says.

"But your arm…" I protest.

"It's fine," he assures me in a cold, determined voice in which there is no sign of a grin, let alone a smile.

This is no time to argue. Scrap needs help now.

"I'll get Tammy and Raul to help you," I say and call the dogs, then lead them at a run away from Scar and Scrap. I start running even faster once I clear the ridge, because I'm pretty sure Scar bit off more than he can chew with his offer to carry Scrap. I need to return with Tammy and Raul, and maybe some tranquilizers, as soon as I can. Thank God we didn't go far into the woods.

Bethany, Tammy and Raul all come running when I call for them as I reach the fence around the ranch.

I explain in as few words as I can about what happened. Raul takes off into the woods right after I'm done talking.

"I'll get everything ready. Poor Scrap will probably need stitches. Maybe he even has a broken bone. I hate those traps, they're an absolute horror," Tammy says, rolling up her sleeves as she heads for the mobile building she uses as her infirmary. "You go back and help Raul since Scrap knows you so well."

"OK, yes," I say as I overtake her and Bethany on the way to it, so I can get the tranquilizers, and the first aid kit for Scar's arm.

I leave them inside to ready the place for Scrap as soon as I get all that, but Scar and Raul are already making their way out of the woods before I even reach the fence. Scar is carrying Scrap, blood dripping down his arm, and I don't know if it's his or the dogs. Either way, there's a lot of it and my heart is racing again.

"Where do you want him?" Scar asks when they reach me, an edge still in his voice, but maybe that has nothing to do with the way I ripped myself from his arms and all to do with the rip in his arm.

"Just over here," I say and lead the way.

Tammy gasps when she sees Scrap's wound, instructs Scar where to put the dog and gets to work. Bethany and Raul help her, but all I'm thinking about is cleaning Scar's wound.

Behind me, my precious Scrap, my baby, is whining in pain, and here I am, locking eyes with a man whose well-being is more important to me. It makes no sense.

"Go help the dog," he says and grins. "I'll be fine."

"No," I say and walk past him towards the smaller room in the back of the building where Tammy keeps the supplies. "Come."

He follows obediently, sits in the chair and puts his arm up where I showed him to, but his eyes are all for me and he keeps smiling. Something inside me is quivering excitedly and warmly under that smile, and from his closeness, and it could just be the aftereffects of the shock, but I'm not sure that's it...

"Owww!" he yelps as I pour saline solution over the bite to clean it. I whimper and jump back, my whole body shaking. But he's grinning mischievously at me as I look at him in fright.

"Just kidding," he says and grins wider. "It's a scratch, just put a bandage over it."

"It's not just a scratch," I say defiantly. "It's still bleeding and it probably needs stitches. I have to disinfect it properly, at least."

"If it'll make you feel better," he says and barely winces as I switch to alcohol to clean the bite. I know it stings, can see it from the way his breathing is deep and his eyes grow angrier, but it needs to be done. Dog bites are the worst when it comes to infections, and if he won't go to the hospital, I need to do what I can.

"I think the bleeding is stopping now," I say as I place a piece of gauze over it gently, then start wrapping a bandage around it equally gently, making up for using all that disinfectant before. "That's a good sign."

He doesn't respond, just watches me tie off the bandage.

I finally look up at him, the quivering deep inside me growing worse the longer we lock eyes. "You'll be fine now, I think."

"Mhm," he grunts in response.

The quivering inside me reaching fever pitch and its cause are his eyes, and this charged air between us which is so hot and disturbed right now it feels like I'm sitting next to a fire.

He grabs the back of my head with no warning, pulls me closer and kisses me hard, and the second his lips touch mine, all that quivering explodes in a shower of happiness and bliss inside me. But the next second, devastating lightning bolts are crashing from the thunderclouds of my fear.

When I finally regain full awareness of my surroundings, I'm way at the other side of the room, leaning against the wall, clutching my arms over my chest and shaking. He's standing in the doorway, silhouetted by the purple and black light of sunset.

"I'm gonna take off now," he says in a calm, timeless sort of voice. "Goodbye, Lynn."

There's such finality in his voice I start shaking worse.

"Will you be here tomorrow?" I ask, even though I'm sure the answer's no.

"What's the point?" he asks and I know what he means. He means, what's the point if I won't let him touch me or kiss me or fuck me.

"You're fucking terrified of being alone with me, and that's not my idea of a good time," he adds, proving me wrong and not at the same time.

I don't know what to say and after a couple of seconds of waiting, he shakes his head and leaves.

A part of me wants to rush after him, apologize, beg him to stay, to come back tomorrow. But another part is very angry and it's clearer and louder and makes more sense.

Who the hell does he think he is?

You don't just grab a woman and kiss her without permission. And you don't get that angry when she pushes you away. Especially if it's a woman who endured what I endured.

Scar's just a brute, and all that safety I feel around him is because he's so damn big and strong and brave.

I can't even stand being touched by a man, let alone get dominated by one ever again. That's what he'd try to do. I know it. Back when we first met I knew it too and kinda wanted it that way, but now, I wouldn't survive it. I'd just lose my mind like I did back then.

It's good that he's gone. It's for the best if he never comes back.

But a tiny part of me wishes he would come back and kiss me again. Because for the split second I let myself feel it, that kiss was out of this world, better than any I ever had, and better than I imagined it could be, back when I still imagined things like that.

8

SCAR

"Come take a look at something," I bark at Doc who's just finishing up his dinner in the dining room. Cross, Roxie and Lily are having theirs too, way on the other side of the room. Roxie looks at me like she's about to say something, but doesn't once she spots my bandage.

"What the hell happened?" Doc asks with his mouth full, staring at the bandage on my arm. Blood seeped through while I rode back, and despite what I told Lynn, I know that it's more than a scratch. But fuck her. Well, I wish I could, but that's not gonna happen.

I gave it one last shot, but it's all inviting looks followed by a-don't-you-dare-touch-me attitude with her and a crap ton of mixed messages in between. She was scared of me when we were in the woods together. She fought me off like an injured animal when I kissed her. I might as well cut my losses while I'm ahead.

"Finish your dinner and meet me at the infirmary," I say and walk back out the room.

Cross looked my way when I spoke to Doc, glanced at the bloody bandage on my arm then at me and went right on eating. He'll want to know what happened later, but for now he's content that I'm handling it and he, for one, never asks needless questions at the wrong time. It's why I'd follow him anywhere and lay my life on the line for him anytime. Which might happen sooner rather than later, since I'm an accident prone motherfucker. I was born that way.

"Scar, wait up," Doc calls after me, jogging to catch up. "It looks bad. What happened? Was it a bull?"

He chuckles as he asks the last question, but turns serious as he glances at my face. I'm not in a good mood tonight. Not even close. Mostly because my cock is still throbbing from that kiss I wish Lynn had returned for longer than half a second, and the dog bite is starting to throb now too.

Being in pain always makes me want to fuck. And right now, no other woman but Lynn will do. At least, I'm not riding anywhere else tonight for anyone else other than her. But she doesn't want it that way, she made that clear now.

"Dog bite," I say through gritted teeth and continue striding towards the infirmary.

He overtakes me and has the glaring white lights on before I even walk in. This place always smells like a hospital, and I hate the smell, especially when it's mixed with the smell of blood. It always reminds me of the day they stitched up my face. You'd think I'd be over it by now, after all the blood I've bled and let from others, but I guess you never forget your first.

The smell grows worse as Doc opens up a bottle of peroxide.

"Let me see," he says and I sit down next to the examination table, since I'm in no mood for lying down on it.

"She wrapped it up pretty well, that beauty queen of yours," he muses as he slowly unwraps my bandage.

"Shut up and do your thing," I snap, since I'm in no mood for anyone's wisecracks either.

He glances at me, turns serious and gets back to work in silence. My arm is throbbing from the bite, especially once the cold air hits it, but I hardly feel it over my anger.

I always get angry when I don't get what I want, be it sex, money or information from someone. It helps with my job. And I wanted Lynn very much for a very, very long time, but couldn't have her, and I only fully realized that the second I kissed her. Lizard took her away from me twelve years ago, so I let it go because I had no choice. But now she's free, and she's here and I'm here, and she's more fucking gorgeous than ever and...what? She pushes me away when I try to kiss her after doing her best to spend lots of time with me and checking me out all day.

Doc clears his throat and looks up at me from examining the bite. "I want to stitch this up, but since it's a dog bite I don't wanna take any chances. I'm gonna disinfect it first and it's going to hurt. You want something for the pain?"

I grimace at him. "Yeah, right, when have I ever needed something for the pain? Just do it."

The pain's gonna be a nice distraction from my anger at Lynn. I didn't even wait for her to say no outright, just like I didn't last night after that dinner, because I don't wanna hear it. Especially now that I know how much I want her. But I already knew the answer was no, because I could smell fear on her when we were alone in the woods. And later when I held her for a second too long.

Doc got a silver-colored basin from somewhere and tells me to put my arm into it. He doesn't say anything, just glances up at me right before pouring what feels like liquid fire over my wound. It burns so bad I'm surprised not to see melted flesh when the pain finally lets up. But I make no sound. I'm used to pain, we're old buds.

"Ten stiches will do it, I think," he muses as he gets to work, producing a curved needle and black thread.

I look away. I can't stand the sight of that black thread. I got enough of looking at it all over my face.

"So apart from this mishap, how did it go today?" he asks after awhile.

"I should've given it a miss," I say truthfully, since even my anger is now dulled by the sleepy aftermath that extreme pain always brings. "She's not interested."

I said it more for my own benefit so I'd hear it said out loud and make it more of a fact that way, but he perks up.

"Yeah, I heard what the Spawns did to her and how you rescued her," he says. "Figures she'd be messed up from it."

"What, you've all been sitting around gossiping about me and Lynn all day like a bunch of hens?" I snap.

He shakes his head as he finalizes the last stitch. "Roxie told me the story. She was real happy to hear that woman was OK. Apparently she remembers the abduction, since it was in her home town, and it shocked her very much at the time. Especially since no one was punished for it."

"Yeah, well, they've been punished now," I say. "As for Lynn being OK, that's a stretch."

Doc nods thoughtfully again then starts bandaging up my arm. "Complex PTSD probably. You're generally OK and can function normally, but there's triggers that can send you spiraling out of control without warning. Most psychiatrists don't know how to treat it, which is why she might still be suffering the aftereffects of what she went through."

"So now you're a shrink too?" I snap. "It all sounds like mumbo jumbo to me."

"I'm not a shrink, but I have personal experience with it," he says rather defensively. "I'm just saying, she probably needs patience. Not sure you're the guy to give it to her though."

He's right. I have no patience for women, especially not ones that reek of fear when they're alone with me, and push me away when I kiss them. Life's too short for that kinda crap.

"She needs to figure out what she wants, that's all," I say and get up since he's done with my arm. "Any more advice, or can I go?"

He shrugs. "Keep the bandage clean and I'll take your stitches out in seven days. Try not to rip them by bumping into anything."

There's some sort of a double meaning in that, but I don't get it. Why the hell would I bump into anything? It's certainly not gonna be Lynn, if that's what he's implying.

I'm staying right here until my arm heals, and I'm certainly not gonna rake up any more of my past. It's always better for the past to stay forgotten. You'd think I'd know that by now.

LYNN

I stayed up with Scrap until past midnight, petting him and keeping him company because he just wouldn't fall asleep. His leg got ripped up badly by the trap, and the bone was broken too. Tammy said it was a clean break and would heel just fine, but I still worried. So worried, I called my mom and told her I was spending the night at the ranch.

Poor Scrap has been through so much. It was touch and go for awhile when he first came to us here, especially since he was so scared of people it took a whole month of coaxing before I was able to pet him. We left him food all over the forest around here, which is how he got his name, since he stayed alive on scraps. I was the only one he'd allow to pet him for months and he's still wary of most people. He's my dog through and through, and I'd take him home with me in a heartbeat, but my mom's terrified of dogs, especially big ones. I hate that this happened to him.

But making sure Scrap was well wasn't the only reason I decided to spend the night at the ranch. I also stayed because I didn't want to be alone and think about what happened with Scar.

At first, I was angry at him for just kissing me, just like that, then leaving in a huff when I pushed him away—as I was perfectly right to do! —but that morphed into sadness very quickly after he was gone. And when I get sad, the regret, depression and "why me?" thoughts settle in, and those have the power to take me under for a long time, if I let them. I'm not strong like my mom, I can't deal with things head on, my only real coping power is being able not to think about things I don't want to think about.

Going home last night would give me time and space to think about all those things, and that's what I would've done. So I slept on the cot in the back room where I patched Scar's arm up earlier. I could hear Scrap breathing from in there, and that made it easier to fall asleep.

But even with everything else to worry about, my first thought when I woke up before dawn was sadness. Sadness at knowing that I'll never be able to return to the life I once had, or be the person I once was. I already knew that, I figured it out a long time ago, and I've come to terms with it. But Scar coming back showed me exactly what that abstract idea means in broad daylight.

There was also hope that he'd come again today anyway, realizing what he did was an asshole move and apologizing. Then we could talk about it. But what would I say? "Hey, sorry, your kiss made me physically ill, but let's just be friends, OK"?

Yeah, right.

Even if I put that into milder terms, it wouldn't go over well. He's a man of action, a man in the most primal sense of the word—he showed me as much yesterday with the way he handled Scrap—and I'm sure mental problems like the ones I have aren't something he understands. He won't change, but I won't change either. Our path together was severed and split a long time ago, and there's no returning to the crossroads to start over.

It's almost noon now, and I'm still waiting to hear the rumbling of his bike approaching, that tiny light of hope I woke up with still shimmering in my mind, even though I know it's for the best that I forget him.

He was my hero and my savior a long time ago, my knight in shining armor when I needed him most, and I will be forever grateful to him for that. But, he's also exactly the type of man I fear the most, and I can't give him what he wants.

9

SCAR

I COULDN'T GET to sleep until almost dawn then I woke up right after it still seething in anger, my arm throbbing like it had actually been burned. It's how it is with me.

When something goes wrong, everything goes wrong. Looking up Lynn and giving her the happy news that the guys who ruined her life got theirs was supposed to make me feel better, not worse. But it backfired spectacularly and her rejection has now been added to the endless reel of shit that's gone wrong with my life, which always starts replaying in my mind when more shit goes wrong. Before this, I could at least pretend things could be different between us. Now she's given me her no.

Tinkering with my bike usually calms me, so that's what I've been doing for the whole morning, but it's not doing the trick today.

I bet Lynn expected me to show up at the ranch today.

But for what? So I can get bit by more of her dogs while she plays hard to get? So I can apologize? For what? Kissing her like I know she wanted me to? Deep down she did, anyway. I'm sure of that.

I've been avoiding Roxie since Ice left two days ago, and doubly so now that I know she wants to talk to me about Lynn. But she tracked me down in the garage and is just standing in the doorway like she's expecting me to start talking first. I'd like to just keep on ignoring her until she leaves, but she's the Prez' old lady and I got too much respect for him to do that.

"What's going on, Roxie?" I ask without looking up from what I'm doing. I expect she'll start by first adding to my bad mood through asking why I didn't ride with Ice like I said I would. I hope to Christ I'll be able to stay civil as I explain that he's a big boy and can take care of himself.

"I heard you visited Lynn Harlow the other day," she says walking into the garage proper.

She's so far along in her pregnancy I sometimes wonder how she even still gets around. I'm also pretty sure she shouldn't be around all these tools I have scattered all over the place, but I guess she can worry about herself.

"Yeah," I say and leave it at that.

"How is she?" Roxie asks, and finds a cleared bit of table to lean against next to me.

"Fine, I guess," I reply and continue doing what I'm doing and not looking at Roxie.

Lynn isn't fine. But I don't understand what's really wrong with her, and I'm probably just adding to it by sticking around. Another reason why it's best I just leave it alone. If only it'd be easier to let her go.

"I knew that it was Lizard who kidnapped her," Roxie says. "I overheard my father talking to someone about it. He was pissed, but didn't think his MC should do anything. But I struggled with the idea of whether I should go to the cops or something with what I knew. I lost over a week of sleep over it."

Was it that much? Lynn lost a lot more than that. I did too. But I'm not gonna start an argument over it with Roxie.

"You were what, sixteen years old? And your father was the president of an outlaw MC that did business with the one that kidnapped her? Seems like you made the right choice keeping quiet," I say instead.

"Put that way, I did, but it still haunted me for all these years," she says. "You saved her, didn't you?"

"Yeah, me, Cross, Tank and Rook got her out. As for saving her…we were a little late for that." I couldn't help adding that, and I peer at her over my shoulder for her reaction. But all I see on her face is sadness. I don't like seeing sadness. I don't like feeling it. Not that I often do.

"At least you got her away from Lizard," she says. "That's a good thing. And she has a life now, which she wouldn't if you hadn't."

I shrug and get back to work, since I don't have anything good to add to that.

"Were you in love with her?" she asks, and I almost run the screwdriver I've been using right through my palm.

The adrenaline of that near miss coupled with the fact that Lynn fucking pushed me away when I kissed her yesterday takes away the last shred of control I have over my anger.

"I liked the look of her, but who didn't?" I snap, throwing the screwdriver at the wall and turning to face Roxie. She flinches, which isn't a good thing, but I'm past caring about offending her. "I know my place in this world, and it ain't with no fucking beauty queen. Wasn't then and certainly isn't now that she's all fucked up by what Lizard did to her. She cares more about animals than she does human beings for one thing, but I'm sure that's not all that's wrong with her. So no, I wasn't in love with her then, and I'm not now. I wasn't made for that kinda thing."

She straightens up from her perch and her face is very hard as she stares me down. Kinda motherly too. But she's pissed right now. "I'm sorry if I offended you, Scar, I spoke out of turn. But I won't be yelled at. If you don't want to talk about this, just calmly tell me so."

"I suppose Cross will wanna have words with me now," I say, not able to stop being an asshole. "That's fine. Send him along."

"I don't need him to fight my battles," she says and really looks like she doesn't right now. I feel myself backing down under that stern look in her eyes. Cross chose a good woman, a strong woman, as his old lady. I guess she has to be, to compete with him. I haven't met many strong women before her, and the ones I did, I just thought were annoying. But not Roxie. She deserves my respect.

"I shouldn't have spoken to you that way," I say, and that's all the apology she's getting. "But my business is my business."

"Yes, and all I wanted was to find out is how Lynn is doing," she says, her face growing softer. "I shouldn't have asked you personal questions. I'd blame the pregnancy hormones, but I'm just a generally nosy person."

She chuckles as she says it and I grin too, since the tension is now gone and so is the edge of my anger.

"Alright, glad we settled that," she says and walks past me, patting my back on the way. "Lunch is in an hour. Ines is cooking, so it should be good."

Ines is Rook's long lost and recently found again lover, and together with Tank and his sheriff's daughter, and Cross and Roxie, it seems all my oldest and closest friends are settling down into domestic bliss. Wanting that for myself never even registered on my radar before, so why am I even noticing it now?

Because of Lynn, that's why.

Back when I first met her was the only other time I thought about being with just one woman. Before that, and afterwards too, I always preferred to keep my encounters with them short and to the point.

But Lynn ain't just gonna fly out my thoughts now, I suddenly realize. She hasn't left them since I saw her again. So I might as well go back to her and see if maybe I didn't just startle her with that kiss last night. She's always seemed to me like a graceful, beautiful doe, so it makes sense that she's just as skittish as one.

Besides, even back when we first met, and I'd go by the diner at least once a day to see her, if not twice, I used to try and convince myself it was pointless to pursue her in any way, since it wouldn't end well. That kinda thinking kept me away for maybe a day or two, but it never stopped me from coming back. When it was on me to save her from Lizard, I went against the then president's direct order not to mess with the Spawns in any way. I risked my place in the MC, and my life by going against an entire MC with just three guys on my side, but I hardly thought twice about it.

So it's pretty pointless pretending I can stay away from Lynn now that I finally have her all to myself.

LYNN

I can't remember the last time I got these happy jitters in the pit of my stomach from seeing someone, but they're dancing now like all the butterflies in the world as I watch Scar make his way across the wide open field between the main gate and the kennel, where I've just brought Scrap so he can be with his doggy family.

"You came back," I call out as soon as I think he's close enough to hear me. I suppose some other kind of greeting would've been more appropriate, since I absolutely do not want to lead him on anymore now that I know I can't give him what he wants from me, but I've never been careful about what I said to Scar. I could always just tell him what was on my mind.

"Yeah, I came back," he replies and leaves it at that as he keeps walking towards me.

All my life up until I met him, I've had to be mindful of my appearance, and how I was being perceived. I was born the sweet girl-next-door type, so there wasn't much pretending needed, but with Scar, for the first time, I felt like I could just be myself, say what I thought, do what I wanted. At first, I started talking to him, because he obviously wanted to talk to me, and I felt sorry for him with that awful scar on his face. But it didn't take me long to realize he neither needed nor wanted my pity, and that I really liked his company. I'd only just started figuring out what that could actually mean when we were so rudely interrupted. Too bad there's no way back to those simple times now.

"I'm sorry, but at the same time not, about what happened last night," he says once he reaches me.

I freeze, drawing a complete blank on how to reply. I'm

sorry-not-sorry too. But if I say the wrong thing, I could either be leading him on again, or pushing him away again, and I have no idea what the right thing to say is.

"Not sure how much help I'm gonna be though," he says, holding up his arm. "This needed ten stitches, and I figured I'd at least know how to handle the dogs. But clearly not."

His arm is freshly bandaged, and not that this is the time to, but I'm admiring how nicely it follows the curve of his shapely forearm.

"I told you it needed stitches," I chide. "But you knew better."

"I knew it wasn't good, but I wanted to spend the evening with you and not at some hospital," he says, winking at me. I don't get sick to my stomach from knowing what he's implying and imagining it in the worst, most painful and degrading way possible. But I do freeze.

"I shouldn't have kissed you just like that. You even warned me against it," he says. "But impulse control's never been my strong point."

"Maybe if you stayed afterwards, I would've told you I'm sorry for pushing you away like I did," I hear myself say, my whole face heating up so I know I'm blushing. But the heat is thawing my paralysis too.

"Really?" he asks, looking at me sideways like he doesn't believe me. "You looked pretty scared and angry."

Now we're at that point where I could explain all about how I get physically sick just thinking about men touching me, never mind if someone actually did. But I don't want to tell him that, and not just because I doubt he'd understand. I don't want to tell him that because his kiss felt so good and right for the half a second I let myself feel it. So maybe, just maybe, he could still be my way out of the prison of my bad memories. Maybe he could be the one man whose touch I can stand, and maybe I just need a little more time. I know I'm blushing worse than ever from thinking that right now, because sweat is breaking out on my forehead from all the heat in my face. And on top of it, I'm frozen again.

He's still looking at me, and waiting for me to say something. But I have no idea what. I was also always the shy girl-next-door, even though I hid it well up on stage. I only had two boyfriends before I was abducted, and I only slept with one of them. To say I'm naive about men would be an understatement of the year.

But the silence is seriously dragging, and I'm not about to explain any of that to him.

"I can find some undemanding stuff for you to do," I say and smile at him, deciding it's best to just keep going like we don't have things to discuss. "But first, come say hello to Scrap. He's doing much better today."

I grab his healthy arm and pull him after me to the kennel, which I've partitioned off so that Scrap gets a part of it all to himself while he heals. He's lying on the bed I made for him with his bowls of water and food within easy reach and his toys scattered around him. The rest of his dog family is lounging near him on the other side of the partition.

Scrap lifts his head and starts wagging his tail like crazy when Scar crouches down next to him.

"You take real good care of these dogs, you know that?" he says and pets Scrap through the bars.

I nod and crouch down next to him. "They're like my pets. Especially Scrap...he was a stray and I nursed him to health from death's door when he was just a puppy. I'm so sorry this happened to him. He doesn't deserve it. I hope his leg will heal back right so he doesn't get a limp from it."

I always get teary-eyed when I talk about Scrap's early days and his injury makes it even worse. I look away and try to wipe away the tears before Scar notices, but there's no hiding from his gaze. He's watching me like a predatory cat would its prey. He always watched me very closely, and I've always felt very *seen* by him.

I can't help but meet his eyes right now, they're just pulling my gaze to them with that quiet magnetic intensity of his.

"You're a good woman, Lynn," he says. "And you didn't deserve what happened to you. So, don't ever feel sorry for putting a brute like me in his place."

I blink hard a few times, and it's not to fight back tears, just surprise. I never expected him to say anything remotely like that. Then again, he could always surprise me, and he could always say the exact right thing to me most of the time.

I nod, and maybe the woman I was when we met might even have hugged him for saying such a kind and appropriate thing. But I'm not her anymore, and he wasn't exactly a gentleman last night.

"You're supposed to ask before kissing a woman," I say quietly.

He chuckles. "Yeah, I remember being told that once upon a time when I was a kid. But in my experience, less talking is better when it feels right."

He's so confident and forward. I wish he was like that when we first met. Then at least I'd have known what real passion was like before the mere suggestion of it made me queasy.

"The Millers are twenty minutes out with the cows, Lynn!"

Bethany yells from the doorway to the kitchen. "We better get everything ready."

I appreciate the interruption, yet I'd also love to stay right here, crouching in the gravel just inches away from him and talking. But that would mean telling him why I wouldn't let him kiss me even if he asked beforehand, and I don't want to repeat it, since maybe, just maybe I'll give it another chance.

"The Millers?" he asks.

"Yeah, the last of the ranchers housing their livestock here until the fires pass," I explain.

"Alright, what do you need from me?" he asks and stands up. "I was kidding about the pain. I can work."

"I knew that," I say and grin at him. "And don't worry, I'll find something for you to do."

It's so nice just joking with him, so much nicer than worrying about all the things he needs to know, but which I don't want to tell him.

So it's not hard to ignore them as I take his hand, and lead him to the stables to find something for him to do that'll keep him here until nightfall at least.

10

LYNN

GETTING the newly arrived animals housed took all afternoon. Scar didn't need many pointers or guidance from me, since the men who brought the animals took advantage of his presence and his strength without needing any urging.

The animals are stabled now and the sun is setting. Scrap is sleeping, but running a fever. Tammy gave him something to bring it down and said the fever's not high enough to worry, so I'm focusing on that and trying not to panic.

I should go find Scar and discuss dinner. We could go to the taco van they roll out every evening in town. That should be safe, since it's not a dark, sit down kind of place. Take out is best, I think, to start things off slow. Then we can bring the food back here, and eat on the ridge as we watch the sun set. I already called my mom not to expect me for dinner. She wasn't too happy to hear it, since it's the second night in a row, but I explained that it's such a busy time and she didn't argue.

Scar is in one of the barns, filling the last stall with hay. He's shirtless, wearing just a pair of jeans, and has a black garbage bag wrapped around the bandage on his arm. His broad back is glistening in the light coming in through the windows and the cracks in the wooden walls, dust he's stirred up shimmering as it settles again all around him. I can make out every muscle in his back as it coils and flexes, then relaxes once his movement is complete, the mesmerizing dance starting up again as he loads more hay onto the pitchfork he's using.

He can't see me, since I'm standing in the doorway behind his back, but I can see him perfectly and I want to see more. The queasiness in my stomach that thinking about men and sex brings is there, but it's more a memory right now than something I actually feel physically.

He turns suddenly, fixing me — all of me—with his predatory and penetrating look, making me shiver and take a step back like I'm trying to run away. But I freeze mid-step, because I don't want to run away.

I want to look at him some more. And I want him to look at *me* just like this.

He grins like he knows it, exits the stall and balances the pitchfork against the wall, and picks up a black bag off the floor. I do back out of the barn as he approaches, but I'm also still watching him, watching his chiseled arms and chest, neither of which need to be flexed for me to make out every muscle. I'm also watching his hard, washboard stomach, the way his six-pack tapers off where his abs disappear behind the waistband of his jeans, marveling at the fact that it's not making me nauseous thinking about what it would feel like to glide my hand across those bumps. The thought's giving me other ideas too, ones that make me feel like I'm standing under the noonday sun and not in the cool evening breeze.

"All done here," he says, the sound of his voice breaking my trance, yet adding to the fantasy. I always liked the sound of his voice, even before I heard it calling my name when he came to save me.

"Would...would you like to get some dinner?" I manage to ask because he's now very close to me and I'm thinking he means to grab me and kiss me again. I can't handle that. *Not yet*, a small voice inside my head says. But I don't believe it. *Not ever,* is more like it. But there's no need to cut up the fantasy just yet.

"Yeah," he says and grins wider, but doesn't come any closer to me. "But I'm filthy. Is there a place I can wash up? I brought a change of clothes."

He shows me the bag he's carrying.

I nod and point at the mobile clinic behind me where Tammy had a shower installed. "Go in the side and then it's straight ahead," I tell him.

"How about you show me?" he says and chuckles. "I get lost easily."

I'm sure that's a bold faced lie and I'm fairly certain he's angling to get me alone in a room again, where he's gonna try for another kiss. But then we'll just have another last night on our hands. I don't know how to explain that to him, so I won't even try.

"It's this way," I say and start walking.

I can hear him following me, and I can feel his eyes on me. It's like a breeze rustling my hair, but a warm summer breeze, not the cold one of terror.

Once I reach the infirmary, I open the side door and wait until he joins me.

"It's that blue door at the end," I say and point to it. "I'll wait for you at the kennel."

He looks me up and down, the unmistakable desire in his eyes sending my heart racing and my stomach dancing, but not from nausea.

"Yeah, 'cause you showered and changed already," he observes and grins at me. "Pity."

"I...I did," I manage to stutter, since I froze up again, and I don't want him to think it means I'd like him to leave me alone. I don't want him to do that. I want him standing this close to me.

"Alright," he says and smiles in a softer way, then slings his bag over his shoulder. "I'll be done in a sec, then you can change my bandage for me. I got it dirty today, and it's better to keep wounds clean."

I nod, since I was planning on suggesting the same thing to him when I entered the stables earlier, but got sidetracked by the sight of his nakedness. It's still catching my eye now, but amid the tattoos and the muscles, I can also make out scars. There's many, more than I can count with just one glance, and if I keep staring he'll get the wrong idea. He'll think I'm leading him on and I better not cause that. But he clearly lives a very dangerous life.

"I'll be happy to," I choke out and turn to walk away.

"Good, I'll call you when I'm done," he says, and I nod without turning and without slowing my steps.

The infirmary is built inside a container and the walls are so thin I can hear the water running as I walk towards the kennel.

Realizing that's so, makes my mind start imagining it running down his broad back and down his legs—which I haven't yet seen, but I'm sure are as defined and hard and formidable as the rest of him. And down his front too.

I'm trying to fight the visions, because if I think about this too much I'll just freak out like I did on our first date. But the image of water splashing across his hard body won't leave my mind no matter how hard I'm trying to ignore it. It's like a memory coming back to me, a dream I have no control over having. A wish I've denied my body for too long.

But the queasiness is there too and my dark memories are getting faces now. Grimacing, rugged, stubble-covered twisted faces of the men who used my body in any and all ways they wanted to, used it in ways it wasn't meant to be used, for days, for weeks, until there was nothing left to use. There's still nothing left to use! I'll go mad if anyone tries. I know it. I went mad in that dark filthy room where they kept using my body, until I lost all touch with my mind, with my reality, any reality, couldn't even go mad anymore, because there was nothing but blackness left in my thoughts.

No, my mind can't handle a man's touch, even if my body wants it!

It's because my mind doesn't know the difference between pleasure and pain, just like it doesn't always know the difference between the past and the present. Even now, the thought of Scar showering also makes me see all those vile men who raped me like they're right next to me. I can't handle even the memory of it, let alone a re-creation.

The body is stupid, it has needs, that's just a biological fact, and Scar is a tall, hunky, good-looking man that I once had very strong feelings for. I wanted him to kiss me, and I wanted to sleep with him back then. That's why I had the reaction I did to seeing him nearly naked. It's not because I could maybe try to let a man touch me and make love to me. No. My mind's too messed up for that. It'll just send me to the black void of no thinking again.

The realization racks through me with all the force of an electric shock, which only grows worse as the dogs start howling. It sounds like they're all doing it at once and it turns my blood to ice. I stopped on my way to the kennel as I processed all that about Scar and me, but I start running towards it now, forgetting the darkness in my own mind, the pain from my past that still hurts in the present and will in the future, reacting only to the distress in their call.

My heart stops dead in my chest as I reach the kennel. Scrap is having a seizure, his eyes rolled back, his tongue hanging from his mouth, blood marring the clean white bandage on his leg.

No! Fifteen minutes ago, he was licking my palm and eating treats from my hand. I was *just* petting him. *This can't be happening!* He *just* dozed off with his head in my lap.

No! The sound of my own silent screams finally brings me back to the present.

"Tammy! Tammy!" I yell as loud as I can, turning all around.

Tammy's now running towards the kennel, Raul limping behind her. But Scar reaches me first.

He smells like the clear water I imagined running down his body not five minutes ago. His shirt is undone, the collar of it wet from the water dripping down his wet curls. There's no predatory desire in his eyes now, only concern as I open and close my mouth, trying to tell him Scrap is dying. My Scrap. My heart. The puppy I nursed back to health from death's door. He's dying. The horrible fear of that happening which I've ignored since he got injured is a reality now, and it hurts so much. It hurts so bad that I can't even say it, can't think it, can't ignore it.

"It's gonna be OK, Lynn," Scar says in a calm voice, his eyes locked on mine, his palms wrapped around my upper arms, as he repeats the words he said to me the last time we saw each other. He was right then, and he has to be right now.

"Let's get him inside," Tammy says and I nod to Scar, who gives my arms one last reassuring squeeze before entering the cage and lifting the no longer seizing, but now unconscious Scrap. He carries him to the infirmary, Raul limping after them.

"It's from the fever," Tammy says, falling in step with me as I follow. "He's gonna be fine, Lynn."

I nod, but don't say anything.

Scar already laid the dog down on the examination table by the time I reach it.

"OK, how can I help?" I ask and go stand beside Scrap.

Tammy and Raul share a concerned look, making me think Tammy lied and Scrap isn't gonna be alright, and they don't know if I'll be able to handle it. *No!* His breathing is hoarse, but it's slowing down. He *is* gonna be alright.

Tammy instructs me to get some medicine from the cabinet, and I rush to get it. She tells Scar to get some blankets and sends Raul to find Bethany.

But Scrap isn't regaining consciousness and his eyes are slightly open and rolled back, only the whites showing.

"We'll have him on his feet in no time, don't worry," Tammy tells me. I nod even though my dark mind doesn't believe her.

I'm petting his head while she checks his heart beat and

listens to his breathing. Scar comes back with the blankets, and I smile at him faintly.

"You'll stay?" I ask and he nods.

"Yeah, Lynn, I'll stay," he says quietly.

And as weird as it is, I feel that whatever happens, everything will be alright because Scar'll be by my side. I don't argue with the thought, don't try to understand it, because I'm so afraid my poor little Scrap is dying despite what Tammy claims, and that's all I can focus on. And because it's a nice thought to have in all this darkness.

SCAR

Whatever's making her push me away when I try to kiss her, isn't preventing her from checking me out when I'm not wearing a shirt, or leaning on me when she's upset. I guess that points us in the right direction. And I feel like an asshole without a compassionate thought in my brain thinking about this now, while she's so worried for her dog she's practically shaking.

I buried a couple of my own dogs back in the day and I know I was upset for months afterwards, but I can't really bring the actual feeling to mind right now. I've seen and done so many worse things since then that I probably *don't* have a compassionate thought in my brain left to think, although watching Lynn this upset makes me wish I had.

Her dog didn't start shaking again after we brought him inside. But he was breathing hard and not waking up, which is never a good sign. I've seen enough men die to know that.

But Lynn was very hopeful he'd pull through regardless, so I left to get us that dinner before I said anything to kill her hopes.

She didn't want me to go, I could see it in her face, but she nodded and let me go anyway. I hope the dog's either sedated by now, or dead, because I'm no good at the gentler things in life nor do I like watching animals suffer. I'll put him down for her, if it needs to happen, and I'll bury him too, but I can't comfort her, because I don't know how.

The light is still on in the vet's office when I get back, but only old man Raul is in there tidying up the place.

"What happened?" I ask, placing the bags with the tacos on the table by the door. "Is the dog dead?"

For all my lack of compassion, I wish I'd been here when it happened. Not sure I'd be able to comfort Lynn, but I'd like to have tried.

Raul turns to me and shakes his head. "No. He had another seizure, so they took him to the animal hospital in town."

I nod, unsure whether I should go track them down or wait right here. I hate hospitals of all kinds.

"Where's the hospital?" I ask.

He doesn't say anything, just looks at me like I've done him some personal wrong and need to be watched closely. He's not the harmless, nice guy the women here seem to think he is, that much has been clear to me since the moment I met him. And that limp of his, that's from a broken kneecap and you don't get that by accident. I know, I've dealt out my fair share of broken kneecaps over the years.

"It's a simple question," I say. "Or don't you know?"

The guy has a pretty heavy Spanish accent, so maybe he didn't understand.

"What are your plans with Lynn?" he asks, the question coming completely out of left field.

I shrug. "My plans are my own."

"Lynn is a very innocent woman. She lives with her mother and working at this ranch is her whole life. She is afraid of men like you," he says.

"She told you she's afraid of me?" I snap, going on the offensive since that's always the best way to deal with nosy bastards like this one.

He shakes his head. "No, she didn't tell me anything. But I see it, and I don't want her to get hurt."

He says it like he's gonna do something about it if it happens.

"Then we're on the same page, old man," I say and chuckle. "Only I've been looking out for her for a lot longer than you. We go way back. All the way to a time before she was afraid of men, as you say."

I probably said too much, seeing as she asked me not to speak to anyone here about her past, but him suggesting I'd ever hurt her pissed me off way more than I expected it to. Probably because I might hurt her, if I keep coming around. But I can't stay away from her either.

He's giving me a hard look, nodding his head slowly and not saying anything. And even though he's about twice my age and has a bad limp besides, I'm on the verge of teaching him some manners.

"I heard about you," he says after awhile. "They call you the Scarred Devil. Does she know who you are?"

I laugh, but I'm not thrilled that this guy knows who I am and what I do.

"That's just Scar for short," I tell him then give him a hard look of my own. He doesn't flinch under it quite as hard as most people do.

"Knowing all that about me I assume you also know it's not wise to mess with me," I add so we're perfectly clear that this conversation is over. "But I don't want any trouble. I'm only here because of Lynn, and she knows all she needs to know about me."

Raul keeps looking at me like he wants me to know that he's put a lot of hardasses in their place in his time. But he's over the hill and works as a stable boy now. I'm not interested in being the one to prove to him he can no longer do it.

"Are we done?" I ask and he looks at me for a couple more seconds then nods. He seems to have decided something during all that staring, and I hope it's that he'll stay the fuck out of my business from now on.

"Then I'll go walk the other dogs if no one's done it yet," I conclude.

"They haven't been walked, no," Raul says.

"After I do that, I'll wait for Lynn to get back," I also tell him. "Is there a place I can bed down for the night?"

He stares at me without saying anything for a good long while.

"There's a perfectly good loft over the barn next to the house," he finally says just as I was about to repeat my question. "Or you can take the bed in the back room here."

He points to the wall behind his back and I nod.

"Lynn will appreciate you walking the dogs," he says as I turn to leave. Maybe I detect a bit of a softening up on his end. But I'll have to keep my eye on this one, and I'll have to watch my back around him.

The last thing I need is this old guy stirring trouble where none is needed. The cops and the press are still hard on our ass from that botched Spawns' killing a couple of months ago. It's getting handled, but not as quickly as Cross would like and he certainly won't thank me if this old bastard calls the cops telling him stories about the Scarred Devil.

That's how I'm known in some circles, mostly the ones made up of our enemies. It's not just the cops I gotta worry about if Raul goes blabbing around that I'm hanging out at this ranch alone. You don't make a career of torturing and killing your enemies without growing a hefty list of your own enemies, and with my face like it is, I don't exactly blend in.

"I'm sure the dogs will appreciate it more," I say and grin at him like we're square now. "And let's keep this conversation between ourselves. You have my word that Lynn is in no danger from me."

I shouldn't have to give my word, since this is none of his business, but it's better we're friends.

He nods and offers me his hand, which I shake. "I'll hold you to this promise."

It's as solemn a statement as I've heard in a long time, and while I have no idea how this limping old man means to stop me doing exactly what I want to do, I have no doubt he'd try. He's also sure he'd succeed. That kind of confidence is rare.

But once I get the dogs out and we reach the darkness of the trees, I start obsessing over the thought that the old man might be right. Maybe Lynn would be better off without me. I got enemies left, right and center, the kind of men who wouldn't blink twice before going after her to get to me.

But then again, when was she ever better off without me? Certainly not on the night she was abducted. And certainly not for the last twelve years that she spent fearing men so hard even geriatrics notice it. I was there to save her twelve years ago and she doesn't fear me now. So maybe I'm exactly the guy she needs.

That thought makes me happier than I remember being in a very long time. And that's worth something all on its own.

11

LYNN

SCRAP WENT into another seizure soon after Scar left and this time he hardly had a pulse once it was over. His breathing was shallow and erratic too. I don't remember much of the ride to the vet clinic and Tammy did most of the talking once we got there. Bethany stood by my side and kept casting me sidelong glances like she wanted to comfort me, but didn't know how. I can't blame her for not knowing. I was completely frozen, my face probably not showing any of the pain and terror raging inside me that was strong enough to stop time itself and leave me in utter blackness.

After I was rescued from my nightmare, it soon became clear to everyone around me, including myself, that I can't handle stress very well. Even a small amount of stress like that time my mom slipped on a wet floor and bumped her head. It happened at the mall, and they called the paramedics for me not her, since it sent me into a paralyzed stupor that lasted almost a week.

That's why Mom makes sure no stress occurs around me. I made sure of it too, by not allowing anything or anyone close. Scrap's accident is the first really painful event that's occurred in my life since I was abducted, and now my whole chest feels like a frozen wasteland. Only there's such a vast sea of boiling, searing pain underneath it, I'm afraid to move because that might cause the ice to break.

They ran tests on Scrap that seemed to last forever, until someone finally determined that a shard of bone must have gotten loose from the break and was now wreaking havoc in his system. To operate would be pointless they said, since there was no way of knowing where it was. It's all on Scrap and his will to live now.

But he's a fighter, I know that, has been since the day I found him. And I kept telling him that over and over again, whispering it in his ear, as I petted him and kissed his head. But he didn't wake up, didn't wag his tail once, and kept having seizures.

I told Tammy and Bethany to go on home, that I'll find my own way back to the ranch. At first they didn't want to leave me alone, but around midnight they finally realized I was serious about spending the night with Scrap and about being perfectly able to handle it.

The initial shock subsided once they had a diagnosis, and I was able to talk and act more normally again, but I'm far from fine. I'm calm only in this bubble, only with my hand buried in Scrap's fur, only in this place where he might still get better. I don't know what will happen when I leave or if he dies, but I've been ignoring that for now and it's working.

I don't know if I'll be able to call a cab and go home. Don't know if I'll be able to just go on with my life if he doesn't make it. I might need weeks to recover. So I don't know anything other than that I'm barely holding on. And that it'd be easier to hold on if Scar was with me. But he's probably asleep in his own bed and who knows when I'll even see him again? But this whole evening, I wanted him by my side even more than I've ever needed my mom there. If I had his phone number I'd call him, but I don't.

I dozed off a couple of times during the night, but woke up with a start each time, scared by different variations of the nightmare that Scrap died while I was sleeping. But each time he was still breathing.

He had no new seizures since midnight, and it's almost five AM now.

"You should go home and get some real sleep," the night shift vet that comes in to check on Scrap every hour tells me. She's said the same thing almost every time she came in.

I rub my eyes and straighten up. I've been sitting on the floor next to Scrap's cage, with the door open so I can pet him, and my whole body hurts as I sit up straight.

The vet smiles at me faintly. "He's out of the woods for now. I think he'll make a full recovery. The fact that he hasn't had a seizure in the last six hours and that his fever is down is a very good sign. Go home and get some rest. We'll take good care of him."

Scrap is sleeping like a furry little angel, his breathing steady and deep. And I'm so tired and drained, I'm seeing two of him.

I get up which makes the pain everywhere so much worse I make a few involuntary grunts to that effect.

"Maybe I do need some rest," I say and chuckle, but the vet is looking at me with a very concerned look on her face. Maybe she sees how fragile the bonds that hold me together are.

Or maybe I just look like a mess, since I spent the whole night sitting on a smelly old blanket next to a dog cage. I was only allowed to stay because Tammy knows all the people who work here personally, and it's likely that I'm the only person in the history of this hospital to do it.

But I can't worry about being seen crazy on top of already feeling like I am all night. I can't worry about anything. Or the ice will break, letting loose all the pain, and I might not be able to be here for Scrap once it does, because I'll need recovering myself.

I leave my phone number with the vet to call me if anything changes and she calls me a taxi.

I remember none of the ride up to the ranch, nor do I have a very firm grip on my thoughts once I reach it.

But that changes as I spot Scar's bike still parked next to my car.

He didn't leave! He's still here!

The thought makes me happy, as happy as I was when Scrap's seizures finally stopped.

But he's not in the back room of Tammy's mobile office. Or at the stables where I watched him shift hay earlier. And I doubt he's at the house, which is still dark. But everyone will be up soon, since there's so much work to do now that our stables are full of animals. They'll know where Scar is and I can wait.

Just as I think it, the light over the kitchen door turns on and Raul comes limping out. He moved into the main house a few years ago, even though him and Bethany both claim that nothing is going on between them.

I rush to him, don't remember my feet hitting the ground.

"Is it Scrap?" he asks with concern in his eyes.

"He's better...sleeping," I say. "Where's Scar?"

His eyes narrow and his lips grow very thin.

"You should be careful of that one," he says.

I wouldn't be standing here talking to you if it weren't for Scar, my mind screeches, but I don't say it, because he asked me not to talk about his past, and I don't like talking about mine.

"He's OK, I've known him for a long time," I say instead. "Where is he?"

Raul shrugs and points at the barn nearest the main house. "In the loft up there, I think."

Dawn starts to break as I reach the wooden door, which isn't latched like it's supposed to be, but that only means Scar is inside, and right now, it's very important to me that I find him. Not sure why, and I'm sure a completely sane person would be lying down in her own bed and trying to get some sleep after the night I just had.

He's sleeping on a bed of hay in the loft, covered by a raggedy, dark brown blanket, like some cowboy from the Little House on the Prairie or some other old Western, which were the only kind of movies and shows I could watch for awhile, since they were drama- and realism-free enough not to trigger me. All that's missing is a candle or an oil lamp for me to light before I rouse him. But I don't need that, since the light of dawn is growing stronger outside, and I can already make out his face clearly.

If I wake him, things will be complicated again. I want it all to be simple, and I just want to be near him.

I don't even think as I lie down next to him in the hay, so close I can feel his warmth. But even so, I'm still just lying here alone. He's sleeping soundly, lying on his back, and I could get closer still, could rest my head on his chest, could get close to him the way a part of me yearns to, but the rest of me doesn't think possible.

But it's actually easy. It's simple. I just have to scooch closer until our bodies are pressed together and then rest my head on his chest.

Memories are bubbling up in my mind, but the loudest, the clearest is the one of him holding me during the ride to the hospital. This will feel just like that. Safe, secure, warm like everything is alright. Dreamlike. Exactly what I needed then and exactly what I need now.

So I don't reason about it anymore.

I get closer, don't stop until his hard body is pressed against me and his chest is rising and falling beneath my head. But his arm is still all the way away from me. So I fix it by pulling it over my back and let his hand rest on my hip.

I remember how strong his arms were when he lifted me from that filthy bed and carried me to freedom, as he held me in the car, as he carried me to the hospital. I felt weightless in his arms, and safe, safer than I ever remember feeling before.

I feel like that now. And for the first time since last night when Scrap had his seizure, I know that whatever happens, I'll get through it just fine. That I'll be fine even if Scrap doesn't survive.

Scar groans and shifts beneath me, opens his eyes just a crack. He smiles once they focus on me. His arm tightens around my back as he brings the other one around to hold me tighter still.

I don't want to, but I feel trapped, like I'm not in control again, like I'm tied down for anyone to use my body as they will. I can't draw a full breath, my heart is racing, blood is whooshing in my ears, and I only know one thing. I have to get free.

The nausea doesn't come until I'm standing outside in the gravel the cold dawn air not cooling my burning face.

"Come on, Lynn," Scar says softly as he approaches me slowly. There's no anger in his face, just a small smile on his lips. "Don't keep running away."

A part of my mind is still in flight mode and the nausea is a real thing, but something else is reacting to the calm, soothing way he's talking in, so I stay put. He reaches me, runs his hand down the side of my face all the way to my neck.

"I want to kiss you," he says soothingly.

"I'm afraid," I mutter, which is whole truth in this matter. I want to kiss him too, but I'm afraid of my reaction to it.

He rests his palm over the racing heartbeat in my neck and smiles. "I know. But I won't hurt you."

I know he means it. But he might hurt me even if he means not to, because I'm broken. But maybe it won't be as painful as I fear it'll be. I should try. That's the only way I'll know.

So I lean my head back, let him support it in his palm.

"OK," I whisper.

He leans down and sparks fly in my mind as his lips touch mine. At first they're just regular yellow ones, but they soon explode in all the colors of the best fireworks display. But that's just the show.

The real magic is the soft warmth of enjoyment and bliss flooding my chest and even my mind that the touch of our lips is causing. Right now, I can rise above anything, survive anything, do anything I want. I know it and the knowledge gets stronger the longer we kiss.

He's holding me tight and I'm holding him too, my arms cinched around his waist, my whole body pressed against his, leaning against it, letting him support me. He's holding me so tight that there's no easy escape for me right now, but I don't need to escape, don't want to. Because this doesn't hurt at all. In any way, shape, or form. It is simply exactly what I needed.

SCAR

Having a scarred face, I spent most of my teenage years at home. Which in my case meant with my father, who thought that with a scar like mine, I better get tough. The old bastard wouldn't let his other son get punished for it, but he did try to make up for it in his own way, so there's that. He was tough as nails already, and to toughen me up he — among other things— took me hunting every chance he got. Winter, summer, rain, snow or shine, we'd be out there with our rifles, sometimes for days at a time, laying low in the middle of nowhere or tracking game in places people weren't meant to be. Those hunting trips were also a way to keep me and my brother apart, because my father never let the two of us be anywhere alone together after what happened.

I was good at hunting, since I guess I was born with the talent for taking life. Only, I would never shoot the does. I had trouble with the female boars and bears too, but not as much as with the does. They were too delicate, too pretty, too graceful, they didn't have to die.

My father tried to change my stance on that. It became a mission for him to make me kill one, and he made fun of me about not doing it all the fucking time. But I stood my ground and didn't let any of that get to me, because even then I figured I had nothing left to prove to anybody. But one overcast winter day, snow already several feet thick on the ground and more on the way, he won. We spotted a doe alone in a clearing, nipping at the frozen buds on the bushes. The old bastard could talk and talk. He could talk a stone into walking. I don't remember what he said to me that day as we lay in the snow watching the doe, but it made me take aim and pull the trigger.

Maybe I just did it so we could go home. I remember being very cold as I knelt beside the dying animal, stroking her neck as her dark eyes lost the light, the snow turning red from her blood as fat snowflakes started falling all around us.

That was the first and last innocent life I took.

Holding Lynn now, kissing her again and again, pausing only long enough to look into her eyes and stroke her long graceful neck, while I savor the feel of her lithe, soft body pressed against mine, I remember that doe as though I only just sent her out of this world. Maybe this is my second chance to do right by her.

But God damn it, I hope I'll know how to.

Right now, Lynn's eyes are blue like the deep ocean and the light in them is floating somewhere very deep below the surface of all that water.

"Let's go lie back down," I suggest and hold her closer, because holding her is a dream from a very long time ago—a dream I've forgotten— come true.

She tenses in my arms, grows harder than a rock for all her softness.

"I..I'm...I'm not sure," she stutters.

"I'm not I'm ready," she corrects herself faintly, since I have no idea what she's talking about and it probably shows on my face.

Her eyes have lost the light. The shimmer's still there, but the rest is not even blue anymore, it's black. As is my mood, once I realize what she's talking about. She's not ready to fuck. I wasn't thinking about that when I suggested what I suggested — odd for me, especially since my cock is rock hard and throbbing for her— but I wasn't.

"I meant you should get some sleep," I tell her too harshly, and my black mood isn't helped even by the surprised, gentle expression on her face.

"I never considered you the type of girl to fuck after the first kiss," I add. "And I still don't."

She might never let me do more than kiss her, might never let me fuck her, and the more I think about it, the more I want to fuck her. But I'm not a gentle guy, I don't know how to be. And I doubt she'll ever be ready for what I have to give her, or to give me what I need.

"Too bad those other men didn't think so," she says growing even harder in my arms, so hard I loosen my hold on her because it's not her I'm holding anymore. It's some stone hard creature they made. I should've kept my mouth shut, because now I've opened a can of worms and all the damn maggots from her past are crawling out.

Fuck Lizard, fuck my brother and fuck all those other assholes who ruined her for me. Ruined her forever. Right now, I wish I could kill every one of them all over again.

What the hell kinda idiot takes a gorgeous woman like Lynn and destroys her? In the sex trade—or at least as much as I've seen of it, which isn't a lot— beauties like her are rare. And degenerates pay very good money for the pretty ones. What MC president in their right mind would give a beauty like her to the entire club to fuck?

"What are you thinking?" she asks in a small voice.

She's let go of my waist so it's just me holding her loosely now, and I can barely recall how good it felt kissing her less than five minutes ago. No that's a lie, I remember it perfectly, and that's why this conversation is pissing me off so bad.

"I don't want you to just leave again now," she says so quietly I barely hear it.

But I do hear it, and I pull her closer again.

"Not gonna happen," I assure her. "But you've been up all night. You need sleep."

And I need to find a way out of this black mood that has me. I hate being reminded I'm not the guy for her, and it fucking happens at every turn, over and over again.

I'm a hard man. My father did his job well and what he failed to teach me, the MC has.

Lynn is a delicate, precious, innocent thing.

Killing the doe taught me something else. It taught me that I better stay away from things I don't want to destroy.

But I meant what I told her too. I'm not leaving her. I can't. Never could.

So I don't even think twice about following her as she smiles at me and takes my hand, then leads me back to the loft where I spent the night and woke up with her in my arms. And I don't think twice about letting her press real close to me and fall asleep with her head on my chest and my arms around her.

We're tied together, her and I. That was decided a long time ago. I've forgotten it, but that doesn't make it any less true. I want her naked, I want my cock inside her, I want her to beg me to stop when it's too much and scream for more as she comes. So we're gonna have to find our way there.

But even if none of that ever happens, I still want her with me.

12

LYNN

I WAKE up with a very dry throat and itchy all over from the straw. My whole body is aching from the hard wooden boards I slept on. I remember coming in here before dawn and nestling in close to Scar. I remember the kisses we shared, my lips and my whole body still tingle from them. I also remember the difficult conversation we had afterwards. And now he's gone.

My memories of yesterday and the night I spent at the animal hospital are a fuzzy mess in a haze of sadness. But Scar's kisses were the first thing I remembered when I woke up, his strong arms around me the second, and poor Scrap in the hospital the third. But he'll be fine, he's a fighter, he has to be OK, he has to. As long as I believe it, I can keep the sadness in the back of my mind where it's not paralyzing me or freezing my heart.

When I let Scar kiss me at dawn, a whole new world opened

up inside me, one I remembered craving when I was younger, before I was abducted and raped. One I haven't dared even think about because of the nausea and flash floods of horrible memories it would always bring.

For all these years, I was sure I'd never have that world or that kind of warm, caring devotion, or just sweet kisses at sunrise and sunset, let alone love. But the bad memories didn't come flooding in and taking me under when he kissed me.

Not even after he kept kissing me.

They only came when my thoughts turned to sex. But not as brutally as they usually do, and not with the paralyzing, inescapable finality that I've been powerless to fight for all these years. Maybe I should try that too with him?

It's with that thought that I finally get up, my whole back protesting as I straighten up. I know Scar is still here, because he promised me he'd stay and because I can feel him nearby.

The sun is already high in the sky, the sounds and sights of a full, working ranch all around me as I exit the empty barn. The horses are out getting exercised, cows are mooing, goats are bleating and dogs are barking, and people are yelling instructions to each other.

Raul is replacing the water in one of the pens. Bethany is with the goats, too far away for me to make out what she's doing, and Tammy is talking to one of the ranch hands that were sent to help by the animals' owners.

I finally spot Scar leaning against the barn to my left, standing shirtless in the shade, only his legs in the sun. Light and shadows play like water across his chest and arms, across his powerful thighs, revealing and hiding, inviting me closer. He's built like some statue in a museum, a living work of art, and if I didn't have a head full of nightmarish memories of large, muscled men slapping me around and raping me every which way, I'd love to get naked with him.

He doesn't see me approach, since he's checking something on his phone. And despite remembering all that brutality, despite those memories roiling black and angry, coming in hot and raging like a vicious storm that hits on a sunny day, I don't freeze, don't slow my steps, don't get sick as I walk closer to him. All the memories that create that black storm are still there, but they're tucked away in my past. Nothing will ever chase them away completely, but I could still have a future. *He could be my future.*

I've never been able to ignore what happened to me quite this fast or this seamlessly. Able to ignore and disregard it, as I can any other unpleasant thing that scares me. Well, almost as easily.

Because I still shiver inside as he finally sees me, the hard look in his eyes turning even harder in stark, predatory desire, for a moment. But his eyes are soft and inviting again once I finally reach him.

"Sleep well?" he asks, grinning at me as he stuffs his phone into his back pocket.

"Reasonably well," I say and smile back.

Everything about him screams, "Danger, Run!" from his bulky, tall body, covered in black tattoos, to the scar on his face and the ones on his chest and arms and probably legs and back as well, which I've yet to notice. But I don't want to run.

I want to get closer to him. I want him to shield me from all the dangers in this world. Including the ones that exist only in my mind. Those are all very naive and romantic notions, and what they all boil down to in this moment is that I want him to kiss me.

He leans forward so only mere inches of space separate us. I lean forward too, expecting to be kissed and held. But that's not what happens.

He chuckles and fishes a strand of straw from my hair, looking at me like I'm a very precious thing that he'd rather not touch, so it won't break. Or like he's waiting for me to make the first move.

I don't know how to. I grew up fantasizing about men sweeping me off my feet and taking charge because they couldn't fight their desire for me. All girls dream that, I'm sure. Only I was dreaming it right up until the night I was abducted. And then I was shown exactly how far men will go to satisfy their desire for a woman.

I rest my hands against his hard, rippled sides, as though to hold on against the dark winds and dark waves of my memories. Maybe if I hold on to him hard enough they won't pull me under. He's not like those other men.

It seems that was all he needed from me in terms of a first move, because he grabs me and pulls me closer. His lips find mine and then jets of rainbow colored light start poking holes in the darkness of my memories, showing me glimpses of what could've been, what might have been, what should've been. Soon it's not just glimpses but full pictures that don't fade. They only get brighter and more vivid.

The nightmares put up a fight, but it doesn't work. The black memories fade into the back of my mind where they belong. They're a thing of the past, not something that can hurt me in the present.

My fantasies are blending and mixing with the very real feelings of bliss, happiness and desire woken by our deepening kiss. His tongue explores my mouth more and more hungrily, and mine tentatively explores his. My fantasies are coming true. No matter how naive and how long ago they occupied my mind, they are reality in this moment.

The bliss ends too soon, yet I'm breathless when we break apart.

"I gotta take off now," he says, then chuckles and kisses me again, disappointment and shock now coiling around the bliss it brings.

"What do you mean?" I ask when he lets me come up for air again.

"I mean, I have to shower and change," he says. "And go to a meeting."

"And I need to go see Scrap," I say, my heart racing, because I clean forgot about him, while we were kissing, and the sadness and pain are ten times worse because of it.

"And then you should go home and straighten up too," he says, fishing another piece of straw from my hair.

"Because tonight, I'll pick you up and take you out for a real dinner," he concludes.

I'm opening and closing my mouth, all sorts of thoughts warring in my mind, like," What if I have to stay with Scrap again?" and "I haven't seen my mom in two days. She'll be upset if I go out again."

But none of those are anything that could keep me from seeing him again very soon.

"I'd like that very much," I finally say and smile because he's already frowning at me, probably thinking I was getting ready to say no.

"You can pick me up at the animal hospital," I suggest and he chuckles again.

"Sure, Lynn, OK," he says. "Not quite the romantic start to the evening I was imagining, but I'll make do."

"Stop making fun of me," I say and smack his arm, which I'm sure hurt me more than him, because he's built like a rock.

"And stop pretending you're some kind of romantic guy," I add for good measure.

He laughs. "Yeah, you got me there. But I kinda want to be for the right woman."

"For you," he adds after a pause, during which I already heard that perfectly well.

I don't want to say anything for fear of devaluing this moment. I feel so special right now, so needed and desired and wanted, for me and not just for my body and beauty, and despite of who I really am—a woman who's afraid of sex. He's probably just saying that, the way men say things they think women want to hear. At least that's what they do on TV, which is where I get most of my relationship experience and advice from these days. Though in the movies and shows I like to watch, they're also sincere when they say things like that. Scar sounds sincere. He always sounded sincere to me, and I think that's because he always was.

"I can't wait," I whisper then wrap my arms around his waist tighter and lean back so he can kiss me some more.

It's only a lot later that I can hear the sounds of the world all around us again. I should be helping out. But I should also be kissing and getting kissed. Because I've gone so long—much too long— without it. And I should be getting kissed by Scar, because with each kiss, each lick and bite and groan and moan and flex of his muscles and shift of my body to get even closer to him, it becomes clearer and clearer that this was always meant to be.

Because I feel just as pleasant, carefree, safe and like my own true self in his arms, as I ever did talking to him, and joking with him and all those other things we used to do together when we met. We just never got to this part. But now that we are touching and kissing, all those things are magnified and a hundred times better. No, a thousand times better. No, a million.

This is how it was meant to be, and this is exactly what I always wanted.

SCAR

It feels good walking into Sanctuary after all that working in the heat at the ranch. Would prefer to still be feeling the heat from kissing Lynn. But she's still far too wary and skittish. I won't get far if I scare her off by going too fast, and I want to go all the way with her. The sooner the better, but I can wait some.

I'm the first to arrive for the execs meeting Cross called this afternoon without giving the slightest indication as to why. But that's how he is, everything is on a need to know basis with him. I don't mind it as much as some of the others do, since just knowing what I need to do and when is simple, and worrying about it is complicated. I'm not, strictly speaking, an exec of the club, mainly because I was never interested in management. I usually sit in though, since my job of gathering intel from people not willing to give is and the backbone of what we do. *Was* the backbone. But now that we're transitioning into running guns, I'll pretty much be obsolete.

Just a couple of days ago that stung like all the fires of hell, but now, as I'm trying to figure out where to take Lynn tonight and thinking up ways of setting her at ease, so she'll let me undress her, it no longer bothers me as much.

I only saw her naked once—on the night I saved her from the Spawns—and fucking her was the last thing on my mind then. I didn't even get a good look before I wrapped her in the sheet and carried her out. I didn't exactly regret it, but I did think about seeing her naked again over the years. I'm thinking about it now, and it's not doing much to help the already painful hard-on all that kissing caused. But she's skittish and I can be patient. I'll have to be. It's another thing hunting with my father taught me. As did all the waiting to get even with my brother.

Rook and Hawk walk in, followed by Tank and Cross, cutting off thoughts of my brother, which always leads me down some dark paths. I'd rather be figuring out where the hell I'm gonna take Lynn for our first night together anyway, since I can't bring her here or the clubhouse in town. I'm certain seeing lots of bikers in one place will make her bolt. On her side, she lives with her mother. Maybe the ranch house, that looks like it has plenty of available bedrooms—

"Christ, it smells like a barn in here!" Tank exclaims way too loudly and with way too much flair for it to be an offhand comment. "It's just like old man Gannon's farm. Cross, remember that time your dad and Ms. Brown decided to try and straighten us out by sending us to help him over the summer?"

Cross chuckles as he takes his seat across from me. "Yeah, I remember. It lasted all of two days though."

"I couldn't take it. I still have nightmares about the smell.

Don't know how you can stand it, Scar," Tank says. "Though for a Miss Illinois, I'd go the extra mile too."

"Alright, alright," I say. "You've had your fun, Tank, now let's get on with this, so I can go back to my beauty queen."

My skittish little doe. She'd be miles away, if she heard Tank right now.

"Yeah, Tank, let the man live his life," Rook adds, since he also has very little patience when it comes to Tank's many and varied jokes.

Tank leans back in his chair and raises his hands in surrender. "Fine, fine. I just wanted to lighten the mood before we get down to business."

His tone suggests the mood will need lightening, and the way they all glance at me tells me it's mine that'll need it after we're done here.

Cross holds my gaze even after all the rest look away.

"What's going on, Cross?" I ask since I could never handle dramatics very well.

It's bad enough he called me here for an execs meeting, which this clearly isn't since not all the execs are present. For once, I wish that man would lay down all his cards at the same time.

"The three jailed Spawns that we could never get to escaped two nights ago," Cross says, obliging me.

"Why did this need a meeting?" I ask as he pauses. "Now we can get them too and our job will really be done."

"Reaper escaped with them," Cross adds and that hard ball of hate that's always there deep in my chest hardens into something cold and jagged.

I refuse to call him by the street name he gave himself— Reaper. My brother always was a pretentious piece of shit. Hell,

I refuse to call him by any name, even the one my parents gave him, which is Reggie.

"If he's a Spawn, he'll have to go too," Cross says almost apologetically. "You know what we always said. You leave one alive and twenty come back to haunt you."

That's one of our MCs wisdoms passed down from our founders, and the goddamn truth besides.

"Reaper never joined the Spawns," I tell them. "He never joined any MC, since he could never play well with others. He had his own little gang. But he was very tight with the Spawns, and as far as I'm concerned that's the same thing as being a member."

The ball of hate keeps growing bigger and colder, until I hardly feel my body anymore, just the hate. I was gonna kill my brother the last time I was in Illinois, back when I met and lost Lynn, and get my revenge once and for all.

Before then, I had my parents to consider, but my father died a couple of months before we headed out on that job, and my mother had been dead almost eight years by that time. They did wrong by me, making me live with him even after he tore up my face, but he was their son, and I have a code.

Though all bets were off once they were dead and buried. The shit with Lynn got in the way, and before I could get another chance, he was inside.

"Reaper dies either way," I add. "And I'm the one who's gonna send him to hell."

They give me a hard look. It's no secret my brother gave me the scar I'm named for, and it's no secret I hate him for it. But I think it was unclear that I'll settle for nothing else but his dead body at my feet as my revenge. That's the only way. Anything else would be dumb, since he'd keep coming after me until I'd be the dead one, if I let him live. It's simple really.

"See, I told you it was like that between them," Tank says to Cross who gives him a very dark look.

"What was?" I ask.

"Cross thought you'd wanna save Reaper, since he's family and all, but I told him there was no love lost between the two of you," Tank says. "You told me all about it that one night you almost had him back in Fairview, Illinois."

"Yeah, the coward left town after he told me where Lynn was," I say, my memory zooming back to that night.

I told Tank the whole fucking story, while asking him to help me save Lynn. My dear brother's parting gift that night was telling me how much he enjoyed fucking her in all holes, and how much she enjoyed it too. She enjoyed it so much she screamed, is how he phrased it.

She'd been missing for two weeks at that point, and I'd never been readier to kill. And right now, the same as it was that night, I want to kill him just for hurting Lynn, never mind the hell he put me through growing up.

"I stay out of personal business, and it doesn't get much more personal than two brothers squaring off their affairs," Cross says. "Do what you have to Scar, and know that Devil's Nightmare is behind you."

I nod curtly, which is my way of thanking him. "I'll keep the club out of it."

It's Cross' turn to nod, then he faces Hawk. "Find the Spawns and keep good tabs on them. Then we'll ride one more time. Find Reaper too and give the info to Scar."

"We should call Ice back," Tank says and like always, it's impossible to tell if he's joking or being serious.

Cross shrugs. "He left without a cell phone, just promised Roxie he'd check in from time to time. I think the man needs some down time, even if he doesn't realize it. Besides, I'm not about to ask her to call him back so he can go kill a few more guys. She'd bite my head off, and I'd never hear the end of it."

They all chuckle and I would too, if I could see past the cold hate that talk of Reaper always brings up. But this time, I'll get him and he'll get his. This time it'll finally be done.

Cross gives out the rest of the instructions, and Hawk assures me he'll let me know the moment he learns Reaper's whereabouts.

I hope the bastard doesn't flee to Mexico, which is a very real possibility. But I'll follow him down there if I have to. I just got my second chance at him, and I'm not letting it slip through my fingers this time.

13

SCAR

I DIDN'T HAVE the best time waiting for evening to roll around. All the ways in which I hate my brother rolled in my head like a very detailed and vivid movie, and nothing I did paused it. Today started out fantastic, but it might not end that way, not at the rate my dark rage is multiplying. He's within my reach again, I can get him this time, but I won't be calm again until that happens. I should stay calm for Lynn, I know that, but it's a very distant consideration right now.

Doc got fresh with me over the state of my wound, bitching about how I, of all people, should know about infection. It almost came to blows, would've if he hadn't backed down just in time. I do know all about infections, the thing on my face is worse than it might've been because the cut got infected before it healed. Just one more reason why Reaper will die soon.

But all that raging shit in my mind quieted down as I

watched Lynn exit the animal hospital. Didn't think that was possible, but it's more or less silent now that we're sitting in this dimly lit Chinese restaurant, because she was in the mood for dumplings. She's happy because her dog is getting better, and I'm happy because I get to sit at a table with her and watch her eat. It's not an experience I usually have with women. But it's something I've always had with Lynn. Pretty much all we had, but I'm planning on that changing tonight.

She's the reason I didn't go after Reaper sooner while I was in Illinois. Somehow, it was hard to focus on killing him when I had her to visit everyday. The night he left, I had the choice of going after him or saving her. I made the right choice. And I'm getting my second chance with him soon, so all is right with the world.

"You don't like the dumplings?" she asks, looking way more dejected than she should over the fact that I forgot to finish my plate, while I was watching her.

"They're good, but I'm sure you'll be tastier," I tell her and grin. She blushes so hard I can see it clearly despite the dim light in here.

I don't feel bad about making her uncomfortable, and she's not freezing up like the first time we had dinner and I said something along those lines. Now that she's given me the green light, I'm having trouble reining myself back in. And the longer I stare at her, the worse I want to see all of her.

"I...I...I don't know—" she starts stammering, but I'll have none of that anymore. I know she wants to fuck, and that I'm the guy she wants to do it with. It's clear from her fluttering eyelashes and her blushes, and the way she presses herself against me when we kiss, not to mention the way she keeps checking me out when she thinks I can't see.

"No need to know," I tell her. "Just finish your food so we can get outta here. Then you'll find out."

She blushes again, but picks up the chopsticks, then starts telling me about her dog again, which I guess is a good sign, since she's neither freezing up nor starting another conversation about those Spawn maggots. I start eating too.

Doc gave me a couple of injections when he checked my wound after we cleared up how fresh he can get with me and when. I suspect one of the injections was a pain killer, because my arm was throbbing all the time before, but I can barely feel the dog bite now. Or maybe that's also from having Lynn close, and the prospect of seeing her naked very soon. She's like a pretty little painkiller, as far as I'm concerned. Better than a painkiller.

I came up with the perfect spot to take her. It's a safe house on the edge of town, one of a couple kept supplied and empty should shit ever hit the fan and MC members had to leave town in a hurry. It's never happened yet, so no one ever uses the safe houses. I got the keys from Fuse whose job it is to oversee them, though with him in charge I'm afraid of the state I'll find it in. But the keys are burning too big a hole in my pocket for me to spend a lot of time worrying about it.

"Did you have any pets growing up?" she asks, still not done with her food.

"Sure," I say. "I had a couple of dogs and we always had a bunch of cats around, because my mom would feed anything that walked by. She even fed raccoons and shit."

She was the exact opposite of my dad when it came to almost everything, including caring for animals. My dad liked killing them and she liked taking care of them. But she stopped feeding the cats once she realized what usually happened to the ones that wouldn't come back. Just one more thing Reggie never answered for, but he's gonna now.

"Sometimes, I'd like to go and visit home," she says. "Do you ever go back?"

I shrug. "Nothing much for me there. My parents are both dead, their house is gone, and my brother's in jail."

I was sure I told her all this back then, but maybe I didn't, since I don't think she's faking that sad slash surprised look on her face.

"I'm sorry," she says and finally picks up the last dumpling from the bamboo container in the center of the table.

"Don't be. My mother didn't speak much, and my father was an asshole most of the time," I say and I wasn't gonna go on, but Reggie's just been too close to the surface of my thoughts tonight, so maybe it's better I get him out before me and Lynn are completely alone together.

"And my brother gave me this to remember him by for the rest of my life," I say and point at my scar, which makes her gasp and drop the dumpling from between her chopsticks. I never told her that story, or anything about my brother, I'm sure of that. Pure pity is in her eyes now and avoiding that is the reason I never talk much about Reggie. I certainly didn't want to see it in hers.

"Don't worry about it," I say. "It happened a long time ago, and he'll get his eventually."

She was struggling to finds some words to say, but as soon as I said that she froze up. Definitely not what I was going for. I can't hide my hatred of Reggie when I talk about him, so I shouldn't have talked about him.

"You ready to go or what?" I ask and wave to our waitress who's just passing without waiting for her reply.

That's enough feeling bad for one day. It's time to feel good. And if how it is when I'm with her normally is any indication, fucking her will be out of this world amazing.

She doesn't say anything as I pay for the dinner, just smiles congenially to the waitress. But her steps are shaky and slow as we exit, and she's practically dragging her feet once we're on the sidewalk.

No one's ever accused me of being a sensitive man and been right, but I know something's wrong and I know all those, "I don't knows" of hers before were referring to this part of our date.

I stop to wait for her, take her hand and pull her to me. She places her hands on my waist and looks up at me with a mixture of fear and hope I've only ever seen once before—in the eyes of the doe I killed.

"Where are we going?" she asks.

"There's this lovely house on the edge of town, where I thought we could go spend the night," I say with a grin. "You know, to avoid sleeping in the barn again."

She tenses in my arms, but doesn't move away, her body still pressed against mine as her eyes—and her whole face, for that matter—go through a bunch of conflicting shit. I see fear in people's faces often, so I recognize that and there's plenty of it. But there's other things as well, so it doesn't piss me off quite as much as it might normally.

"I...I..." she starts stuttering again.

"Just say it, Lynn," I interrupt and she tenses some more, her eyes growing harder, probably to match mine.

"What if I say I'm not ready?" she asks, and sure it's a question, but it's also a statement of fact and I hear that loud and clear. And if she were any other woman, I'd be having a different reaction right now.

Because on top of all those highlights of my past my brain's been showing me all day, I really hoped Lynn would be more willing to make the evening and night worth forgetting everything else for. But she's not ready. That's just fucking perfect. But OK.

"So that's what you're saying?" I ask to make sure. Even though I already know.

She lets go of my waist.

"I'm not ready," she says in a quiet voice. "Can we just talk?"

We've done a lot of talking already. Maybe not tonight, but back then. I was hoping we were done with that for tonight, but then again…

"Sure, Lynn, if that's what you need," I say before the idea to do it even fully forms in my head. No one's ever accused me of being mindful of the needs of others and been right either.

"But it's not what *you* need," she says quietly. "Or want."

I hold her tighter because she's starting to back away from me, and I can't let her slip from my arms. Not again. Not ever.

"To tell you the truth, yeah, I want you. That much you already figured out," I say and smile at her, because her face is so damn stony and serious, it's unnerving. "If you were any other woman, we'd be done by now, because I'm usually not very interested in talking."

It's the truth too. Not that I ever looked for women to talk to. I looked for women to fuck. And with the ones I found, the talking usually consisted of them either crooning like young girls, or cracking jokes about my ugly scar to piss me off, so I'd hate fuck them. There was no need for it. Rough and hard always came naturally to me, and I'm always happy to oblige.

"But you're different," I add, since even though she's perfectly still, that's flight in her eyes. "I always liked talking to you. Why'd you think I did so much of it?"

I grin, but she frowns back. "Not tonight, you didn't."

"I got some news today," I say. "But seeing you tonight made it all better."

"Right, and now I'm playing hard to get and pissing you off, is that it?"

I shrug, but don't say anything, because she's completely right. She feels so damn good in my arms and she looks and smells so damn good, and I will never get enough of just looking at her, and I'm about to fuck everything up for the second time with her, if I don't find the right thing to say. She's already moving away from me again.

"I thought a lot about tonight too. I thought about it all day and that was probably a mistake, but I couldn't stop thinking about it," she says once she reaches the point where my arms are preventing her from stepping away any further. I don't release her and she doesn't try to break through, but it's an awkward position.

"I was hurt very badly by those men you saved me from," she says more quietly than before. *Here we go again.* But I'll hear her out.

"So badly, I couldn't have sex afterwards," she continues. "It was a choice and a necessity for me. And I thought, I truly believed and I really hoped I could break through that for you… to be with you. I wanted to be with you back then, and when you showed up now, I couldn't believe it, but nothing had changed. I still wanted to be with you. So I thought I'd try, but—"

"That's a lot of talking, Lynn," I say and chuckle although

almost none of what she's saying makes me happy. The fact that she wanted me to fuck her back then does, and that's about it.

"You should've asked me out then," she says. "I would've said yes. And then I'd have given you what you want. But now—"

"Are you saying it's never gonna happen?" I ask, beating her to saying it, because I don't want to hear it from her mouth.

She looks into my eyes, but doesn't speak. I take that as a, "No" and pull her closer again.

"Lynn, you're too damn gorgeous and sweet and good to kiss to waste on just talking and thinking about," I say and grin. "I made that mistake the first time around and I'm not making it again."

She frowns at me like I've said the wrong thing again, but I have more to say.

"I get that you went through hell, but you know what, fuck them, fuck all those assholes. Don't let them keep ruining your life more than a decade later. There's almost none of them left to blame anyway." There's at least one more left, and he's getting his shortly, but she doesn't need to know that right now.

She relaxes in my arms and there's more fire than fear and sadness in her eyes now. The fighting kind.

"It's not about how hard you get hit, it's about how much you can take and keep going," I add, borrowing some of my father's wisdom, but paraphrasing so it's fit for her ears. I hope it makes as much sense to her as it does to me, since this is that key piece of advice I've gotten that always keeps me moving forward. She seems to be getting it, her eyes softening like she's once again thinking about doing it with me.

"So unless you say you wanna just go home and forget all about tonight, I'm gonna kiss you now," I say and she smiles, parts her lips but doesn't say anything.

I kiss her before she can think of something to say. She kisses me back. And with all the talking and remembering we did just now—and that I've been doing all day— I'm imagining us kissing on that dark parking lot behind the diner she worked at. Or on those rocks by the river where I had plans to take her after our first date, since it was a hot summer that year and she said she liked swimming.

She's holding onto me tight now, her whole body pressed against mine so completely I can feel the hard nubs of her nipples against my chest, so whatever she's about to say, as she pulls away from the kiss and looks up at me, won't be bad news, I'm sure of it.

"Is it really that simple?" she asks. "Just say fuck it and move on?"

I shrug as best I can with her standing so close and get a nice treat of her nipples rubbing against me.

"Life's real short, Lynn, and we already missed a lot of it," I say.

"What if I can't?" she says. "I still have nightmares about it."

"I have nightmares too, so fucking what? That's just dreams," I say. "In real life, it's gonna be so good."

I'm tripping over my words, but I think she knows what I mean. She's not saying anything though, and I can't read a damn thing from the look in her eyes.

"My nightmares sometimes come when I'm awake," she whispers.

I'm all out of sage advice. "Just go for it. You can always stop me, though I hope you won't."

Hell, I'm not sure she can stop me, but I think she needs to hear it, and I know I'll try my hardest to stop if she wants.

"OK," she finally whispers.

"Alright, let's go then," I say and waste no time releasing her, though I keep my arm wrapped around her shoulders.

I feel as excited as I did the first time a girl agreed to get naked with me back when I was a teenager. More so, since I waited for Lynn way longer than for that first one—my whole life, it seems right now— and I always wanted Lynn more than I ever wanted any other woman.

14

SCAR

She's not very talkative anymore, and she's gripping the steering wheel so hard as she drives that her whole hands are stark white. Her face is very white too, glowing in the moonlight. I can't wait to hold it in my palms. My bike is still at the animal hospital parking lot, since she insisted on driving to the restaurant and I didn't argue. I didn't argue when she wanted to drive to the safe house either, even though it'd be much faster if I drove.

We're almost there, and she turns a few more shades whiter as I point out the house at the end of the street lined with other houses in various states of disrepair. She gasps as I tell her to turn into the driveway, but does it anyway, though very slowly.

Beyond this house there's nothing but a field of dried grass with a tree here and there, then hills in the distance. She's afraid, I can smell it, and maybe I should suggest we can go back if she wants, but it's beyond my power to do that, and I'm not gonna hurt her. I'll never do that.

I don't talk either, and give her plenty of space to follow me from the car to the front door, fearing she'll bolt, hoping she won't. She follows.

But she whimpers as I close the front door behind her.

Tonight, her fear doesn't piss me off like it did that day in the woods. It just makes me want to protect her that much more, even more than I already do, than I already always have.

I'm a scary, dangerous guy, pumped up with a lot of anger and hate. But Lynn has never had anything to worry about from me. And she never will.

The safe house is a small, one level and one bedroom home, and thankfully Fuse didn't neglect paying the power bill, because all the lights work. I turn on the one in the hall and walk towards the bedroom, hoping she'll follow, hoping I won't hear the front door open and close any second now.

I wanted to grab and kiss her as soon as we got out of the car, carry her to the bedroom and toss her on the bed once we entered the house, then give her all I got to give fast and rough. I have no idea what gave me the strength to fight that urge. Probably the knowledge that she'll bolt if I get too rough too fast.

She stops in the doorway to the bedroom.

"We can leave if you want to," I tell her even though all I want to do is rip her clothes off and make up for all the time we lost from now until dawn, or better yet, 'til sometime next week.

She doesn't say anything, just walks over to me with a very determined hardness in her step. Seeing someone this afraid of doing something they clearly want to do, something that's as natural as breathing, makes no sense to me. I don't understand the demons she's fighting in her head right now, but the battle is fierce, I can see that much in her set face and her eyes that cycle through so many emotions the look in them is impossible to read.

"I want you to kiss me now," she says once she's near enough to grab. I don't grab her, but I do kiss her, deep, long, slow.

She molds to me, and I once again have to fight the need to rip her clothes off, throw her on the bed and take her the way I need her. She'll bolt if I do that, I know she will. And I want to keep her for a long time.

So I go slow, stroke her neck instead of grabbing it. Kiss the path my palm just took, her racing heartbeat tickling my lips. Then I slide my hands across her breasts, don't clutch, just caress and pull her t-shirt up slow, wish I could watch her skin getting revealed as she does it herself, for me, but there's time yet.

I pull her t-shirt up and she helps me get it all the way off. Then I kiss her neck some more. Her skin is like velvet, something I barely noticed before with other women, because I'm always in a hurry during this part. Always racing to the finish line, just satisfying my hunger. But she's different, always was.

There's no beginning to her, just as there's no end. It's a weird sorta thought, but it makes perfect sense to me right now, as I taste her lips some more, caress and play with her breasts some more, not grabbing or slapping, exhibiting a gentleness I didn't know I was capable of.

Soon she's no longer stiff, no longer stinks of fear, and my cock is throbbing hard and pulsing with the kind of need I've never experienced before. I never wait for much permission from the woman I'm with. I take what I need. But I'm not that guy tonight.

Right now, every one of Lynn's moans, every one of her muscles she relaxes, every kiss she returns is a reward in itself. I don't know this guy she brought out of me, but I kinda like him, because he's the one she needs. The one that's not gonna fuck all this up.

But I don't know how much longer he's gonna stick around, because her smell and her softness, her beauty and her pureness, her grace and her gentleness are already fogging up my brain with one thing and one thing only: the need to make her mine. And I don't think she's got long before I lose control.

I want to break her, make her give herself to me completely, make her scream my name, but I need her to stay whole afterwards. And I don't know if she can.

LYNN

To say I was shaking inside as we drove to this house is an understatement. There was an earthquake going on inside me! Once we were inside the house, it got worse, so bad I was surprised not to hear my teeth chattering.

I don't know what force gave me the ability to follow him to the bedroom, because everything in my body and mind was screaming to run away, run and hide back home with my mom where it's safe, keep hiding from the world because that's best. And yet I do know.

I've wanted to be with Scar for a long, long time. I've yearned for the kind of passion I know we'll make real for a long, long time. And I wanted to sleep with him, since the day he showed up at the ranch. My mind is protesting, but my body is doing its own thing, because it's completely sure it wants this, that it needs this. I'm just following its lead. And what he said before made such perfect sense that even my mind is almost completely onboard too.

The men that kidnapped me and held me captive took something from me, something precious and very fragile, but I just let them keep it for years afterwards. I never took it back. This is my chance to take it back. This could be my only chance.

I want to feel loved, I want to feel wanted, desired, want the physical pleasure that love and desire brings.

I want Scar, the man who saved me from my nightmare, the only man who sees me for me and not just my beauty, and I want to give myself to him. I wanted that for a long time. But I forgot just how much.

Yet, I'm afraid. Afraid that the dark, nightmarish memories swarming my mind will take over if I let him touch me. That they'll take me under and bury me in darkness if I feel a man's touch on my naked skin, his cock in my body. I'm afraid that once we take this further, no ignoring will keep those memories from blasting right back from the corners of my mind I've managed to sweep them into. I'm afraid they'll drag me back down into that black hole of madness, of unawareness that became my world when they raped me again and again. Which was my world for weeks afterwards as I tried to climb and claw my way out and find my way back to the light. I never completely succeeded.

This is my second chance, but
I'm afraid my memories will destroy it.
Scar was my light then. He'll be my light now. I know it.

"I want you to kiss me now," I tell him as I reach him by the bed.

He was looking at me like he expected me to call it all off and run away, right up until the moment I spoke. Now his eyes are happy again. But that playful light is quickly drowning in his dangerous and predatory stare that's full of desire, which makes my stomach quiver in fear. But it also makes me feel like I'm the only woman in the world and the perfect one at that.

He grants my wish, and as his lips touch mine, as his tongue enters my mouth looking for mine, it becomes easy to ignore my fears. Even though I can hardly breathe, I feel as though I've finally been able to take a breath of fresh air.

He doesn't stop just at my lips this time, but trails kisses down my neck, my racing heartbeat and his becoming one for a moment as his lips glide across it. I can feel all his burning, pent-up desire for me right under the gentle touch of his hands as he runs them down my neck. All his strength is coiled around it to prevent it from exploding out. I don't know where he gets his strength, but it's formidable, it's out of this world, it's godly. I can trust him with anything. Even with my body and with it my sanity.

A new wave of cold, paralyzing blackness hits me as he slides off my t-shirt, but I let him, I even help. And the warmth of his touch, of his kisses on my naked skin as I'm standing before him in just my bra and my jeans is enough to keep it at bay.

My bra follows and his hands grow rougher, the coiling of his muscles more ominous. But his strong presence, the light of his desire, his gentleness that masks his ferocious need to have my body, is protection enough against my fears, is like a fire in the dead of winter on a cold snowy night. It's all I need.

So I surrender, stop fighting the memories because I wish to just enjoy the present. The blackness starts to recede and the paralysis begins to lift as I stop focusing on them.

My skin tingles from his kisses and his touches, and my mind is burning from the magnetic, deep looks he gives me every once in awhile as though checking if I'm alright, if I'm still here, if I'm enjoying this. I am.

He's still fully dressed as he guides me down on the bed and pulls off my jeans. The chill that hits my nakedness is just in my head, because it's perfectly warm in this room, turns hot even, as his lips find my bare thighs.

He keeps his eyes locked on mine as he pulls down my panties, and I start shivering, my thighs taut because I can't relax them. His vivid green eyes, so much like a cat's, yet soft like a field of wild grass, promise summer will come, that even after this winter, the sun will come out and melt the snows.

I've longed for a man's touch, yet I've spent years terrified of it. I'm still terrified.

As he glides his hand down my stomach and doesn't stop, as his palm slides across my clit and his strong hands spread open my taut thighs, a jolt passes through me, painful and electrifying, frightening and jarring.

But also necessary, just what I needed.

The war my fear is waging against this pleasure Scar wants to give me, that I want him to give me, starts to wane. He kisses my clit, gets bolder as I sigh and moan. His lips and his tongue soon start sending more jarring jolts through my body, and my mind, and my soul too. Each one tears chunks off my fear, until it becomes just memory, becomes inconsequential against the need and desire and heat that is the right now, this moment, with this man, the one who knows me and knows what I need even when I don't.

And that realization becomes even more solid as his lips and his tongue and his fingers too, start pulling me higher and higher along this fiery path of pleasure to a peak I never even imagined existed.

I'm not just moaning but shrieking now, as all those memories, all those fears I didn't know how to shake, that I kept locked away behind soundproof walls, shatter beneath this searing hot mountain of pleasure rising inside me. The bliss is already breaking the barriers of its origin and flooding the rest of my body, entering my blood, which carries it everywhere.

I scream out when I can't take it anymore, when I come as I never have before, the room spinning all around me, my body pulsing and shaking and radiating all the heat it could no longer contain.

He stops playing with my pussy, but I don't move, just squeeze my thighs together—not because I'm afraid, but because I want to hold onto this heat, this pleasure, this bliss, which is already fading now that he's moved away and is standing over me.

"How was that, Lynn?" he asks and chuckles when I just smile, my voice too cracked to speak.

He rips off his shirt and removes his boots and jeans with the precision born of practice. Seeing him standing over me like this, his wide, strong, muscled, tattoo-covered body half in light and half in shadow brings some of my fear back to center stage, fires off memories I don't want to have.

But he only looks like those other men, the men who kept me tied up on a dirty bed in a dark room. He's not those man, he's this man, the one who saved me, the one whose naked body

I wish to look upon, have covering me, the one I want inside me despite what all those other men did to me.

My body and my mind are in sync on this knowing, so even those thoughts of running away and hiding are just a memory now, a bad one—a memory I want to forget.

His cock is raging hard, wide and long. I want it inside me. And I don't.

Because I'm afraid, afraid of the pain and the memories coming back. They're never quiet when I dream of being with a man, never quiet when I think about it. They couldn't possibly be quiet when I'm with a man for real.

Yet all those thoughts are just fading echoes of the screams they once were.

I want this. I want him.

"You're so fucking gorgeous, Lynn," he says hoarsely, still just looking at me, his face in darkness, but his eyes alive. "I can't believe you're here with me."

He says it like me being here is an honor, a gift, something he's always wanted, but didn't think was for him. And hearing it is an amazing feeling, reminds me of my life before, when I was happy and admired and loved, of the time when I was sure the world was mine for the taking, and I couldn't wait to live in it. The time before I hid so hard from the world it was like I didn't even exist anymore.

"This is exactly where I want to be," I tell him. "Then and now, this is where I always wanted to be. Alone, with you."

The light in his eyes shifts, becomes edgier yet softer at the same time.

"Good," he says as he walks over.

He lays his palms on my folded up knees and spreads them

apart. "But I gotta warn you. Before...that was all the slow and gentle I got in me."

He kneels on the bed, spreading my legs almost as wide as they'll go with his strong hands. My heart is racing so hard I'm sure he can see it pulsing in my chest and my neck. I'm breathing hard too, but I don't know if it's from fear, or desire, or what?

A lot of it is desire and a lot of it is fear. I didn't lie before. When we first met, I wanted him to make love to me with all that passion and desire he had for me and I for him then. It's this same passion he has for me now— the passion he's kept locked away inside until now by some sheer power of character and internal strength I'll never have. He's still keeping it locked away even now that I'm naked beneath him, completely under his power if he wants it that way.

"Can you take it?" he asks, the force of his gaze so magnetizing I couldn't look away if I tried.

"I hope so," I whisper and nod, because it's the only true answer I can give him.

"You hope so?" he repeats and chuckles. "Alright, that's good enough for me."

His voice is already different. It's deeper, harder, and now I see little but the hard, burning desire for me in his eyes. But I know I'm safe in his hands. I know I'll always be safe in his hands.

He keeps his eyes locked on mine as he slides one hand up my stomach, twisting my nipple and making me yelp a split second before he thrusts his cock into me, hard, angry, but not painfully.

My mind is full of conflicting thoughts as he starts thrusting his cock in and out of me, each jab faster and deeper, each opening me up a little more. But none of them are clear enough to hear as the ceiling above us becomes bright with all the stars of the night sky, and we're once again climbing that mountain of pleasure, which is all that matters in this moment. All that should matter is how good he makes me feel. And right now, that *is* all that matters.

His palm is cradling my face, his thumb sliding across my lips, his eyes boring into mine, his breaths jagged and loud, as I kiss it, lick it, suck on it as he pushes it into my mouth. His cock seems to grow inside me, his thrusts shallow and hard now, getting faster and faster, taking my breath and messing up my sight, making me see stars in his eyes shining down on that peaceful forest I always see in them. Beasts are roaming in the darkness of those trees, vicious and ferocious ones, but they're there to protect me, never harm me.

His hand is wrapped around my neck now, his thumb massaging my racing heartbeat. Like a cat, he's watching my every move, my every wince and grimace and blink, as his cock bangs against my barriers, pleasure and pain and fear and bliss all rolling into a ball—a wrecking ball that will leave nothing whole once it swings and crashes.

He sees me, he knows me, and he won't hurt me. He isn't hurting me.

The pleasure he gave me before, the pleasure I tried so hard to hold on to, is winning. Each hard thrust is bringing it closer back to me. My need to catch it, to feel it once more, is pushing all those other fearful, painful thoughts farther away, so far they don't come back even after his hand closes around my throat, even after his thrusts get so fast and so deep I feel like he's splitting me apart. The pleasure turns searing, its edges painful even though its center is pure bliss.

His thumb is on my lips again, demanding entrance and I open, let him in, bite down as his deep thrust almost takes me under. He's pumping his cock into me so deep and hard and fast my body's bouncing around on the bed. His hand on my throat and the other one now spreading my legs apart are the only thing keeping me in place, keeping me where he wants me, how he wants me. But I wouldn't move even if he let me go. No, I'd stay right here, waiting for this explosion of bliss he's bringing to tear me apart.

This pleasure rising inside me, fueled by the passion, the wild primal abandon radiating from him and multiplying as it mates with my own, is a force of its own. Nothing can stand in its way. Not even me and my fears.

There's no room for fear and doubt in this kind of pleasure, this kind of desire and passion, this kind of bliss. No room for anything but enjoyment and surrender to it. This is how it was meant to be. Always. For everyone. And for me too. For us.

As my orgasm explodes inside me, the room and everything in it shatters into uncountable shimmers of multicolored dust. My memories shatter too, become just black specks among the shimmering ones. Inconsequential. Unneeded. Swallowed up by the good, the pleasure, the bliss, the way it was meant to be. Gone.

15

LYNN

SOMETHING IS BUZZING in my dream, and it doesn't stop even as I wake up fully and open my eyes.

I can't move! I'm being held down! The room is dark!

But my fear subsides before it has time to fully explode, just gets carried away on the waves of the realization that it's Scar's arms around me. He's not holding me down, he's just holding me. Both his arms are wrapped around me the way they were when I fell asleep, which seems like a lifetime ago, but was probably just a couple of hours ago, since I'm still very sleepy.

The buzzing that woke me is still going strong.

It's my phone ringing, I suddenly realize, since the sound is coming from my purse, which I left by the door to the bedroom.

Scar opens his eyes as I try to extricate myself from his arms and pulls me closer, so close I couldn't move if I tried.

"Where you going?" he mutters, his voice thick with sleep, but I hear the hard accusation in it too like he thinks I was trying to sneak away.

I glide my hand down his cheek, since I don't want him to think I'd ever just slink away from him, don't want him to think I'd rather be anywhere else but in his arms right now. "My phone's ringing, I have to get it."

"Yeah, do that," he says and lets me go so fast and so completely, I sway from having my support taken away. "That vibrating is annoying as fuck."

"Why didn't you wake me, if you heard it before," I say as I climb off the bed.

"It wasn't annoying enough for that," he says and laughs, then turns on the nightstand light. "But I would've woken you up eventually, don't worry about that. I might've even mentioned you had a missed call. Or a couple."

Who'd call me a couple of times in the middle of the night?

The question sends my heart racing, has my hands shaking, as I rummage through the bag looking for my phone. It was Mom. She called five times already, and it's only just past three AM.

"Lynn? Where are you?" she asks breathlessly, in a pinched and panicked voice, as she picks up before the first ring even fades.

"I'm...I'm fine, Mom. I'm out," I answer her unasked question, relief that something bad happening wasn't the reason for her phone calls mixing with my shame for making her worry.

"You said you'd be home by midnight," she says shrilly. "I've been worried sick."

She sounds it too. "I'm so sorry, Mom. I should've let you know I'd be home late."

"I was imagining you hurt and God knows where again, I couldn't sit still and you weren't picking up the phone. I was just about to call 911," she rambles off breathlessly. "You have to let me know if you'll be home late. It's all I ask."

I don't appreciate this stark reminder of why she's in such a state of panic right now. It turns the room cold, makes the night outside the windows seem much darker than it is, brings all the fear and pain I could finally forget for the first time back to the forefront of my mind.

"I'm sorry," I say anyway, because I am. "I forgot to call. It won't happen again."

"Will you come home now? I have to see you to know you're alright," she says and I know she really wants me to. I also know that would be the only thing that'll make her stop speaking so breathlessly and in such a panicked voice, which almost scares me more than the memories that are its root cause.

My mom spent every minute by my side as I recovered and every minute since. I should go home and set her mind at ease to thank her for that. But I should also return to bed and let Scar hold me as I go back to sleep by his side, because that's what *I* want to do.

"I'll be home in a couple of hours, Mom," I say. "Don't worry about me. I'm fine."

Scar grins and nods as I say it, and I smile back. My mom says something else that I don't understand, because the call of his bright eyes, of the comfort only his strong arms and his kisses give me is too loud, louder and more urgent than my need to make my mom feel better.

"I'll see you soon, Mom," I say. "Bye."

She gasps, but stays silent. I hang up the phone, then walk

back to the bed. Scar is still grinning as he makes room for me by his side.

"You missed your curfew and your mom got worried and raised hell in the middle of the night. Is that what just happened?" he asks mockingly. "Gotta say that's a first for me."

"My mom gets worried if she doesn't know where I am," I answer defensively, since, yeah, I know I'm a grown up, thirty-three year old woman, who just got scolded by her mom, but I'd still be a sniveling mess afraid of being alone in the dark, if my mom hadn't propped me up and took care of me for all these years. She nearly lost her mind too when I went missing, and when I came back in the state I was in, but she stayed strong for me, because she had to, because each other was all we had, and I wouldn't even eat for the first few months. "She has good reason to worry."

He nods like he understands perfectly and keeps grinning as he takes a lock of hair that's fallen over my face and brushes it back behind my ear. "Yeah, I know. But neither of you got anything more to worry about now. You, especially. Because I'm here now."

"Just like you always were," I whisper, take his face in both my hands and kiss him.

I'm not annoyed with him anymore, or worried about my mom. I'm just happy, happy like I haven't been for the past twelve years, happy because he's here, because he was there when I needed him most, because he found me again now, and because I found the strength in myself to let us have this second chance.

I'm not ready to sleep. Scar isn't either. We had different reasons for that to begin with, but now his kisses and caresses, gropes and bites, licks and nips are pulling out moans of pleasure from deep within me, from a part of me I've ignored for so long I forgot it existed, a part of me that's still whole and untouched. The pleasure of it all is pushing against the fears my mom's panicked call brought back to life in my head and back to the present.

They're no longer confined to the past where they belong and where Scar chased them by showing me pleasure in sex is possible, by showing me how much I missed it.

The first time it was easy to ignore them, but they're putting up a fight now, even as his skilled fingers find my clit and start making bubbles of bliss pop in my head. Not pop, explode. I hold onto the fireworks, try to think of nothing but how good his lips feel on my skin, or the strength in his muscles coiling beneath my palms, pulsing under my hands as I close my fingers around them. That is all I need to be safe. He is all I need. Because his passion and his desire for me, and mine for him, can take me to a different world, one without sorrow, without regret and nightmares that overtake my waking moments and which I cannot fight on my own. It can, but it's not doing it now.

I yelp in surprise and pleasure and fear all rolled into one as he pushes his cock into me, the intrusion unexpected, unannounced, yet welcome, but also too much like before, too much like those dark, scary, horrible nights and days.

I need to get out, need control, need to be free!

But he's holding me down, thrusting into me, his cock finding that pleasure button inside me each and every time. I forget the bad for one glorious moment each time he presses it, making my brain and my body explode in bliss for the split second it lasts. Then his cock retreats.

I writhe to get away, surrender as the pleasure explodes, fight again once it fades. The push and pull of pleasure and fear, of terror and bliss is ripping my mind apart. Each of those emotions is too strong, too stubborn, none will let go, and I can't take it. I can't take it, but I want to. I want the pleasure and bliss to win. I need it to win. But I can't take it. I won't survive this fight.

My writhing annoys him, breaks his rhythm, speeds up his thrusts, makes him miss.

"Stay still, Lynn," he says as he does exactly that with his cock buried deep inside me. It's throbbing against that pleasure button, keeping me right at the edge of another explosion of pleasure, withholding the fireworks, letting the fear get the upper hand, driving me mad.

He grips my wrists, pushes them into the mattress and holds them there. It's no different to being tied down. He pulls out his cock and thrusts back in, but this time even the explosion of bliss isn't strong enough to fight back the fear.

"I can't!" I yell even as I moan. "Not like that! I can't, please!"

I'm twisting my arms to free my wrists, and he lets them go. He stops thrusting into me and the wide fast lane to world-shattering bliss we were speeding down comes to an abrupt dead end.

His eyes are like two peaceful pools in a deep, untouched forest, reflecting the trees surrounding them. The beasts hiding in the trees are scary and many, but they can't touch the waters, and they're not where he looks at me. They're just there to protect me.

"Alright, you scared little doe," he whispers, replying to

whatever he saw in *my* eyes, because I have no idea what he's talking about.

He leans down and kisses my neck, then starts pushing his cock in and out slowly and steadily, calmly and deeply. The two paths of soft pleasure—from his lips on my neck and from his cock caressing my pussy—are meeting in my center now, as deep as the calm pools in his eyes and more glorious than the first rays of sunlight at dawn.

There's no more push and pull between the desire and fear in my mind, there's only bliss, only sparkling pleasure, and that's all that matters. This moment is all that matters. I'm safe, I'm secure, I'm protected and cared for, and I feel good, I feel great, I feel better than I ever had in my whole life.

I caress his arms and his neck, touch his strong back and powerful thighs, his face. I need to feel all of him and I want to see his eyes, because I'm so close, so very close to coming, and I want to look into his eyes as I come, want to see him and feel him at the same time, want him to know how much this means to me, how much he means to me. He's my savior. My protector. My lover. And I want to be his too.

But he won't lift his head.

His kisses grow more urgent as his thrusts speed up, his breath fast and hot on my neck, my whole body vibrating under the volleys of pleasure that keep coming in stronger and faster, driving me towards the edge. His groans are blending with my moans and whimpers, and I know he's close too. I want us to fall over that edge together. But I can't hold back much longer. I can't hold back at all anymore.

I wrap my arms around his neck tight, as though to brace against the fall. But he's right here with me, falling too, landing now in a field of pure pleasure. The impact shatters the last of my defenses, sending them crumbling into the depths of my past with the bad memories and the nightmares, into the black nothingness of oblivion where they belong.

    I'd tell him to look at me, but my voice is hiding somewhere and I can't find it. But we don't have to look at each other. I see him clearly even with my eyes closed.

16

LYNN

It's almost ten AM and I'm only just driving Scar to get his bike. By no definition of the word, will I be home "soon" like I promised Mom I would be. I should feel worse about that, but how can I? The sun is out, everything is sparkling, Scrap will be released from the animal hospital later today, and the news on the radio just said that they've managed to stop the raging fire threatening the area and have called off the red alert. Apparently there are now only a few isolated patches of the fire left to extinguish.

Scar is sitting by my side, still kinda grumpy since he's clearly not a morning person, but it's endearing to watch him grumble. Besides, I have enough energy in the mornings for the both of us. I love dawn, I love watching the sun rise, I love the freshness of the world as it begins to wake after a full night's sleep.

And probably most importantly, for the first time in twelve years, I feel like a woman. A woman with a body that's made to be worshipped, not used and abused. A woman who enjoys offering her body to be worshipped. Last night, despite all his roughness and gruffness, I never, not for a split second, believed that I was just a vessel for his pleasure, a thing to be used and discarded, which is how my ordeal made me feel.

For the second time in my life, the man sitting next to me, being very quiet and grimacing as he squints from the glowing sun in his eyes, saved me.

"That's great news that the fire is under control," I say.

He grunts something in answer, but I can't for the life of me figure out what he said.

"What?" I ask, giggling as I do.

"There'll be another one soon enough," he says. "There always is. California's that kinda place."

"Alright, Grumpy," I say as I park the car next to his bike at the parking lot of the animal hospital. "Why don't you go wake up fully, and I'll see you later in a good mood."

He chuckles and runs his hand down my cheek. "You wanna put me in a good mood? Then how about we go back to the house?"

I shake my head, but smile and lean my cheek against his palm. He didn't want to leave the bed yet, I forced him too, and that's a huge part of the reason for his grumpiness right now.

"We'll see each other soon," I say. "I'll just go home, then come back here to pick up Scrap, and then we'll have the whole day together at the ranch."

He nods along slowly. "Yeah, about that. I got some things to take care of first. It could take all day or it could take an hour, I don't know. But I'll see you tonight, count on that. I'll pick you up and we'll go for a ride."

Back when I was just a waitress and he was just a biker who'd come in to talk to me every day, we sometimes talked about going for a ride. I said I wanted to know what it was like, he'd invite me, and I'd make up an excuse. Thinking back, me saying no to a ride was probably the reason—or at least part of the reason—why he never asked me on a date. But now I still want to go for that ride, and nothing is stopping me. Nothing except the fact that my chest still freezes when I hear a Harley and I get nauseous right after hearing it. But this is Scar. This is my savior. And I won't refuse him again.

"OK," I say and smile, since he's frowning at me now, probably because I took too long to answer. "Pick me up at the ranch and we'll go."

"I'd love to go for a ride with you," I add, since the expression on his face is telling me he's not entirely satisfied with my answer.

He grins, smiles almost, then kisses me so deeply and so thoroughly I feel as though the morning sun is now inside me too, calling everything awake, warming things that have been left forgotten in a cold, freezing darkness for far too long.

And as I watch him ride away later, there's no nausea, no fear, only the freshness of a new dawn, of a new life, one where memories are just that—things that were done, that happened, and that can and will be forgotten. For the first time in more than ten years, I dare to believe that love in all its forms is possible for me too.

The house is quiet as I enter and smells sickly sweet, like from flowers only worse. Mom is probably in the garden shed, which she uses as her workshop and I should go find her, but she's not gonna be happy with me, and I'm too happy for an argument.

"You said you'd be home soon, Lynn," she says from behind my back, before I even reach the stairs leading upstairs.

Her hair is a mess, and she's wearing her favorite robe, which she's owned since I can remember and looks it, over the clothes she must've worn yesterday, because they're very crumpled. There are dark blue bags under her bloodshot eyes, which are glowing with an unnatural brightness. That only ever means one thing. I know now why the house smells sickly sweet.

"I'm sorry, but I was having fun," I say.

"Having fun?" she says, more to herself than to me, and retreats back to the living room where she came from.

I sigh and follow her. As I enter the living room, she's already pouring herself another tumbler of whiskey, mixing it with the amaretto liqueur she likes so much and which is the source of the sweet smell all over the house. This isn't her first drink since last night, that's for sure.

Mom started drinking after my dad died. I'm pretty sure his death was the reason. She's tried to quit many times over the years, but it never sticks, not for long anyway. I know that I only added and continue to add to the problem, but I don't feel guilty over it like I used to. Well, I feel a little guilty right now, as I sit down on the sofa next to her.

"So, who were you having so much fun with that you forgot to call me?" she asks taking a long sip of her drink.

I shouldn't have said "fun". I did that because I was planning on telling her about Scar, but going by her curt tone and that unnatural, angry gleam in her eyes, I think she'll try to spoil it for me. And last night was too perfect to allow that.

"We got to talking up at the ranch after the work was done, you know about the future and everything, and pretty soon it was two AM," I start saying, the words sounding very stiff as they leave my mouth, because I don't like lying. "You already know that Bethany is thinking of selling, but she doesn't really want to, so we were coming up with alternate plans. And then it was so late and I was too sleepy to drive home, so I just stayed there. I should've called. I'm sorry for making you worry."

That could all be true. But if that's how things had gone last night, I'd never have forgotten to call her and tell her I'm not coming home.

"Why didn't you call me?" she asks shrilly, picking up on it, but not quite, because she's drunk. "Do you know what I went through when you went missing? I almost went mad. I was almost hospitalized because I couldn't eat or sleep or do anything but wait by the phone for news about you."

And do you know what I went through? I was hospitalized for three months afterwards, and I've been a prisoner of those bad memories ever since. Until last night.

I don't say any of those things, because I know it's the alcohol talking right now, not Mom, and I probably wouldn't be in any position to take my life back last night if she hadn't been by my side, propping me up for the last twelve years.

"I really am sorry, Mom, it slipped my mind," I say. "But I'm a grown woman after all and shouldn't have to tell my mom where I am every second. Nothing's gonna happen to me ever again."

I can be certain of that because Scar's with me now. He promised me as much, and I don't plan of letting him go anytime soon. I can't tell her that yet, but by the look on her face I just said the wrong thing anyway.

"How can you be so sure? Those men could still be after you? There's a big gang of bikers just two towns away from here," she says, telling me what she's told me a million times, since she found out about that biker gang. When we first came here, we didn't know about them, and by the time we found out we had already started our lives here, so we stayed anyway. But she worried.

Yet she had no reason to. I think Scar is a member of that gang. He still doesn't tell me much about his life, but I sorta read that between the lines of what little he lets slip. So he was near me all along, as though still watching over me, even though neither of us knew it. With us, it's fate, I have little doubt about that left.

"I'm not worried about them Mom, and you shouldn't be either," I say and continue smiling at that thought. "I was never really in any danger after I was freed, you know that."

"Have you completely lost it now, Lynn?" she snaps. "You were in no danger because we always took every precaution. How can you not worry?"

I don't stop smiling, because I'm happy and even her dark mood and aggressiveness can't spoil it. I won't let it spoil it. I've lived with the paralyzing terror of what happened to me twelve years ago every day of those years. My mom going off like this —which isn't a once in a while occurrence— reminding me of it, warning me, perpetuating my fear even after twelve years of living such a boring life I'm sure old people in nursing homes had more fun than me, is a big part of the reason why I couldn't let go of it, couldn't forget it, and I'm only just fully realizing this.

It's not her fault and she wasn't doing it on purpose, so I don't blame her. She had to deal with it too. But it's time I start living my own life. I appreciate all she's done for me, but it's time I stand on my own two feet.

"No, Mom, I'm thinking very clearly," I snap instead of telling her all that, since I don't even know how to begin saying it.

She blinks at the harshness of my tone.

"I'm sorry I didn't call you last night. It was a mistake, but it happens," I say and stand up, since this conversation is over. "Now get some sleep, Mom. You look very tired, and I have to get back to the ranch."

She opens and closes her mouth a few times, but makes no sound. Her eyes aren't gleaming with that alcohol-induced anger anymore though. She finally nods.

"You're right," she says. "I am very tired. We can talk more tonight. I'm making Quiche Lorraine. You like that, right?"

It's my favorite dish and she knows that.

"Yeah, I do," I say anyway.

But I don't add that I won't be home for dinner. I'll call and tell her later, because if I bring it up now, she'll go off again, and I'm already not nearly as happy and carefree as I was when I woke up this morning.

17

SCAR

"So, you find Reggie for me yet?" I ask loudly as I barge into Hawk's computer room. He slams the lid of his laptop shut, causing a woman's chipper voice to cut off mid-sentence. Maybe I was right last time, maybe he does watch porn in here all day. But that's none of my business.

"Knocking, Scar, it's polite," he says harshly as he turns.

I shrug. "Yeah, I heard about that once or twice. Polite's not part of my skillset though. So, Reggie?"

"Reggie who?" he asks looking genuinely bewildered before he figures it out. "You mean Reaper?"

I nod. "Yeah, but that's one pretentious fucking name, and I don't use it. It's completely undeserved unless you count the hoards of domesticated animals he killed. And we don't count that."

He grunts something that sounds like agreement, but

doesn't say anything, which is for the best since I hate discussing my brother more than is absolutely necessary. I pull up a chair, but he shakes his head at me like there's no need.

"I haven't found them yet," he says. "They're laying low real deep somewhere. And the FBI is hard on their asses, they made the top ten most wanted list. Well, the Spawns who escaped with him did anyway. Not your brother though. Go figure, since he was inside for first degree murder."

I sit down anyway, since maybe I have some info that'll make it easier for Hawk to find Reggie. I want him found and I want it done soon. I've waited too fucking long for my second chance at him, and I'm not sitting around twiddling my thumbs while waiting for him to surface.

"Reggie was always a charmer, kinda like our Tank, but with a whole lot more psycho," I say. "I wouldn't be surprised if he made like a puppy dog in prison, that was always one of his favorite tricks."

I've seen first hand the depths of psycho that run very deep in my brother's mind. My reflection in the mirror is a lasting reminder of them, but everywhere else, you'd have a tough uphill battle to prove he was capable of something like that.

"He's a fucking coward is what I'm saying," I say. "He only ever dared to show his true face to a select few. The rest was just a lie."

Hawk nods with this weird expression on his face, like he's willing to hear me out if I want to chat, but he has other things he'd rather be doing. Don't we all? I managed to tear one of my stitches last night with Lynn, and Doc said no more farm work until it stops bleeding and closes up again, unless I want to get sepsis. So I have the whole day to get through before I can see her again, and I could be spending that time productively, as in tracking down Reggie.

"He won't stay with the Spawns he escaped with," I add, since this is where I was heading with this conversation. "He'll try and find his old gang, if he can. If not, he'll search for someone else who'll take him in and shelter him. Like I said, he's a little pussy. He also knows me and him have unfinished business, since I've made it quite clear to him that I'll kill him one day. That either means he'll try to get to me first, or that he'll run as far away from me as he can. I can't tell you which it'll be, since Reggie is very unpredictable like that."

"Alright, yeah, that's good info," Hawk says and wheels his chair away from the laptop he's been using to his large, three-monitor setup he usually works at. "I'll see what I can dig up in that direction."

I nod and stand up. "I'll leave you to it and check back later."

"Could take awhile," he says and grins at me over his shoulder. "In the meantime, go enjoy your downtime. How's that beauty queen of yours doing?"

A couple of days ago that suggestive question would've pissed me off no end, but I had her now, had her twice last night and once this morning, so it doesn't even sting. "She's just fine."

"I bet she is," he says and that does piss me off.

It's a throwaway comment, the kind I'd make too if a brother said a woman he'd fucked was fine. But Lynn isn't just another piece of ass that come a dime a dozen for us. I won't be starting shit over it though, so I let my hard look and silence do the talking as I leave the room.

I hoped I could start tracking Reggie today and making plans, but instead I have the whole afternoon of not having jack shit to do, but kill time until I get to fuck Lynn again, or see her for that matter, which is all I want to do anyway. I've never experienced anything like this before.

Women were always just there for the plucking when I felt like it, and I never spared them much thought, while I wasn't plucking them. Unless maybe I used to feel that way back in high school when all the girls looked at me with pity and disgust and none wanted to be alone with me.

But Lynn does, and that makes up for every other rejection and then some.

LYNN

I brought a change of clothes for tonight with me, and used the main bathroom in the house to shower and change an hour ago. I even picked up some new makeup on my way to get Scrap from the animal hospital and did a pretty stellar job applying it despite my lack of practice.

Bethany and Tammy have been giving me sidelong looks and making all sorts of comments about where I'm going so dressed up, but Raul's just been frowning.

I smiled at their questions and didn't tell them anything about my plans. I tried to keep the conversation pointed to whether it's a good idea to let the owners come pick up their animals now that the fires seem to be under control, or whether we should keep them for a few more days.

"If I have the maps and reports figured out right, that riding school near Sycamore Ridge is still in danger even with the main fire under control," I say. "They have ten horses, I think. We should convince them to bring them down here."

Raul grumbles something, and Tammy snorts derisively. "I tried one more time a couple of days ago, but the woman that runs the school is an arrogant fool. You can try convincing her if you want, but I've had enough of her."

"Alright, I'll call her in the morning," I say and check my watch, which is something I've been doing practically every minute for the last hour.

It's almost seven thirty and the sun is setting outside. Scar said he'd be by to pick me up in the evening for sure, but didn't give me a time. It's the evening and he's not here yet. I'm growing afraid he won't show up at all, since I expected him to be here a lot earlier, if I'm honest with myself.

"Don't let us keep you, if you have somewhere to be," Bethany says with a smile as Tammy and her exchange a look.

"No, no, it's fine," I mumble and I know I'm blushing because my face is very hot.

"Or maybe…" I add and stand up, pushing my chair under the table awkwardly and so clumsily the screeching noise echoes across the kitchen and makes hair stand up on the back of my neck.

"Have a good time," Tammy says and smiles at me. I smile back, thank her, say bye to the others and leave.

I left so quickly because I'm worried and their questions and looks were making it worse. I'm worried Scar won't show up, worried last night was just a one-time thing. Worried he just used me.

We didn't talk about the future at all, didn't even exchange phone numbers, just made this one date to go for a ride. I have no idea about what he does with his life. For all I know he could have a family. I could've just been a bit of fun for him, a little trip down memory lane.

The failing light outside, as I stand by my car out of sight of the kitchen and the three inside it, waiting for him to come isn't helping my mood. My thoughts are turning blacker and bleaker with each minute that passes, and he doesn't appear.

If he just used me it's because that's all I'm good for. Getting used. Paying for my beauty and attractiveness with my body. And I paid with all I had.

And as hard as I try to fight it, pretend all that is done and gone, the grimacing faces of my abusers are coming alive before my eyes even though they're wide open. I kept my eyes shut while they raped me. Got slapped and punched for lying there like a log. Got choked and bitten and pinched and punched until I screamed.

Scar well and truly used my body last night, but I loved it, loved also that he stopped when I asked him to. Loved it because he showed me the pleasure in rough sex, showed me the passion in it, so now I don't see just pain and degradation like I did before last night. He made me believe I could put all that behind me and start fresh, because he showed me the path to pleasure and led me to its breathless, earth-shifting end.

But right now, as I wait for him to meet me in the twilight, I can't tell Scar's face from the grimacing ones of those other men and it's making my heart race, making my skin cold and clammy, and my breaths hurt.

Then I hear the rumbling. The whole earth shakes from it. My thoughts shake too, so hard they crack then crumble into the ashes our passion made of my bad memories last night.

My racing heartbeat takes on a different pitch as I approach him.

"You came," I whisper.

"I said I would, didn't I?" He's grinning, but his eyes are serious. "Ready to go?"

Despite all the fear and darkness I was experiencing a minute ago, I don't think twice, don't hesitate for even a moment before climbing onto his bike and cinching my arms around his waist.

Maybe it's because the absolute terror unfolding inside me moments before he came is rapidly getting replaced by a gorgeous song in my heart, which started playing the second I saw him driving towards me. Or maybe it's just how strong and big he is, how solid, like a rock, like a whole castle made of rocks built just so I can be safe, just to protect me. He even smells like rocks, and leather, and wood, all things hardy, hearty and earthy, natural and eternal, everlasting.

"I'm ready. Let's go," I say and hold him even tighter, press my whole body against his broad back, feel his laugh as well as hear it, and I know that we don't have to actually go anywhere, because we've already arrived. To the place I always wanted to reach, that I yearned and longed to reach. But it's not a place and it never was. It's him.

18

LYNN

"So, your plans for tonight are takeout and bed?" I ask coyly as we climb off his bike near the taco truck in town.

Joking and flirting with him this way comes so naturally, so effortlessly. I'm surprised I even still know how to do it, since I spent so many years cooped up at home and avoiding men and all and any mentions of sex. But his sly grin back just confirms that I haven't lost my touch at all.

"No, who do you take me for?" he says and offers me his arm. "I was thinking we'd have a picnic up in the hills. But if you'd prefer to just go straight to bed..."

"No, no," I say and wrap one hand under his arm and clutch it with the other. "Your idea is better."

He laughs again, and I love the sound. It reminds me of birds taking off after being startled in the forest, their chirruping and flapping of wings a sudden burst of life in the calm.

Eating under the stars and kissing in the moonlight is something I've never done. But I always wanted to. I used to be a sucker for romantic things like that, used to imagine perfect dates with my perfect knight in shining armor in my head all the time before I was kidnapped. I was one of those girls who had a pink secret diary with a lock and I'd write things like that in it. Scar's not perfect, and he'd probably laugh from here to the end of time if I called him a knight in shining armor. But that's what he is, he's my knight, and for me he is perfect.

There's no line for the tacos and ten minutes later I'm clutching the bag of food as we speed up another hill, the rumbling of his bike echoing off the trees lining the road, sounding and feeling like an earthquake. Not the scary kind, a good kind, the best kind, the kind that only destroys what has no reason to exist, only destroys and buries things that should've been destroyed and buried a long time ago.

He stops at the start of a dirt road, but even though it's completely dark now, the end of the path seems illuminated, glows a whitish orange like the setting sun, and I'm not sure if I'm really seeing that or it's just in my imagination. Either way, it doesn't matter and I don't think of anything else but how happy and light and content I feel as I take his hand and let him lead me towards that light.

I've been worried and afraid and anxious for so long, didn't know how to escape those dark feeling that trapped me in an endless circle of pain. But they're gone now, replaced by this blissful elation, this glowing light of a future I look forward to so much that I hardly feel my feet touching the ground as we walk.

The path opens onto a clearing at the top of a ridge. He

leads me to the very edge, to the stony part where grass doesn't grow. The light wasn't just in my head. It's coming from the fire raging in the distance, beyond a dark valley and beyond another, smaller hill. The fire is so large that the sky above it is orange. My light of hope was this monstrous wildfire destroying all in its path, hot and ferocious, annihilation made thing.

"Isn't it gorgeous?" Scar asks. He's already sitting on the ground, the paper bag he took from my hand when we arrived rustling as he takes out his food.

I manage to tear my eyes away from the fire and sit down next to him, and even take my own taco out of the bag he's holding out to me.

"It's mesmerizing, that's for sure," I say. "But I can't call it gorgeous. Animals are dying in extreme pain in that fire right now."

I'd save them all if I could, I'd risk my life to do it in the blink of an eye. But there's nothing I can do. And I can't look away either.

"Oh, yeah, the animals," he says. His mouth is full, so I can't tell if he's making fun of me, or if he's actually concerned for them too, now that I mentioned it.

I look at my taco, but can't bite into it. I lost my appetite, would probably retch if I tried to eat.

"Well, I still think it's gorgeous," he says, so I suppose he was poking fun at me before.

"People are losing their homes too. Everything they worked hard for all their live is getting destroyed, is disappearing like it never was. Many of them will never recover. How can you call any of that gorgeous?" I ask quietly.

"Because it is," he says and chuckles. I'm sure he sees my point, he has to, but he's clearly refusing to join me on my level, and maybe I should stop forcing him to.

"I come here to watch the fires sometimes, this place almost always offers the best view of them," he adds. "I like watching the world burn. It's nature showing her teeth and taking her own back. You know, like the ultimate punishment, and there's nothing any puny human being can do about it, or any animal for that matter. I thought you'd appreciate the idea too, given what you've been through."

I glance at him, and his face is illuminated just enough by the fire so I see it's actually very serious. In his own rough way, he brought me here to help me, not because he thought I'd like the orangey glow in the sky. And on some level, I understand what he's saying. But I don't feel the same way.

I'll never be able to look beyond the pain and suffering this fire is causing, despite the pain and suffering I went through. I've never longed for revenge on anyone for what happened to me, nor did I ever want anyone else to suffer like I did. The suffering of others won't make mine any easier to bear. That's what I know. Maybe I can help him understand it too, because he sounded so angry and yet so darkly satisfied when he spoke about the world burning.

"You're talking about the scar on your face and getting revenge for that," I say. "You've had it for a long time, haven't you? Since you were young?"

It's like a breeze of very cold air hitting me from the side as he turns to face me.

"You been doing a lot of thinking about my scarred face, haven't you?" he asks harshly.

I shake my head, have the sudden urge to touch his scarred cheek, but his stone cold eyes and the hard set of his jaw tells me he won't allow that right now.

"We can talk about something else if you want to," I say. "It's just…"

"Just what? I already told you how I got it," he says. "But I suppose you won't be happy until you hear the full story."

His voice isn't as hard and cold as before, so I offer him a sheepish little smile. "Most likely, yes."

He grins and shakes his head. "Fine, Lynn. There's not much I can refuse you anyway, for some reason I don't understand. I mean, I spent the last week shoveling hay and horse shit, for fucks sake."

This time I grin. "Hey now, you did that for the animals, not me."

He gives me one of those piercing, exasperated looks he'd sometimes give me while we joked around on slow afternoons at the diner. The ones I grew addicted to. The ones that made me fall in love with him back then. Because he saw me those times, me for me, and not just me the local beauty queen, didn't see me as an object, a thing to have, like those other men who came in to watch me did. He's still looking at me like that right now.

"My brother cut up my face when I was twelve, because I played his video game without asking," he says, his story driving a sharp stake right through all the butterflies fluttering in my stomach from remembering those fun times we used to share.

I gasp, try to say something, then just end up gasping again.

"Yeah, it's a fucking terrible story, Lynn, not much more to say about it," he says. "It's made even worse by the fact that I had to live with him in the same house for the next six years, pretending I tripped and fell on a saw, which was the story my father told everyone when he brought me to the hospital."

"Your parents just pretended it never happened?" I say after another gasp.

No wonder he wants the world to burn. Me, I'd probably hide in the basement for the rest of my life, alone with my pain and my grief, but he's different than me. He's angry and he needs revenge.

He shrugs and frowns. "Well, yeah, to everyone else. Not at home. But I still hated their guts for it. They're both dead now, so that doesn't matter anymore. And my brother will get his any day now."

The venom, the cold hate in his voice as he says it, strikes me like the coldest gust of wind, strikes me right through. His need for revenge is eating him up inside like a wound that won't heal. I know this very clearly right now, and it hurts me too.

"I understand that you're angry. You have every right to be," I say quietly after a few seconds of silence. "But revenge and thinking about it all the time will only make you angrier, and it'll only make you feel worse. What happened, happened. It's no one's fault, it just happened."

"It's my brother's fault," he snaps. "And what happened to you is Lizard's fault. It happened because they're both sick motherfuckers who need to be put down."

For the second time in the space of five minutes, I'm hit with that cutting, cold wind his anger brings. And it's harder to recover this time, because he reminded me of things I'm not really good at forgetting yet.

"You're a gentle and sweet woman, Lynn, and I hate it that

what happened, happened to you of all people," he adds, holding my chin with his thumb and forefinger, so he can look into my eyes. "I'm also amazed that you're still as pure as you were before it happened. But I don't know how well it's all worked out for you these last few years that you spent living at home with your mom, and hiding out at a ranch in the middle of nowhere. It's not something that makes a whole lotta sense to me."

"It worked fine," I say, kinda hurt by his mocking tone, but not really, because he's wrong and I know it. "I found peace with what happened to me. I could've been an angry and resentful mess, like some of the women I met in group therapy were, and I'm not judging them, but they had no peace. Maybe I had a boring life, but at least I had a peaceful one."

"Not judging, huh?" he says, but despite his mocking tone, his eyes are thoughtful.

"Not at all. It's just my way," I say. "But it's a good way, and it worked for me."

"It's never been my way," he says after a longer pause, which he spends looking very deep into my eyes, like he's searching for something in them.

"And I'm too old to learn new tricks now," he concludes.

Then he leans down and kisses me, making the earth spin, bringing the heat of the wildfire raging in the distance much closer. But destruction isn't what I'm afraid of now.

I hold him very tight as we kiss, tighter that I've ever held onto anyone, even the teddy bear I still keep on my bed and hug when I'm sad.

He needs me. Needs me to give him the peace that he can't find for himself. Just like I needed him so many times before.

He always gave me what I needed, and I will give him this. I just hope I'll know how.

He doesn't stop kissing me as he picks me up and carries me back from the edge of the ridge, into the grass and flowers growing wild and unfettered there. I can smell the grass, smell the flowers, smell the rocks and the trees, but not the burning. His scent explodes all around me as he takes off his jacket and shirt, accentuating it all, bringing new ones to the mix.

He does stop kissing me long enough to pull the dress I'm wearing up over my head, nothing sensual about the action, nothing slow, seductive or romantic, but I don't need that, I don't *crave* that. I crave the passion, the feel of his naked skin pressed against mine. His scent and mine are mixing in the air, becoming one with the other wonderful scents of the world all around us.

The world is beautiful, the world is whole, and it's mine for the taking. No, it's ours for the taking.

But the world is burning all around us too. It's getting destroyed just over that hill in the distance. That fact strikes home in my mind when my knees collide with the hard earth beneath the soft grass, as he turns me and forces me down on all fours.

His passion is as wild and unbridled as the nature around us. As destructive and rough as the wildfire raging just beyond the next hill. He yanks down my panties until the elastic is digging into my thighs just above my knees.

"I want to look at your face," I whisper as his fist closes around my ponytail, and he leans down for another kiss.

He says nothing, his fist tightening in my hair as he kisses me. And the gentleness of his lips against mine, and later against my neck, belie the roughness of his hand gripping my hair and pulling my head back, of his rough thrust as he gives me his cock.

He starts riding me fast and hard, until even the gentleness of his kiss fades in the raging furnace of pleasure his cock is stoking up inside me. Before long I'm screaming and writhing, my nails digging into the dirt, breaking on the stones buried inside it.

But I miss the gentleness mixed with this roughness, I miss his eyes soaking me in all the wild passion and desire he has for me, bathing me in the recognition, the appreciation of *me* that I only ever see in his eyes and no one else's.

"Please," I shriek and moan more than say. "I want to look at you."

He gives me one more vicious thrust that nearly makes me come, then freezes with his pulsing cock buried deep in my pussy.

"No you don't, Lynn," he says gruffly. "No one wants to look at me."

I never expected this kind of self-consciousness from the rough, strong and tough man he is, but here it is, plain as day for me to see.

"I do. I want to look at you," I tell him and gaze at him over my shoulder as he loosens his grip on my ponytail. "I never want to stop looking at your face. It's the most beautiful face I've ever seen, because you're the man who gave me back my life."

The distant fire is illuminating his face, hiding nothing, not a single jagged edge of his scar, nor the softness of his eyes, which see only me right now, the way no one else ever has. The way I don't think even he's seen me before.

"You mean it?" he asks, and I can hear it in his voice that he's sure I was just saying that.

I gasp and moan as I slide off his cock then turn to face him, not breaking eye-contact as I glide my hand across his cheek, across his scar like I should've done when he told me how he got it earlier.

"I mean it," I say. "Your scarred face is the most beautiful face I've ever seen."

He just looks at me for a good long while after I say it, frowning, and if it weren't for those peaceful forest pools in his eyes bathing my face and my body and my soul in their calm waters, I'd be sure I said exactly the wrong thing, even though I know it's what he needed to hear, and I meant every word.

He chuckles suddenly, the smile staying on his face even after the sound fades. "Then you haven't been looking in the mirror much, because your face is the most beautiful face that exists."

"No, I'm pretty sure that's yours," I say and smile too.

"You're wrong," he says, but kisses me before I can keep this little back and forth game going.

His kiss is as soft as the grass he lays me down in, as everlasting as the earth beneath my back as he spreads my legs apart and enters me, slowly, almost gently, making us one, joining us in body, the way we're already joined in spirit.

He gives me what I wanted, looks deeply into my eyes, as his cock brings me to the brink of an abyss of pleasure so vast and deep I might never reach the bottom. He keeps looking at me as I topple off the brink into the abyss, into the sweet, bottomless expanse of pleasure and bliss, of devotion and passion, which shines brighter and burns hotter than the fire devastating the world in the distance.

But it's not too much to bear, because I'm floating in the peaceful waters in his eyes, they're washing over me, caressing my skin, giving me what I've yearned for. Peace and belonging. And love. I think.

19

LYNN

When I arrive home in mid-afternoon, Mom is sitting at the kitchen table, fully dressed and wearing shoes. The room reeks of her perfume, because she put on too much of it like she always does before going out. She always insisted I wear just as much of it too, because she's convinced there's no point putting it on otherwise as it just fades too fast. I never liked wearing perfume, it masks all the other scents. Like Scar's scent, which is still all over my skin although I haven't seen him for hours.

We spent the night at the house. I dozed off in his arms after we made love again—true, pure, lasting love, not the rough and passionate kind, which is great too — and afterwards I had the best sleep in years. I think he did too, because he wasn't grumpy at all this morning when he took me up to the ranch.

He wouldn't stay, but he gave me his phone number, so we can make more precise plans from now on. I planned to message him as soon as I got home to ask when we can be together again. All day, I felt like I was walking on clouds, and I still do. Something very heavy was weighing me down all these years, not even something I was carrying but more like a very heavy winter coat I wore year round. It's gone now, Scar removed it for me. Or more precisely, he gave me the strength to finally toss it off and live again.

"I thought we could go grocery shopping today," Mom says after I greet her cautiously.

She reacted with curt silence to my text that I couldn't make dinner yesterday and that I wouldn't be spending the night at home again. She also didn't reply to the one this morning when I told her I'll come home in the afternoon. I have no idea what kind of mood she's in.

"We're out of everything," she adds.

I hope my sigh of relief wasn't too audible. I think she's in a normal mood.

"Sure, Mom, let me just shower and change and then we can go," I say and rush upstairs.

I'd much rather be setting up an early date with Scar, but my mom doesn't drive very well, and besides, she needs the car to get to the store and we only have the one I use to get to and from the ranch.

I also wanted to take a long bath before tonight's date with Scar, maybe curl my hair the way I used to every time I went out, but haven't for more or less the past twelve years. But this works too. I'll be able to buy some more makeup and maybe even a few new dresses.

"I'm ready," I say as I come down to the kitchen less than a half an hour later with my hair still wet. I'll set it later, when we get home. "Let's go."

"You're so chipper lately," Mom remarks as she gets up from the kitchen table.

She didn't say it, but I'm pretty sure I heard a, "How is that possible?" at the end of that sentence.

"Things are going well at the ranch," I say. But maybe I should stop keeping her in the dark about Scar.

"And I met a man," I add rather quietly, but she heard me well enough. She turns to me so sharply she loses balance in her high heels and sits back down in her chair with a thump.

I giggle at the sight of her reaction, which is straight out of some slapstick comedy. "Wow, Mom, are you alright?"

She smiles too. "Well, that was quite possibly the last thing I expected you to say. Come, sit down, tell me more."

She taps the table next to her, urging me to take a seat. "Who is he? Where did you meet him? I want to know everything."

There's a very wide smile on my face as I take a seat. "I didn't think you'd be this happy about the news, Mom."

She shrugs and keeps smiling. "Of course, I'm happy. You need someone by your side, and you need to shake your fear of men."

We didn't discuss that part of my lingering affliction much over the years, mainly because it was too painful for both of us to talk about, so I didn't know she felt this strongly about it.

"He's not someone I just met. I met him a long time ago. He's the one who saved me from the men who abducted me. He came back to tell me..." I pause, realizing I probably shouldn't tell her exactly what Scar's news was. "To see how I was doing."

"That guy?" she says pensively, the expression on her face no longer happy or excited. Now it's just worried and dark. She doesn't say anything more, but I can see she's thinking about saying more. Thinking about saying things I probably don't want to hear.

"Yes, *that guy*. The one I owe my life to," I say.

"That's no reason to just jump into bed with him," she muses, and I have no idea how she can think I'd do that. Does she know me at all?

"That wasn't the reason," I counter. "As I already told you, we spent a lot of time together before I was abducted. We were friends, but I was kind of in love with him, and I think he was kind of in love with me too."

"What's kind of in love, Lynn?" she says with a tone that suggests I'm the most naive woman in the world. I get the feeling sometimes that this is how she perceives me, but I know it's probably just in my head, so I try to ignore it.

"It's like when you're friends with someone and then you start falling in love, but there's that period of time before you realize you're actually in love, as in when your heart already knows it but your mind doesn't yet," I say, my words not coming together the way I want them to. "It's hard to explain…"

"Oh, like when your hormones overtake your reason?" she says harshly.

"What's that supposed to mean?" I snap back, since I don't like her tone at all right now, and this time I'm not ready to ignore it and start convincing myself it's all just in my head.

She looks at me thoughtfully, frowning as though she's trying to decide how to continue this conversation.

"I don't think he's the right man for you," she finally says, clearly not willing to let me down easy. She's completely wrong. He's quite possibly the only man for me.

"He's the perfect man for me. He's the only one I wanted to kiss me in all this time for one thing," I say, oblivious to how the words are coming from my mouth, because they're coming from my heart. "And he's the one who rescued me, in case you forgot. So I don't think I have anything to worry about from him, and I don't know how you can think that I do."

She shakes her head and purses her lips. That's never a good sign. "I never said this to you, since you were intent on putting him on a pedestal, and I thought that maybe you needed to do that, that maybe you needed the idea of a knight in shining armor coming to your rescue, so you could get better after your ordeal. After all, you were always prone to daydreaming and such. But I think he was with the ones who abducted you, and probably just felt remorseful enough to save you, because clearly you did have some sort of friendship."

Some sort of friendship? We were in love. She thinks Scar abducted me? That's nonsense. Absolute nonsense. And I know that. I know it because the only reason he came to see me now was to tell me he helped kill all the men who tortured me. But I can't tell my mom that. In fact, I don't want to tell her anything more at all.

"Why can't you just be happy for me, Mom?" I snap and stand up. "I've barely lived these last twelve years, and now that I'm finally living again, you're trying to spoil it for me. I know you think I'm a naive, defenseless idiot who can't take care of herself at all, but you're wrong. I know my own mind, and I know he's a good man. I'm certain he cares about me very much and that he'd never hurt me. And it's enough that I know it. You don't have to know it too, you just have to take my word for it."

I was going to fly out of the room after I gave her this piece of my mind, but the expression on her face as I finish speaking is so puzzling I just stare at it.

"You can't take care of yourself, Lynn," she says after a few seconds of dead silence. Her face looks angry, but her voice is very calm and cool. "You need someone to guide you, and that someone has always been me."

"You're wrong, Mom," I say, shaking my head in disbelief that she just said that. "I can take care of myself just fine. I was just never given that choice, since you were always right there, insisting I take your hand and let you lead. It's been like that since I was a little girl, with all those beauty pageants and later when you wanted me to continue doing it. I've lived my whole life according to what you wanted from me. I appreciate all you've done for me, but I *can* take care of myself, and I *don't* need you to guide me. I don't need anyone to do that."

My voice is shaking by the time I finish speaking, and I know I'll burst into tears if she says just one more hurtful thing to me. So I bolt out of the kitchen, run straight to my room and plop down on my bed, trying not to start crying.

All I told her is true. I've known it for a long time and ignored it to keep the peace. This is the first time I've ever voiced it, ever even came close to it. It's pathetic to be doing it as a thirty-three-year-old woman, but here I am. It needed saying, and it's time I start living by those words too.

That calms me down enough to chase away the tears. I text Scar, asking him if he can pick me up soon, then call when I don't get a reply.

The house is quiet and I'm starting to feel guilty over the way I spoke to Mom. She sacrificed her life to take care of me. And for awhile that *was* absolutely necessary. I shouldn't have spoken to her like that.

I can't tonight, doe. Scar texts after he doesn't return my call.

I wait for a full five minutes for more to come, but it doesn't. I want to know why, I want to know when I'll see him again. I need to see him soon. But instead of asking that, I just text back, *OK, pity*, and add a smiley to the end, so he'll know I'm not too upset.

He doesn't reply to that and after fifteen minutes of staring at my phone I finally toss it away from me to the edge of the bed, so I'll stop. He has a life. He's busy. I get that. But I also need him to hold me, need him to reassure me what my mom said about him isn't true. I already know it, but I'd still like him to say it.

Mom's walking down the hall outside. She stops by my door and knocks. "Come on, Lynn, let's go get that shopping done now."

She sounds happy and boisterous, the way she always does when trying to cheer me on and up. I guess she's sorry for the way she spoke to me too.

"OK, yeah, give me a second," I tell her.

That's how arguments at my house are handled. We ignore them and then forget about them. And I'm a pro at ignoring the things I don't want to see.

SCAR

Hawk was nowhere to be found when I got back to Sanctuary this morning, and by the time Cross finally told me that he'd gone to do some hands-on inquiring about our latest prey's whereabouts, I'd pretty much given up on finding out where Reggie is today. Hawk could've called me so I could ride along, but that would cut into my time with Lynn, so it's not as infuriating as it might've been a couple of weeks ago.

She's still a little skittish if I get too rough, but that's part of the fun by now, and I'm loving the chase. Not that I felt like getting rough with her last night after she said what she said about my face. She meant it. And it's hard to admit it now, in broad daylight, but that shit touched my heart the way nothing has in decades. I just wanted to make her feel good after that. Didn't know I was capable of it, never thought I'd enjoy it as much as I did.

What's pleasure without pain? Not as good as it could be, that's for sure. At least that's what I always believed. She taught me different last night, and I'm not sure exactly what to make of it. But I do know I want more of what only she can give me. Much more.

The rumbling of bikes returning snaps me out of my daydreams of Lynn. I do a lot of thinking about her when we're not together, all the time really, and I don't know what to make of that either. I'm prone to thinking about fucking while I'm not doing it, but before Lynn, I never daydreamed about doing it with any particular woman. It's odd, sounds kinda girly, but there it is, and I kinda enjoy thinking about her all the time.

I exit the garage where I've been working on my bike for the past two hours while waiting for Hawk. The choppers returning are kicking up a lot of dust, since it hasn't rained in ages—another reason for the fires that upset Lynn so much.

Hawk is the first one to reach me, just in time to stop me from regretting taking her to see the fire last night. I think she got my point by the end of the evening, but what's more surprising, I think I got hers too. Those damn wildfires really are the devil's work for some. I just never saw it that way so clearly, since I was too deep in doing the devil's work myself.

"Scar, have you been waiting for me?" Hawk asks mockingly as he dismounts in front of me.

"Cut the shit," I snap. "You got any news for me?"

"Easy now, where's the fire? Let me get settled first," he says, grinning at me. "Or are you in a hurry to go see your beauty queen? Don't worry. She'll wait for you if she's worth it."

The brothers who were with him have all dismounted by now and more than a few of them chuckle at his joke. Hawk's not the best judge of what he can say to who and in which situations, I've noticed that about him plenty of times before. It makes for some interesting conversations when he's interrogating people, and it's a good thing he's a big guy who knows how to protect himself against the fallout that results from him running his mouth off. It also makes him a good intel getter, since he asks the questions others—even tough-as-nails bikers—would avoid asking straight out. But all that aside, he's just pissing me off right now.

"Alright, Hawk, that's enough of your shit. Just tell me what you found out then I'll let you get back to watching porn in your dark room," I counter and that earns me a bunch of chuckles from the others too.

"You never could take a joke," Hawk grumbles and starts walking towards the house. "Come with me."

"Did you find him?" I ask before we reach the front door, since I figure he's heading inside to find Cross and brief us both at the same time, but I can't wait that long.

"I don't know where the three Spawns are yet, and Cross ain't gonna be too happy about that," he says. "But I'm fairly certain Reaper is laying low with the Renegade Knights MC over in Santa Lucia. In fact, I'm almost 99.9 percent sure of it. I didn't see him when I visited them earlier, but those dumb fuckers don't know how to keep a secret and more than a few of them started whispering amongst each other like a bunch of schoolgirls when I asked if they knew where he was."

I stop dead and he halts too. "Santa Lucia as in the town an hour south of here?"

Hawk nods. "That very one. But don't go looking for him on your own. He's under the Renegades' protection, so you won't get him without starting shit with them. We'll tell Cross about it. Maybe he can get him out for you," he says, but I'm already heading for my bike.

"At least take some backup, Scar," he calls after me.

"I don't need fucking backup to deal with my brother," I snap and keep on walking.

Lynn texts me as I'm mounting my bike. She wants to meet, but it ain't happening tonight. She calls just as I reach the front gate in the wall surrounding Sanctuary. So I stop aways beyond it and text her back to keep her calm. I do want to meet her, but this is important.

I'm not daydreaming about her anymore right now.

Right now, all I'm seeing is my brother's scared eyes as life leaves them. That's something I've daydreamed about for a lot longer than I've known Lynn. And tonight, it's finally gonna become reality.

20

LYNN

Scar might have given me his phone number, but we're communicating less now, not more. For a day and a half, all I've gotten were short, curt answers to texts and no returned calls. He doesn't have time to meet. And on the face of it, maybe he really doesn't.

But maybe he just doesn't want to. Maybe Mom is right about him. Maybe I'm wrong and all he wanted from me is sex. Maybe it was like that even back then.

I don't want to believe it, but I'm starting to.

It's the evening and after I walk the dogs, I'm going home for another night of Mom's sidelong glances as we first eat dinner and then watch TV. Minus her questioning gazes, it'll be the same exact night I've lived every night for the past twelve years.

She hasn't mentioned Scar at all since our argument a

couple of days ago. There really was no reason to, since he's been gone from the time I finally told her about him. I'm sure she has her own ideas about why that is, and I'm sure she thinks it proves her right. But she's not saying it, and I'm ignoring it.

The rest of the pack is running around the woods, but I'm keeping Scrap close, because he's not well yet. He keeps looking at me with huge eyes, probably asking me why he can't run like his brothers and sisters.

"Just a couple more days, and then you'll be all better again," I say and scratch him behind the ears, which always sends his tail wagging like crazy.

He tries to stand up on his hind legs to give me a hug, but yelps terribly, the sound piercing my heart. I should be more careful with him. I would be, but my mind's not really here. It's too full of questions about Scar and memories of him. I hope that's not all I get — just memories. I have enough of those.

Scrap's yelp was almost as terrible as the one he gave when he was injured, and he's still whimpering even as he wags his tail, while I comfort him. Scar was with me when Scrap got injured, and he took care of it. I wish he was here now.

But he's not. And maybe he never will be again.

Just as I think it, the wind brings the sound of a bike rumbling in the distance, sending my heart racing, my stomach filling with warm frothy waters like it does whenever I see Scar. I no longer get sick when I hear the sound. I just get the butterflies. But the rumbling cuts off abruptly, the forest silence restored, and if Scrap wasn't intently staring at the direction it came from, I'd be sure I just imagined it.

Any minute now, Scar's gonna walk through the trees to me. He parked and now he's looking for me.

"I'm over here, Scar!" I yell out in the general direction of where I heard the bike stop.

But seconds tick by, and he doesn't appear.

Scrap is still staring at the trees where the sound came from. Lucy and Butch returned too. They're walking towards me, but looking at the trees where the bike stopped.

Scar walked the dogs a couple of times, so they know him, but they don't look excited like they're about to see him. They look wary and I'm growing scared, the frothy waters of happiness turning to something darker and angrier as the fear starts to surface.

Why would Scar drive his bike into the woods? It makes no sense. He'd park by my car and call me. He wouldn't come looking for me in the forest, since he'd have no way of knowing where I am.

I'm watching the trees as intently as the dogs are. My heart is beating so fast I can hear it in my ears. Someone is there, but I don't think it's Scar.

There's a rustle in the bushes, Scrap growls, Lucy barks, and the branches move.

"Who's there?" I yell. "Is it you, Scar?"

But I know it isn't. He wouldn't play this kind of game with me. Besides, no part of my body thinks he's near and it always reacts when he is. And whoever is there is scaring the dogs. I try to fight them, but images of the night I was abducted are preparing to play in my mind. I feel watched and it's making my skin crawl like I'm covered in spiders or maggots or some other nasty thing like that. The other two dogs have returned too, so my whole pack is surrounding me now, keeping the worst of my panic at bay. I'm sure they'd try to protect me. But can they?

Memories of getting grabbed from behind in the dark

parking lot of the diner all those years ago are forcing their way to the front of my mind, forcing their way out of my past and into the here and now. I'm cold just like I was that night, and the woods seem darker than they were a second ago. In another second, a strong arm will grab me from behind, a meaty palm will be slapped across my face, making it hard to breathe and impossible to scream.

I'll try to scream anyway. I'll kick and fight and claw at the arm clutching me, breaking fingernails and drawing blood. But it won't help, the man will carry me away from my car, into the darkness, and my fighting will be about as useful, as if I was fighting a boulder. And then I'll be tied to a bed in a smelly dark room, raped and beaten, visions of my own death the only thing before my eyes for hours and days until I can't take it anymore, until I break again.

No! I'm back. I'm safe. I'm well.

The dogs all start barking ferociously at the trees. Maybe they're just reacting to my fear. It's so strong now, I'm not entirely sure that I'm not still locked in that dark smelly room.

No! I shout at my own thoughts. That was then. And it will never happen again!

The sound of a bike rumbling starts again, but this time it's retreating, growing fainter. The dogs stop barking and Scrap bumps my hand to be petted, so I know the danger is past. If there ever was any to begin with. The more I think about it, the more I'm sure I just heard a helicopter and my mind did the rest. And then the dogs reacted to my fear.

I'm shaking, my teeth chattering from the shock of remembering the night I was abducted. This memory was so vivid I relived it all, right down to the moment my mind broke. But it's easier to come back to the present now. Easier to know all that is the past.

I was never able to fully face those memories. All my therapists suggested I should, but I just couldn't replay them in my mind. It was too painful. All I saw were glimpses and felt some of the emotions, but I always stopped it before it got too involved.

Yet as my breathing and heart rate start returning to normal, I feel lighter like something hard and unyielding finally broke inside me—some barrier holding my worst fears intact and locked away from me, so I wouldn't have to face them. It protected me, but also created a burden of unresolved things I could hardly carry, but stubbornly did anyway, because ignoring is what I'm good at, and I believed I was too weak to face the full extent of my ordeal a second time.

This was one hell of a bad experience, but I think I needed it, desperately, because I feel like I've just climbed the tallest mountain and can finally shout, "I'm free!" from the top of it.

"Good boy," I say, scratch Scrap behind the ears and give him a treat.

"You all did a great job," I tell the others, and toss them the rest of the treats.

I wish Scar was here with me. Then I'd throw my arms around his neck and kiss him and thank him for showing me the way back to a normal life. I'd also tell him I love him, because I do. Then I'd give myself to him the way I haven't yet. Because it was him, his presence, his touch, his strength that gave me the courage to face my worst nightmare and defeat it.

I text him right away. *Where are you? I need to see you today!*

It's the most forward text I've sent him yet, and everything inside me is quivering with excitement as I press send.

But he doesn't reply right away.

There's still no reply half an hour later when I'm giving the dogs their dinner at the kennel. Nor an hour later as I park the car in the driveway at home. Or two hours later as I'm sitting next to Mom on the sofa, watching some movie I've seen five times already, ignoring her glances and the icy air in my chest, because all the excitement is gone now.

Scar doesn't want me the way I want him.

And I'd ignore it, make up excuses, believe that maybe he really is just too busy with something else.

But ignoring painful things only makes them hurt worse. I learned that today, and I won't put myself through that pain ever again.

SCAR

I reached the Renegade Knights MC clubhouse at six PM and have been in this same position—lying in the dirt up on a ridge overlooking it— trying to spot Reaper for almost two nights. It's six AM, and the sun coming up woke me. I only saw Reaper appear twice, and I couldn't get close to him on either of those times. Hopefully I'll get him today, but if not, I'll wait right here until I do.

The first time he left with a group of five Renegades, and I decided not to follow, since six against one meant I'd fail. The second time he left on his own, but I lost him on the road to somewhere out of town. This was yesterday afternoon, he left at two and came back at dusk. Clearly he's afraid to be away from the safety of the clubhouse past dark.

I blame my lack of sleep and the heat for losing him yesterday afternoon. It's also been awhile since my work involved actively staking out someone. Other brothers do that, I just come in when it's time to get some answers, crack a few skulls and otherwise finish the job. I got lazy, but it's all coming back to me.

I'm the hunter again, he's my prey. All those hunting trips with my father prepared me for this, taught me to be patient. This is no different than laying in the snow and waiting for a deer to come by. And me and Dad did plenty of that.

The next time he comes out, I won't lose him.

I'll run him down on some deserted stretch of road and then we'll face off. Then he'll pay. With his life.

Lynn kept texting and calling, and I've replied as much as I could. But there's no place for her in this, although I'll also be avenging her when I kill him. But that's not something she agrees with, yet this is my task to finish.

Where are you? Lynn's last text reads. *I need to see you today!*

She sent it last night.

I heard my phone buzz, but I didn't even look at it, because I was still seething over the fact that I lost Reggie. I was waiting for him at a fork in the road he'd have to pass to get back to the clubhouse, but when he finally rode by again he wasn't alone anymore. For hours after that, I spent all my mental energy convincing myself not to storm into the clubhouse and drag him out so we can get this shit over with.

Twelve years ago, I would've done it. But if I do that now, it'll just end in both of us dying. Twelve years ago, I wouldn't have cared. But now a gorgeous, gentle woman wants to know where I am, because she misses me and wants to be with me. No, *needs* to be with me, is how she put it.

I'll come by the ranch tonight. I text back. I should've checked the text last night. Then she'd be waking up in my arms right now, and that'd be a whole lot better than this.

Awesome, she writes back a split second later. *I can't wait to see you.*

I can't wait to see her either, and that realization hits me like a bolt of lightning from a clear sky. It's been two days. I want to see her more than I want to keep lying here waiting for an opportunity to kill my brother. It's something I've been fantasizing about for damn near twenty-five years, but right now it's not nearly as important as seeing Lynn.

Same, doe.

My brother will keep. Lynn might bolt. Of the two, I know which I'd rather pursue, it's no contest. That answer surprised even me. Of the two, it's Lynn I want to keep close. More than I want revenge on my brother. A couple of weeks ago, my answer would've been completely different.

But now it's as clear as the day rising before my eyes as I ride home to see her.

21

LYNN

I'M CLEANING out the goat stall when a pair of strong, stone-like arms grabs me from behind. I scream out, fear turning my vision black despite the mid morning sun in my eyes. But a second later, as Scar twirls me around and kisses me so deeply and so magically, all that darkness is gone, replaced by the feeling of standing under the rainbow, bathed in its light.

My heart is still racing once he stops kissing me and just holds me in his arms. His eyes are enveloping me like soft wild grass, just like the one that rustled when we made love on the ridge a couple of nights ago, with the fire raging in the distance, but no match for the one we sparked to life.

"I didn't expect you until this evening," I chide breathlessly.

He grins. "Yeah, and you won't see me again until then. I need a shower and fresh clothes. But I couldn't wait that long to kiss you."

He's not wrong about needing a shower, but I don't know if I can wait until the evening.

"I thought you weren't coming back to me," I say quietly, although that fear is about as insubstantial as a breeze right now and just as fleeting.

"You did?" he asks and chuckles. "I'm not sure there's a force that could keep me from coming back to you."

His voice sounds so light as he says it and his eyes are so bright, like two green pools glowing in the light of the sun, their calm waters washing over me like a healing nectar. The beasts are nowhere near the pools right now. There's no doubt in my mind that what he's saying is the absolute truth.

I lean against him and he wastes no time kissing me again, which is exactly what I wanted and needed. And I know I'll wait for him for as long as it takes just so I could see him again, kiss him again, feel his arms around me one more time.

And I know it still, much later, while I wave him goodbye as he drives off, the rumbling earthquake the sound of his bike is causing making everything inside me shake and topple, then fall back into its right place, its perfect place.

I'll see him again in a couple of hours and that's a long wait. But I'll be waiting.

"What, take out again?" I ask as he stops the bike by a small roadside burger place that has no tables or chairs that I can see, and isn't exactly in a spot I'd choose for a sit down dinner, given that it's sandwiched between the highway and a dirt-lined country road.

"Yeah, and tonight I thought we could eat it naked," he says and winks at me. Then he grins and offers me his arm like the perfect gentleman. I take it gladly, since I've only not been holding on to him for like two minutes but I already miss it.

"This place makes the best burgers," he adds as we get in the back of the long line, which could've told me that on its own. There's a woman with small children in front of us, a couple of men and women in business suits, even an old man with a cane, and a couple of bikers.

"I guess this place is famous," I say. "I never heard of it before. But then again, I never went out much before I ran into you again."

He smiles and just looks at me for a few seconds with a very soft expression in his eyes that I can't quite read. But I don't have to read it for it to make me feel so wanted and appreciated that something melts into wide flowing rivers of joy in my chest. He kisses me just as I'm about to ask him why he's looking at me like that. But I think I already know. And I feel the same about him. But it'd be nice to hear it spoken.

The rest of the wait for the food is like a good, pleasant dream, one where things don't happen linearly, but all lead to the same place. A place where all is good and all is right.

In our case, the dream leads us to the bed in a small house at the end of a dark street. He wasn't kidding about the getting naked first part. The bags of food are forgotten where he let them fall by the door, as he took off first his jacket then his shirt, then unbuttoned my dress and kissed and licked and bit me from my neck down to my thighs as he removed the rest. My skin is sparkling from his attention, my soul glowing bright.

He picks me up suddenly, and I feel lighter than air as he carries me to the bed.

"The food will get cold," I moan as he lays me down on the cool sheets.

I missed this bed, I suddenly realize, during the days he was gone from me. I missed our bed. The bed I was reborn in.

He grins at me. "Yeah, but we're gonna start with an appetizer."

I smile too, but it's wiped clean off my face as his lips and his tongue and even his teeth get to work on my clit, replaced by something that can't be attractive, I'm sure. But I don't care about any of that as the fiery bliss only he can coax from deep inside me starts to mount and mount, until I can't draw a full breath anymore, let alone worry about anything else but riding this fiery river of pleasure he's filling me with.

My moans and my shrieks, my hands in his hair, my nails digging into the muscles of his back and his stone strong arms all urge him on, his licks growing faster, more ferocious, wilder, creating pure heaven inside me.

He pushes two fingers into my pussy with no warning, making me yelp in joy or surprise, pleasure or pain, I don't know which. All of them at once! He pumps his fingers in and out, his tongue still wild on my clit, not slowing at all. And that's all it takes for my whole being to unravel around his fingers, like the skin of an orange peeling off all at once, revealing a soft, tender center that's exploding with joy and bliss and all the things I feel when we kiss, only times a hundred, a thousand, a million.

He's kneeling between my wide spread legs when I open my eyes, my vision still blurry.

"You ready?" he asks, running his hand down the side of my face and his thumb across my lips, before letting his palm come to rest right over the heartbeat in my neck.

There's something very dark and dangerous in his eyes right now, but it's wrapped in that softness I saw there before—that love—so I nod, don't dream of doing anything else. Because his eyes also hold a promise that I'll feel all that bliss from before times a billion in a second.

His eyes still locked on mine, he lines up his cock with my pussy, making me sigh as its head brushes against my still throbbing clit. His eyes grow even darker as he thrusts his cock into me, drawing out a scream from beyond my conscious awareness, my body talking now, and my soul, but my mind too, because no part of me doesn't want him inside me right now.

He picks up the pace, his hand closed around my throat, but not too tightly, just tight enough to let me know I'm his, that he's my man. That he'll protect me and care for me and love me, make me feel so good I forget myself, but that he'll also take me the way he wants to, the way he needs me to be his.

After a few more thrusts, even that awareness fades, and all I feel is his cock opening me up, joining us together, hitting my walls and my barriers, breaking them down, going deeper and deeper until he's so deep he's truly a part of me like he was meant to be.

I'm shrieking and moaning with every thrust now, my hands on his hips urging him on, my mind losing it's last hold on my awareness, as my body fills to the brink with the fiery, sparkling expectation of the explosion to come. My blood is glowing, my breaths are fire releasing. He glows too, towering over me, holding me down to keep me from writhing away from this almost unbearable wildfire of pleasure he's causing inside me.

But I see his face perfectly clearly, see his eyes, see the love and devotion in them. It's that calm softness in them that pushes me over the edge, makes me scream out his name, as wave after wave of molten pleasure wash over me, before receding into memory, leaving behind sparkling pools and lakes on my soul that I'll remember forever, and which I'll always want to revisit again and again for as long as I live.

22

LYNN

THE RUSTLING of a paper bag wakes me later, and it's not until the smell registers that I realize where the noise is coming from.

I'm lying on one side of the bed, covered by the sheet. He must have placed me here after I passed out before. He even covered me, and it's such a small gesture, but my heart is melting into puddles of mush as I roll over to look at him.

He's leaning against the headboard and eating a hamburger, not caring where the crumbs fall, looking like he's in ninth heaven.

"Did you leave any for me?" I ask, sitting up and peering into the bag he's still holding.

"Here, I didn't touch yours," he says with his mouth full and offers me the other, still unopened bag. "But it's a good thing you woke up, else I probably would've. You gave me quite an appetite."

He grins and I grin back, then take my burger and unwrap it. I lean against the headboard next to him, sitting so close our sides are pressed together.

"Now that you mention it, I'm starving too. I don't even care that it's cold."

"A good burger is good hot or cold," he observes and reaches into the bag to pull out a wad of napkins, offering them for me to take some first.

I grab a bunch, then unwrap my cold burger, not really sure I want to eat it since I'm not a fan of cold meat, but I am starving.

"Next time, we'll go to a real restaurant," I say.

He shrugs. "I'm not really the "going-to-restaurants" type. Those two times with you were an exception."

"Same for me," I say and giggle. "But we can change that together."

"Why would you want to be seen around town with a scary-looking guy like me?" he asks in an offhand way and laughs right after.

But I think he was serious and I thought we covered this already. Not just around town, I want to be everywhere with him.

"Come on, you know I don't care about that," I say. "Besides, I'm pretty enough for the both of us."

I giggle after I say it, since I'm kidding. I know I'm pretty, but despite all the pageants and the crowns I won, I've never completely identified with any of that. Not in my heart and my soul. There, I was always just a simple girl who wanted a simple life.

"You got that right! You're pretty enough for a hundred people," he says and kisses me, making me forget all about how hungry I am. Making me forget about anything else, but how right this moment is, how perfect, how unforgettable. How I don't need anything else but this. Absolutely nothing at all.

I thought the kiss would go on for much longer, but he pulls away, grins at me and takes another bite of his burger.

"You're tasty, but I'm fucking hungry," he explains with his mouth full. "Didn't get much to eat these last couple of days."

"OK, you can have some of mine too, if you want," I say. "Where were you, anyway?"

I meant to say it as an off-hand kinda question, but it came out very serious and pointed anyway.

"Did you miss me, Lynn?" he asks, eying me from the corner of his eyes.

"You know I did," I say and smile. "Didn't you get my texts?"

I take a bite of my burger, more as a distraction from his burning, piercing gaze than because I want to eat.

"I got your texts," he says and leaves it at that.

It takes me awhile to chew the piece of burger I took, mainly because I can't stand the taste of cold meat and I'm only just realizing how true that is.

"Did you come up to the ranch the day before yesterday, while I was out walking the dogs?" Ever since, I've been switching between thinking I just imagined hearing the sound of a bike, thinking it might have been him, and worrying that some biker from my past was stalking me. "You should've just come out of the bushes and said hi."

The blank look on his face tells me he has no idea what I'm talking about, and the spark in his eyes says he'd do more than just say hi, if it were him. I probably just imagined the whole thing.

"It wasn't me," he says. "I was in a town called Santa Lucia an hour away from here waiting for my brother to come out of hiding. You sure you didn't just hear a helicopter? They've been flying around constantly because of the fires."

The way he mentions his brother chills my blood for some reason.

"It was probably a helicopter," I say. "Isn't your brother in prison?"

He crumples the burger wrapper and tosses it in the bag. I offer him my burger automatically, and he looks at it like it's the most disgusting thing in the world but takes it from me anyway.

Something switched inside him the moment he mentioned his brother, and now it's like there's a wall of ice between us, the temperature in the room dropping fast. I want him to still be grinning and kidding and laughing and kissing me, but I fear he never will again. An odd fear, but I'm prone to exaggerated extremes when I start panicking over something.

"He's out," he says. "And now I'm finally gonna send him to hell."

His voice, what he's saying, and the icy, stony look on his face make the room even colder. My heart is racing, but the blood it sends whooshing through my veins isn't warming me. I wish I knew what to say, wish I knew how to call him back from where ever his mind took him now, so we can start having fun again. I know he needs that as much as I do.

"Does me saying that scare you, Lynn?" he asks, breaking my trance.

"Yes, it does," I say automatically. "Violence and death scare me."

His eyes turn a fraction softer, a fraction warmer, the calm forest pools no longer black from the ice covering them. A glow is starting deep inside them, and I want to spark it higher, I want it to crack the ice, melt it.

"I'm a scary guy, Lynn. I thought you knew that already," he says and grins. "Do you want me to take you home now?"

I think he's just joke-offering that, but he sounds so serious that I'm not entirely sure. I shake my head, because of all the things I want right now, that one isn't even on the list.

"I know your brother hurt you very badly," I say. "But is killing him really the answer? The best revenge is walking away and forgetting, showing the people who hurt you that they didn't beat you down, kinda like what you told me the other day."

I'm one to talk. I spent the last twelve years hiding inside myself because of what happened to me. But now, I do know that what I just said is true, because I've finally been able to put it all behind me. He's frowning at me like he thinks I said a very dumb thing.

"The best revenge is death," he says. "I thought about giving him a taste of his own medicine, but, bottom line, my brother should either be locked up in a cage or he shouldn't be alive. He's not fit to be around other humans. Just like the guys who hurt you."

"Killing is never the answer," I say, the thoughts of black death, which I thought was a certainty when I was held captive rising to the surface of my mind. I'm trying to beat them back, but I'm losing. "Even just thinking of death rips apart your soul."

I know this, mine was torn to shreds and it took me a long

time to put them back together. And *he* was the thread that let me sew my soul back together.

"Then mine's too far gone to save," he says wryly, darkly, the ice around him no longer just frozen water, but frozen stone, impossible to melt. But I want to melt it, I want the temperature to rise again, I want the loving, softness in his eyes back, not this blackness.

"How can you even say that?" I say. "Your soul is pure and good."

"Yeah, Lynn, right," he says and laughs, but not with the kind of happiness I was aiming for.

"You're a good man," I say. "You rescued me. More than once. And it chills me to hear you say you have no soul, because it's just not true."

The look in his eyes is softer now, almost, almost back to the color of the soft wild grass I want to lay in forever. Just a little further and we'll reach it again.

"And…and, I love you, Scar," I say in a shaky voice, since damn, those words are hard to say. They're three simple little words, but they just rip your heart wide open.

And his silence isn't helping. Nor is the fact that his eyes are just stuck on disbelief right now. This isn't how it's supposed to be. He's supposed to say it back, because I know he feels it too. I thought I knew it. But maybe I was wrong.

"You're better off without me, you do know that, right?" he finally says, after I've given up all hope he'll even grace me with a reply.

"I love you, and I will show you that you're worth it," I add. Not quite the answer to his question, but I think that's what he was actually asking.

"I'm not the settling down type, Lynn," he says with a

defeated sort of sigh. "And I'm not worth your love, I never was."

"How can you say that? After all we've been through, after all you've done for me, how can you believe that?" I no longer know what's going on or what we're really talking about.

"I can say it, because it's true," he says. "You're gorgeous, and I like spending time with you way more than I do with any other woman. But you deserve better than me, you know you do. You deserve a normal, quiet life with someone who worships you. I live a dangerous life, and there's no place for someone like you in it. So let's not complicate this with all of that. Let's just have some fun together. We waited long enough, didn't we?"

I can't believe what I'm hearing. He worships me, I want him in my life forever. How could I have misread the signs so badly? I was sure he loved me.

But it makes sense. I am a very naive, inexperienced, soft and sensitive woman, who really is just a girl in a woman's body, and who still often thinks in terms of fairytales, because she's been locked up inside her own mind for so long. And I've had the fantasy about Scar being my knight in shining armor for a very long time. My mom wasn't wrong about that. I needed that fantasy to keep me going. Did I let it blind me now into thinking this is love?

"We have a good thing going here, Lynn," he says after I don't reply. His eyes are softer now, kinda apologetic, but I'm not really seeing them.

"All you wanted with me was a good time," I whisper. It's not really a question, it's a realization.

He shrugs. "I have an amazing time with you, every minute of it. Much better than I ever had."

He grins after he says it, and I understand he's trying to make light of it all, trying to have fun again, the way I tried to cheer him up when he was talking about death. And I also understand that I've succeeded. But at the expense of opening up my heart and letting it fill with nasty blackness of the kind I really hoped—really believed— I'd finally left behind for good.

He just used me. Used me for my body and my looks and my naivety. Used me the way those men used me when they tied me to a bed and raped me over and over and over until I lost my mind. He didn't force me, he made me feel good, made me want it, but the end result is the same. He did just use me, and he'd like to continue using me like I'm just some pretty toy he likes playing with. I'm barely holding onto my sanity right now.

"I'd like you to take me home now," I say, ignoring his confused expression as I get up and start to dress.

"What? Just like that, Lynn?" he says.

"Yes," I say. "I want to go home."

And be alone with my thoughts, be alone where it's safe. I suppose a lot of women would shrug and move on past even this with barely a second thought. But I had a lot riding on it, more than others do.

I can't be his plaything. I've been that to other men in the worst possible way, and I never want to be that again. I can't be that again. Not even to a man who makes me feel as good as he does. Because even the memories of those fantastic nights and days we spent together are curdling now in light of this.

He watches me dress for a couple more seconds in silence, a very hard expression on his face, then he shrugs and gets dressed too.

"Alright, let's go," he says when he's ready, letting me precede him out the bedroom and then out the house.

We don't speak, and the wind hitting me as he drives me back to my car, which I left at the ranch, is full of razorblades. Huge, sharp razorblades cutting me open. I should be holding onto him, but I'm not. I can't.

"So, you'll call when you calm down, or what?" he asks as we're standing in the dark by my car.

I know he wants to hold me and kiss me, the heat coming off him now is almost as unbearable as the ice was before. Neither concern me anymore. I'm already alone. The way I was meant to be.

"I won't be your booty call," I say, hoping I'm using that word right, since I've never used it before. "I've been that in the worst possible way and...never again. So thank you for all you've done for me. Goodbye, Scar."

I turn and open the door to my car.

"You're fucking over-dramatizing, Lynn," he calls after me. "I'm not just using you. You can always count on me. I'll always be around if you need me. All's I'm saying is, don't expect to make a home with me. You know I'm not the guy for that. So you just go and calm down and think about this, then call me."

He sounds angry now. But I don't care. I get in my car and drive off, leaving him behind in the dust.

I'm doing this for me, to protect my sanity, to not open myself wide just so he can rip me to shreds. I can't go through that a second time. I thought he loved me, but it was all in my head. It's what I needed to believe, so I could heal, so he could heal me. But I can't let him undo it all by keeping me around just for sex. Which is probably the only thing he was after from the beginning.

I can't stick around to find out that's what it really was. Can't go deeper into loving him only to find out he just wanted my body. I don't think I'd survive that, I know I wouldn't. The mere idea of it is making me nauseous right now, the way it hasn't in years and certainly not since he came back into my life.

He doesn't follow me and I don't go home. Because I can't face the life that was my prison for so long, can't face any more of my mom's knowing glances, can't face knowing that what I thought was love wasn't.

So I circle back to the ranch and sit with Scrap in the kennel, just petting him until the dark fog in my mind finally starts lifting.

This is my life. Taking care of these animals and earning their love is my life. I don't need a man's love and I don't want it. Not if losing it hurts this bad.

SCAR

I expected her to call as soon as I drove off, definitely figured I'd have at least a text by morning. That was one helluva flip she did last night. And why? Because I didn't tell her I loved her back. Hell, I do love her. More than any other woman, that's for sure. Maybe I should've just told her that. But it's more likely she flipped out, because I told her the truth. My love ain't worth shit.

She must've figured that out when I told her the truth about myself. About what I do, who I am. Right up until the moment I told her I'm gonna kill my brother she probably still pretended that's not the guy I am. But she couldn't pretend no more after I told her. So she bolted. Just froze up and left the bedroom even before she asked me to drive her home.

It wasn't because I didn't say I love you back. It can't be. She can't be serious about accusing me I used her the way those maggots used her. She knows that's not true. How can she not know that's not true?

No, she bolted because I'm a killer, a monster, and she never really thought that through all the way until I made it plain last night. I shouldn't have laid it all on her like that and then we'd probably still be kissing and fucking right now. I had no plans of taking her home anytime soon once I got her in the bed last night.

But she can't be with someone like me. I knew that all along. It's why I never pursued her back then, and why I shouldn't have done it now.

It's for the best that way. Probably. Feels rotten in broad daylight, but lots of shit does. I'm used to feeling rotten.

She's right where she's supposed to be. With her animals and her mom. And I'm right where I'm supposed to be too, laying in the dirt behind a bunch of rocks, waiting for my brother to show up so I can finally kill him. That's what I am. A killer. And maybe she made me stumble a little, made me think there might be more to it than that, but there isn't.

And I'm over it. Or I would be, if it wasn't for her sweet, soft little voice still chirruping inside my brain, telling me she cares about me, that she wants to be with me forever, telling me I'm worth all that. But it's fine, her voice is already fading. She's wrong. I'm not worth anyone's love, least of all hers.

I'm good for one thing and one thing only. To kill and torture. There's no way out for me anymore and no way back. The MC will provide new opportunities for me to be me, I no longer fear it won't. And women whose faces I won't remember will provide what I should never have taken from Lynn.

She's a tasty, graceful, soft little doe, but she's not for me and never was. I have to leave her alone, in the wild, like I should've left the one I shot and killed all those years ago.

My brother walks out of the Renegades clubhouse, slicing right through my thoughts of Lynn, pushing them to the other side of a thick wall in my mind. I'll be avenging her too when I kill him, but she's no part of this. I never should've made her a part of it.

Reggie is alone. This is my second chance and I won't waste it again.

23

SCAR

I LOST HIM AGAIN. At that same railroad crossing where it happened the first time. He crossed, I got the train in my face. Last time, I sped off after him as soon as the train passed, but couldn't find him again. This time, I'm hoping it'll be different. God damn trains, what the fuck are they still good for?

The wind tunnel caused by the freight train is a tornado against my face, but I don't move back, not even an inch. I hardly feel the wind anyway, all the rage I called up for my brother together with Lynn bolting are creating a wall with me on one side and the rest of the world on the other. Nothing but cornering my brother will change that. It might not change even after I corner and kill him.

The rest of the world hasn't held much meaning for me in a long time, and I haven't been interested in being a part of it either. With Lynn way on the other side of that wall now, what's the point of it coming down at all?

What the hell does she want? A two-story house with a picket fence and me as a husband? So that she'll what, cook and clean for me while I fix shit around the house and mow the lawn? She wants that with me? With the Scarred Devil? Bad men are scared shitless of me. I'm not meant to have a normal life. That shit isn't for me and never was. And why'd she wanna get tied down to something like that? She wouldn't!

Now if only that voice in my head saying, "Maybe she knows what she wants", would shut the fuck up everything could go back to normal.

Even before the train's done passing, I concede that I'll have to ask the brothers for help getting my hands on Reggie. He's holed up too tight with the Renegades, and I'm out of patience. This shit's got to go my way. Nothing else has in a while, so this has to.

My phone's vibrating in my pocket and I hate the sweet anticipation of seeing Lynn's number on the screen as I fish it out. Especially after it turns more sour that curdled milk once I realize it's not her calling. Unless she's calling from some other number...

"Hello, Bobby," Reggie says, that queasiness in my stomach from a second a go pleasant compared to what I feel now. It's a good thing I pulled up to the side of the road to answer the phone.

"I heard you've been looking for me, so I decided to give you a call," he says in that charming, pleasant voice he uses when he's tricking people into thinking he's not a psycho monster. It doesn't work on me.

"Yeah, Reggie, I've been looking for you. And you've made your final mistake stopping off so close to my home," I say.

There's no harm letting him know I've already found him. It might even make him turn his bike around and head back in a panic. Head back right past where I'm waiting.

"That was no mistake," he says and laughs. "Never mind hiding from the cops, I knew you'd keep coming after me once you found out I was out. You always were like a dog with a bone about that. And as far as I understand it, your best friends are now running your MC, so I figure you'd get their help like you did when you snatched that waitress from us."

He shouldn't have talked about Lynn, but this is the last time he's gonna.

"So face me one on one, once and for all. Stop running from me and face me," I say. "Or are you too scared?"

He laughs again. "You don't scare me, little bro. You might scare everyone else, but you'll always be that screaming, crying little weakling I cut up to me. Don't worry, I'll face you, it's why I'm calling. But first I got an errand to run."

What fucking errand? Either he's gone off the deep end completely in the last twelve years, or he's playing a game with me. It's the latter, because he was born insane. But I'll bite. I need a time and place.

"An errand? What, the Renegades got you grocery shopping for them like some bitch?" I ask.

He laughs like I've just said the most pleasant funny thing in the world. "Not groceries, but I am getting them a present. It's the least I could do to thank them for letting me stay at their clubhouse."

He's telling me this because it concerns me, I get that, but I have no idea *how* it concerns me.

"Alright, so you are too scared," I say. "Then just enjoy your shopping trip and me and my friends will come to you."

"You'd like the present I'm getting them," he says, this weird conversation starting to mess with my mind. He's a talker, I never was. I like things plain and simple, he likes the sound of his own voice. "In fact, you already do like it very much. Or should I say her. Although there won't be much to call a she after we're done with her this time."

All the air's gone from the world, replaced by burning hot sand. My mouth's full of it, my throat's full of it and my eyes are too.

"Stay the fuck away from Lynn!" I growl. "Or I'll kill you slow."

He laughs again, and it lasts a fucking long time. "You and your buddies shouldn't have taken her from me the first time. She was the Spawns' property by then. Me and Lizard wanted to go against you, but the Spawns' old president didn't want to move against the entire Devil's Nightmare MC and the Wolves too. Fucking coward. But she wasn't yours anymore, she was mine."

The way he says, "mine" takes me right back to that rainy afternoon when he cut up my face. But I'm not that screaming, scared boy anymore.

"She's mine now," I growl. And I mean it. No part of my mind doubts it in any way. I'll never let her go again.

And right now, the only thing that matters is keeping her safe from Reggie. The only thing. Fuck just protecting her. I want her by my side all the time.

I just hang up. There's no more time for threats and there never was any reasoning with Reggie. He doesn't have her yet, and he can't be more than a couple of miles ahead of me. I can reach her faster. I better reach her faster. Because if anything happens to her, the whole world will burn.

LYNN

I woke up at dawn, feeling just as lousy as I did before I fell asleep last night. That feeling of being used, of being just a piece of meat for anyone to ravage is back with a vengeance, and I can't shake it. Even the man I love, have loved for a long time, the man who saved my life, the man I've esteemed above all others even when he was gone from my life. He just used me too. Didn't force me, didn't tie me down, didn't beat me into submission, but he used me just the same. The only difference is, I let him. How could I not see it?

I only texted my mom briefly, telling her not to expect me home today or tonight. Didn't give any reasons, didn't even check for a reply from her.

I can't go back to the life I lived before Scar came back into it, and I can't move forward with him to the life I wanted, the life I craved, the life I hoped we would have.

That's not for me.

The life for me is on the ranch. Taking care of abandoned animals no on else wants.

That's why I volunteered to go speak to the people who run the riding school when the reports this morning said the fire is raging again, and that it'll cut right through the area where the school is.

They need to take those horses to safety, and I'll make them understand that. Bethany and Raul were against me going, but

Tammy agreed with me, although Bethany wouldn't let her come along. I heard the shaking in her voice and the pleading in her eyes as Tammy stood her ground, so I said I'll be going alone, got in my car and that was that.

Tammy has a life to live. As for me, I'm just a broken woman with no real life. Pretty much everyone is better off not having to put up with me, including myself. The only ones who truly need me are the animals, which includes those poor horses.

The heat outside starts rising the higher up the hill I get on the way to the school, and the smoldering patches of foliage are close to the road here. But there's no flames near yet. I still have time to save the horses before the fire comes.

I've crested the hill atop which the school stands, will reach the stables in another couple of minutes. I'll outrun the flames and the horses will too.

"Is anyone here?" I yell as I get out of my car in the wide driveway in front of the ranch house. The air is hot and smells like it shouldn't be breathed. There are no other cars in the driveway and from the stables just to the left of it, I can hear the horses neighing even over the weird hushing sound in the air. That's gotta be from the fire getting closer, but I hope I'm wrong.

"The horses need to be transported off this property!" I yell. "The fire will pass here."

Still no reply.

I run up to the house to bang on the doors, even though I'm pretty sure I'm the only human being up here. The door gives way as I slam my fist against it. The house isn't just empty of people, it's empty of furniture and appliances too. There's a broken plate on the floor in the foyer, along with a lady's dress, shoes with no pairs and some jeans just lying there. The owners left in a hurry. They took their valuables, but they left the most valuable thing. The horses.

I run to the stables, even though I know I have almost zero chance of getting all of them down this hill to safety before the fire comes. Not on my own anyway. I'd hoped the owners would be here, that they'd help. But I'm gonna give it my best try.

If I hurry, I can make a couple of trips up and down, I'm sure I can. I'll have to. Because the transporter trailer parked at the side of the stables is only big enough for two horses. Maybe I can fit three in there—

"What's such a pretty lady doing up here on her own?" a man's voice asks behind my back.

I know that voice. I fear that voice. But I don't recognize it.

When I turn, I'm facing a huge man with a large smile that's anything but inviting. He's wearing a black leather biker jacket and boots. Another biker is standing by my car. A third is near the trees, the chrome handles of his Harley gleaming red from the flames now raging just beyond the ridge.

Maybe these are Scar's friends, maybe he sent them to bring me down from here. But he'd never send strange bikers and not come himself. He knows my fears, he knows what men who look like these did to me, he saw it. And I fear this voice. I know this man.

I'm frozen in place as the memory surfaces. I should run, sprint all the way until I reach those flames, because burning alive would be a better death, a kinder death that the one which awaits me once this man grabs me.

He's the one who grabbed me in the parking lot. I remember his voice from the ride to that vile dark room where they kept me, telling me how pretty I am, how glad he is to finally meet me.

I remember his face too now, grimacing as he raped me later that night, and probably on many nights after, but all those are still congealed together into a black mass of pain and sorrow in my mind.

"It's time for you to come with me," he says and grabs my arm.

I have to run! I have to fight him off this time! I'm not going back to that room!

And the voice in my mind that's been telling me this since I laid eyes on him finally gets through to my legs. I yank my arm out of his grasp and bolt to the trees. But another man is waiting there too, and I watch him get off his bike to block my path as though it's happening in slow motion. I know I won't get past him, but I don't stop sprinting.

And then not even that matters anymore. The one who spoke, my kidnapper, catches up and slams into me. My knees collide with the ground, my palms scrape against the gravel as I use them to break my fall. He lifts me as though I weigh nothing. For all my kicking and screaming, his grip on me remains like a vise. Just like it was that night.

My body's defense wasn't enough, so my mind is already taking over, sending me to that black nothingness where I feel nothing, see nothing, think nothing. To that dark void where I spent the better part of my captivity and a long time afterwards too. My safe place. I wish I'd made more of the twelve years I had outside it. Because I'm not coming back from it a second time.

24

SCAR

I LOST precious time going to the ranch looking for Lynn. She wasn't there and the directions as to where she went — up some hill, to some fucking riding school, right into the fire—were skimpy at best. These damn hillbillies know these hills like I know the ones around Sanctuary, based on what tree grows where and what type of rock formation to keep an eye out for so you know the turn to take. I lost even more precious time getting up here, because the fire was already blocking my way on two separate roads I tried. Lost time I didn't have to keep her safe, time Lynn didn't have.

Reggie didn't come here alone. Six Renegades are hiding in the trees surrounding the property that I can see, but there could be more. They must've been following her before Reggie even left their clubhouse. How did I not see this danger? But it's too late for regrets now. It's time for action.

Reggie's talking to Lynn who's just standing there, so still she might as well be a statue.

"Run, woman!" I mutter to myself, but even yelling it would be no use.

I can't see her face well since I'm looking at her from the side, but I see it clearly anyway. It's that same one she got the first time I suggested we go back to her house. It's almost the same one she wore when I barged into the room where they kept her. Living but dead. Paralyzed with fear. Why the fuck did she come up here on her own? Why the fuck didn't I kill my brother before now?

He's the one who took her twelve years ago, and it's my fault it happened, because he was doing it to mess with me. It makes perfect sense now why she was gang raped by the club and not sold to the highest bidder. That's a guilt I don't even know how to begin unraveling. But there's no time to try now.

No time for much else either. If I storm in, I'll get killed and she'll be taken anyway. I know that, but it's still nearly impossible not to just do it. And it's growing more impossible by the second, as I watch Reggie talking to her.

I pull my phone out and call Cross. Whatever happens here today, he should know about it from me. And if I die here, I need his promise that the MC will still do right by Lynn and save her from the Renegades if she gets taken again. I'll do my best by her, but my best might not be enough today.

"No time to explain, but shit is about to go down," I tell him as he picks up. "It involves my brother, and at least six Ruthless Renegades MC members. Some of them will die and I'll kill them. I know you don't want us starting shit with anyone right now, but it can't be avoided."

"What the fuck are you telling me, Scar?" Cross asks the moment I pause to take a breath.

"You know the waitress we saved back in Illinois? They're after her again, so I gotta save her again. This time I might die trying. If that happens, I'd like you to get her away from the Renegades for me. I love her. You might as well tell her that too if I don't get to do it today."

That's important for her to know. I'll do my best to tell her myself, but just in case I can't, I know Cross'll take care of it.

"Back the fuck up, Scar, and don't do anything stupid," Cross says in a hard voice. "We'll ride for you. Just tell us where to go."

"Don't come here, the fire's about to sweep over this place," I tell him. "I'll do my best by her, because I can't watch her get taken again. But if I fail, then I'll need you."

I'd give my life to prevent Lynn from going through any kind of pain ever again. Gladly and without a split second of regret, unless it's over the fact that we won't get to spend any more time together. I know that with greater certainty than all the times I've done the same for my MC.

I just hope my death will buy her freedom now. But if it doesn't, Cross and the guys will save her later. So I just hang up, because it's time to give it my best shot now.

I start creeping up on the guy closest to me, coming at him from the side. He's on his bike, focused on the scene in the driveway and completely ignoring everything else. The sound of the fire approaching is masking all other sounds anyway, so I don't even try very hard to walk quietly.

He's wearing the Satan Spawns MC club colors, I see once I'm right behind him. He's not even a Renegade, but one of the Spawns that escaped from prison with Reggie. Killing him is high on my list of priorities too. That's like a sign from above that I'm on a right path here, that I can't fail. The second sign is Lynn finally waking up from her frozen paralysis. She frees herself from Reggie's grasp and bolts for the trees. Good girl.

Her flight doesn't last long and her scream as Reggie grabs and lifts her pierces my very soul, but makes me certain I will save her. There can be no other way. I don't even have to aim to shoot the Spawn in the back of the head. I'm armed with a fully loaded handgun, minus the bullet I just fired, and years of experience hunting down and killing scum just like these. It should be enough to take them all out by myself.

I also have a knife with me. But I'm saving that for Reggie.

LYNN

The shot ringing out, echoing off the hills stops time. It makes the man holding me freeze and in the silence I can hear the whooshing of the fire again.

"Your buddy Diesel is down, Reaper!" the man who was grinning at me a second ago, while he thought he'd prevent my escape into the woods, yells. "Let's get the fuck out of here! Leave the bitch! The Devils are here!"

"Fuck, no!" the guy holding me—Reaper —yells, grabs me harder and starts me dragging backwards away from the house.

He's here. Scar. The man I could always depend on. The man I should never have chased away. I can feel him near.

And in this moment, even despite the black nothingness that already started rising in my mind, I feel nothing but happiness, nothing but relief, nothing but love. And it explodes into a shower of warm sparkling rain as I hear his voice calling for me.

"Hold on, Lynn! I got you!" Scar yells and I start kicking and screaming again, clawing at the arm holding me.

"Fuck this! You're on your own, Reaper," the guy by the trees yells and mounts his bike. "We ain't fighting Devil's Nightmare over some spent old bitch. Brothers, let's ride!"

It's like the rest of the bikers encircling the driveway were just waiting for this command, because the roar of their bikes as they start them up is deafening. But it fades quickly, its echoes blending seamlessly with the whooshing in the air.

"Let her go, Reggie," Scar says.

He's approaching me from the trees, the most welcome, beautiful man I've ever seen, despite the rage twisting his features as he stares at the man holding me. "Let her go and I'll let you live."

The man laughs a very amused laugh, and despite the fact that it's coming from my worst nightmare, it sounds mirthful and happy. But it makes me feel cold despite the heat in the air.

"That's a tall offer coming from you, since you've been plotting to end me for the last twenty-odd years. But I'm not gonna do that, Bobby," the man says. "At least not until I give her something to remember me by. Something like what I gave you, maybe. Yes, I think that'd be fitting. Then you two would match."

It's like the man doesn't really know where he is, because he's talking like we're just sitting in some living room somewhere having a chat. But the eeriness of that realization fades as something cold and sharp presses into my cheek—a knife, I realize with horror. He wants to cut up my face!

But even that wouldn't be so bad as long as he let me go

afterwards, so I could run into Scar's arms. He's standing so close I could be in his arms in less than five steps. But he's too far to save me.

This man won't just cut my face, he'll kill me. This time I will die. This time Scar can't save me. It's too late. Like it always was for us. Always too late. Always the wrong time, never enough time. Always too late.

Scar lifts the gun he's holding, his hand shaking for a moment as he points it directly at me. But then he aims it right above my right shoulder, his arm perfectly still.

"Last chance, Reggie," Scar says. "Let her go and leave."

If there's any doubt in his mind that he'll miss the shot and hit me, it doesn't show in his voice. So I have none at all either.

The guy holding me takes the knife away from my face, and loosens his grip on me like he's about to let me go. It's just enough for me to get my elbow free and get him in the Adam's Apple. The self-defense classes that I took obsessively for years after I was rescued prepared me for this moment. But the last one I took was ages ago, and I never had to use what I learned in real life. I didn't do it right, I missed the sensitive spot, got him in the collarbone. The guy just grunts and grabs me again, harder and tighter this time.

"Feisty bitch, but I'll tame you soon enough," he grunts. "Just like last time."

He brings the knife to my face again. It's so close to my skin I can feel its coolness against my cheek. Any moment now, I'll feel the pain as it cuts into my flesh.

A shot rings out. Its path ruffles my hair, the jet of hot air passing so close to my head it burns.

But Scar didn't miss.

The guy screamed, and I'm no longer being held. I'm free. I

don't look back, don't think, just run to Scar. He yanks me to him and gets in front of me, his gun still aimed at the guy who tried to abduct me.

He didn't kill him, just shot him in the arm to prevent him from cutting my face. The man is cursing, clutching his right arm to his body with his left, trampling the knife he threatened me with into the dirt.

Scar is like a rock now, pure magnetism radiating off him, but it's all laser focused on the man in front of us. This is his brother, I'm sure of it, and Scar is getting ready to kill him. I'm sure of that too.

I hate this man and I fear him and he just tried to make my life living hell again. But killing him won't change any of that. And it won't help Scar any either, it'll just tear another piece of his soul away.

"Don't do it, Scar," I whisper into his ear. "He's not worth it."

My words break his laser focus, I can feel it shift to me like a gust of hot air, even though he's still looking at his brother.

"He's the one who kidnapped you," he says. "He did it to fuck with me, because he knew I liked you. Loved you, even, I think. What happened to you is all my fault."

The apology in his voice pierces me to my very soul. He thinks I'll never forgive him for this nor that I should.

"It's not your fault, it's his fault," I tell him and I mean it. "But his death won't change any of that. It'll just weigh heavy on your conscience, along with all the crap he's already put us through. Look up and forget."

"Lucky shot, Little Bro," the guy says breathlessly through gritted teeth. It's clear he can't move his right arm and that he's in pain. "Now finish it."

"Get the fuck outta here, Reggie," Scar says. "Just walk away and leave the state. Or better yet, leave the country. If you ever come near me or mine again, you die."

The man grimaces, then grins. "You been promising you'd kill me for a long time, but I'm still alive. You're threats ain't worth shit."

Scar shrugs and aims the gun more accurately at his brother's head. "Stay and see what happens, or run away now, while you have the chance. I'll give you to the count of five. One."

The man frowns again, his whole face twisting like he's really struggling with the decision. The blood dripping from his arm has already created a puddle by his feet.

"Two," Scar says.

His brother grimaces worse, but then turns and walks back towards the trees, without saying anything more, kicking up dust as he goes.

Scar's magnetic steel resolve starts vibrating as the guy starts his bike somewhere in the bushes, but he doesn't lower the gun, not even once the sound of his brother's bike fades and the only sound in the air is once again just the whooshing of the fire.

"I never thought I'd let him go," Scar says and glances back at me, still keeping the gun trained on the target that's not there anymore.

Then he finally lowers his gun and turns to me fully, his whole face slack and shocked, showing me the truth of what he just said.

"He's not worth a piece of your soul," I whisper and glide my hand over the scar on his cheek, stand on my toes and kiss him. His lips are dry from the sand and the heat, but the kiss is still the most nourishing thing I've ever experienced.

He grunts the way he does when his pleasure and enjoyment

are at their peak, grabs me and pulls me closer, kisses me back. He loved me then and he loves me now, whatever else he says, that's the truth. It's right there in his kiss and his embrace. It feels like he'll never let me go, but he does, abruptly.

"We gotta go, Lynn, the fire's almost here."

The horses are neighing in the stables and the fire is so close now, I can make out the flames amid the trees and hear wood burning. It's too late to save the horses, but their cries are piercing my heart.

"Lynn! Come on! Move!" Scar says with urgency. He grabs my arm, and I let him start pulling me to the tree line.

"No, wait!" I halt and he nearly pulls me to the ground.

"I can't just leave the horses!" I say, looking back at the stable.

The air is whooshing worse than ever and I can smell wood burning as the fire engulfs the trees around us. The flames are so close I can't believe they haven't reached the house yet, and the horses aren't just neighing anymore, they're screaming. They know they're about to die, and I know how that feels like. I can't let them suffer like that.

"It's too late, Lynn. We have to leave them," Scar says, but for all the harshness in his voice, his eyes are very soft as he looks at me. I can make sense of what happened here today—or how it's possible that he claims the soft care and devotion in his grass green eyes isn't love for me—later. But I can save the horses now.

"Please, I can't just leave them," I say in a shaky voice, because I know he's absolutely right, but I still can't just walk away.

"Alright, let's go let them out," he says, then runs beside me to the stables, reaching them first.

"How we gonna get them down?" he asks, looking around. "There's no truck."

"There's the transporter..." I say, but let my voice trail off. There's no way we can make more than one trip up and down with it.

"We'll let them out and herd them down, that's the best we can do," Scar says with finality and opens the stable door.

He pulls me out of the way just in time before the horses bolt. I whistle and call them, but none even slow before they disappear into the trees. They're running away from the fire, so at least there's that.

"Let's go now, Lynn! You did all you could," Scar says, grabs my arm and starts pulling me away from the stables.

I did all I could, but it wasn't enough. I didn't save them. But Scar did save me, like he keeps doing, like he's always done.

So it's easy not to be so very sad as I wrap my arms around him on the back of his bike, and lean in so close it feels like we're one person.

Heavy smoke is rolling in from our left as he starts the descent. If I listen real hard, I think I can hear horses running alongside us as we ride down the hill. We're going fast, but they're keeping pace. Maybe I did save them. Maybe they'll be alright.

"Whoa, shit!" Scar yells and breaks hard, plastering me even closer to his body.

I peer around his shoulder and my heart stops. A wall of fire is blocking the road in front of us.

"We can't go back 'cause it's coming in from that direction," he says. "Is there another way down?"

"From the other side of the hill," I say. That's the road I came up on.

"No good," he says. "It was blocked when I was coming up."

He saved me, but we might still die on this hill. I should be more panicked about that, but I can't be very panicked about anything as long as I'm holding onto him.

"Nothing for it," he adds with determination. "We gotta ride through this fire and hope it's narrow."

"We'll die," I mutter.

He grins at me through the rearview mirror. "Don't look so scared, it'll be fine, Lynn. And if not, you're first on the list of people I want to die beside. And that list is pretty long."

I know what he's saying even if he's not quite saying it. At least I think I do.

"OK, let's do it," I tell him just as two of the horses pass us at a gallop, racing towards the wall of fire.

The rest of the horses are close behind, their galloping forms an explosion of life and freedom racing towards certain death. There's no one else I'd rather die beside than Scar.

He revs the bike and takes off towards the fire.

The horses are running on either side of us now, and I hold on even tighter to him as he speeds up. Just a couple more paces and we'll reach the fire.

I want to close my eyes, burrow my face in his back so I don't have to watch. And at the same time, I wouldn't dream of looking away. This could be our death. This could be the last seconds we have together. It's enough.

We reach the wall of fire, the heat so unbearable it burns all other thoughts from my brain. The horses are still running with us. No, they're flying. And we're flying too, flying right through the angry orange flames eating up the world around us, our world, mercilessly and without reason.

The fire is terrible, but beautiful too. Time has slowed, a

whole eternity passing in the blink of an eye. Our eternity, the life we should've had. But we will have it, something is promising me that, a voice speaking outside myself, and I believe it. I know it's the truth.

The heat burns my eyes, but I keep them open anyway, focused on the horses silhouetted by the fire as they fly free.

I'm sure this is the end, but just as quickly as the temperature rose it drops again, and time once again moves.

We're on the other side of the wall of fire, behind us the last three horses flying through it. Smoke is billowing from their manes, but their gallop is perfect and their eyes are alive.

We're alive too.

I feel more alive than I ever have in my entire life, and I'm holding on tight to the man who wants to spend the rest of his life with me and die with me. I feel the same way. Always have, always will.

And I'd tell him so, but we're still riding fast, the wind too loud to allow speaking. But I'll tell him the moment we stop. Tell him I can't imagine my life without him by my side, so he better stop pretending it's any different for him.

25

LYNN

"My car's gone," I say, only just realizing that fully as we stop in the driveway at the ranch. Of all the things that have happened, that's not the most important thing, not by far. But the fire we rode through burned off the last traces of what held me locked in my pain, the last charred pieces of it finally crumbling away. I'm finally free of my past. Completely and utterly. Finally able to live in the present.

The girl I was is back and I missed her so much.

"Yeah, but you're safe," Scar says, his eyes alight with all the fire we just witnessed, but none of its destruction.

"Thank you for saving me. Again," I say and smile at him. "I'm sorry for the way I acted towards you the other night. I love you, I've always loved you, and I need you in my life. I was wrong to send you away."

He grabs me and pulls me close. He's a rock—my rock— put on this earth to keep me safe. Just as I was put here for him. No matter what happens, that will always be true.

He stares so deep in my eyes I'm transported from this place, from this world even, into one where all is perfect, always was, always will be.

"I need you in my life too," he says and grins at me like maybe he has more to say. But I won't push him, and I won't pull him to me too hard either.

"Good, because you have me," I say and smile, cinch his waist in my arms to prove the truth of my words.

He laughs and wipes something off my cheek, maybe dirt, or maybe soot from the ashes that fell on us as we rode here, the ashes of my past. He's covered in them too.

"No, Lynn, you're not getting it," he says. "I mean, you're the most important thing in my life, and I was an idiot for not realizing it sooner. I love you, and I've loved you for a long time. I just didn't realize it. So what I meant is, I need you in my life all the time."

What he's saying isn't romantic, isn't rehearsed and well spoken, probably isn't what every girl wants to hear. But it's exactly what I want to hear.

"I knew all that already," I say and chuckle. "I knew it before you did."

He shrugs. "I'm sure there'll be a lot more of that kinda thing down the road."

"As long as you catch up eventually," I chide, but smile at him afterwards, my winning smile, the one that never fails to make him look at me like I'm the only one worth looking at in the whole entire world. And he's the only one who can make me smile this wide.

"We got some other catching up to do, " he says and kisses me before I can ask what.

But his kiss and his hug and his groping hands give me the answer quickly enough. I'm not far behind, and I would undress him right here, but we're in full view of the house.

"What?" he asks as I pull back, looking worried but kinda exasperated too.

I smile coyly and wink. "They can see us here and I don't want an audience. Let's go to that house of yours."

"Gotcha," he says and grins. "But the house is too far away, the barn will do."

He doesn't wait for my reply, just picks me up and carries me towards it like a cowboy might a farm girl for a quickie, but in reality, like a lover would the woman he can't be without.

By the time he sets me down next to the ladder that leads to the loft where we spent our first night together, the only thing I know is that I need him, need him naked with me, on top of me, inside me, with his lips pressed against mine. No part of me is reluctant, all parts of me are on fire for him.

He slaps my butt to hurry me up the ladder, but I needed no urging. Just as I need no urging to start ripping his clothes off as soon as he joins me.

"You're in a hurry," he observes and laughs.

I nod and pull on his belt, which he then undoes by himself. I kneel before him, because I also need to taste him first. I feel so light and so free and so full of life I'm ready to burst, and that's the only thing that's missing right now.

He sees where I'm going with this, and needs no extra urging before he frees his already rock hard cock. And I need no extra urging before I wrap my lips around him, this first taste of him exploding inside me and all around me like a million birds taking flight at once, singing as they do.

I take more, savoring the taste, pull back, lick just the head like its a lollipop, only it's better, sweeter, divine. I bob back down, and he grabs the back of my head, groans as he feeds me more of his cock. The action is jarring, but the sudden shock of it releases another hot river of pleasure inside me.

We play like that together for awhile, me licking and kissing softly, him invading my mouth and my throat from time to time. Soon, we settle into a dance, each taking what we need from the other, each giving back exactly what the other needs.

He grabs a fistful of my hair, pulls his cock out all the way and makes me look up at him.

"I want some of that pussy before I come," he says hoarsely.

The way he says it is rough and uncouth, but his demand just makes me feel wanted, desired, needed the way no one has ever needed me and never will.

I stand up and move a step away from him, smile and pull my t-shirt off, then unhook my bra and let that fall too. I feel so comfortable standing naked in front of him, even more comfortable than I feel when looking at myself in the mirror.

"Don't stop now. Keep going," he says as he ditches his jeans without taking his eyes off me.

I do the same, unbuttoning my jeans slowly, but then getting them off fast. He's right next to me when I look up after kicking my jeans away. He grabs the back of my head and kisses me deeply, his other hand slipping into my panties. Before I can even draw a single breath, he has two fingers pumping into me as his thumb flicks across my clit. By then I don't even need to breathe anymore, I just need this pleasure he's giving me.

My whole body turns soft like jelly as his fingers keep up their assault on my pussy, and his kiss opens up glorious, sun-filled worlds I've never seen before, but which we'll explore together soon and forever.

But it all ends abruptly as he releases me and sits down on the floor. He leans against the wall and grins at me, his huge cock standing to attention.

"Get on, cowgirl," he says. "I don't want the hay prickling you, but I expect you to ride."

I wouldn't dream of doing anything else. But I still remove my panties very slowly, then walk up to him seductively, placing one foot in front of the other like a runway model or a cat, basking in the desire, the raw, pure need in his eyes.

He pulls me down into his lap as I reach him, the action abrupt and jarring, such need in it, I giggle. But that's cut short as he thrusts his cock into my pussy as soon as I'm straddling him. I scream out instead. Not in pain, in pleasure, which rose from high to nearly unbearable with just that thrust alone. And it just keeps on building as he keeps thrusting.

He's pinching my nipples, stroking my neck, groping my thighs and my ass, slapping it to keep me bouncing, the pain and pleasure of it blending into blinding bliss. I'm holding onto his shoulders, whimpering and moaning and screaming in no particular order, as I offer him my body that's already sparkling and crackling in anticipation of the explosion of pleasure I know is just beyond his next thrust. But it doesn't come, just keeps building and building, growing hotter, sucking up all the air in the room.

I'm slamming back, meeting thrusts now, riding him for all I'm worth, just like he told me to, just like I want to. He's entering me all the way, I feel his cock everywhere inside me, but my whole soul is concentrated on the burning center of the explosion we're creating. The one that will destroy the world, so we can remake it together. I hardly see his face, but I feel him with me. In this room as well as in spirit, we are one.

I meet his thrust one last time and the air whooshes as my orgasm sweeps over me. The pleasure burns hotter than wildfire, yet is sweeter than taking a breath after ages of going without. He keeps his cock deep inside me as blast after blast of searing pleasure, of fiery bliss racks through my body, each more devastating, each better than the last.

"We have to do that again sometime," he tells me breathlessly later, once I finally find my mind, which got lost in the force of the explosion we created.

His cock is still inside me, but getting softer.

"Oh, we will," I say, take his face in my palms and kiss him, which makes his cock twitch back to life and start growing again.

One month ago, I'd be having panic attacks if someone mentioned sex to me. But maybe not, if I knew this is what they meant when they spoke of making love. Because this oneness, this is love and life in it's purest. I've wasted a long time running away from it, but I now mean to make up for all that lost time.

And as our kiss deepens and my heartbeat slows to the steady, happy rhythm it always has around him, time stands still. We lost none of it. The past doesn't matter, the present is glorious, and the future is open before us. We belong together and we have all the time in the world.

I'm his cowgirl, I'm his beauty queen, I'm his lover, I'm

everything he needs me to be. And he's my knight in shining armor, my protector, my lover, my everything.

I'm softness and he's hardness, I'm gentle and he's rough, and together we make a perfect whole just as we are. Like ying and yang. Light and dark, night and day, beginning and end. Two parts that fit together perfectly. In all things. Always.

EPILOGUE

Four Months Later

SCAR

Me and Lynn have been pretty much living together in the safe house for the past three months. She still goes home to her mom from time to time, but those times are growing shorter and farther apart. That woman hates me, but she loves Lynn, and that's all that really matters.

This place is a shit hole and she deserves better, but she won't move in with me at Sanctuary, because being around large groups of bikers still terrifies her from time to time. I won't force her.

Besides, I've enjoyed this domestic bliss we have going on here way more than I ever imagined I could. And she's fixed up the place real nice, it's almost like a home already.

She's awake, since she got a phone call a couple of minutes

ago, and I can hear her moving around in the bedroom. I've been awake since dawn, thinking about shit and waiting for her to wake up. It's a special day today.

I just got off the phone myself. With Cross. It's been some time in coming, but I finally told him I want to tone down my involvement with the MC. What I did for them is no longer required, not the way it used to be, and we both know that. I'll still ride whenever he needs me, but I'm moving out of Sanctuary.

I've seen enough death and caused enough pain. I have to find out if there is anything other than that out there for me. Lynn gives me hope that there could be. Cross listened, didn't say much, but I think he understood. Then he wished me good luck.

"Bethany sold the ranch!" Lynn informs me as she barges into the kitchen.

Even when she's angry like she clearly is right now, her voice is soft and inviting like a sweet little bird chirruping. She's so damn pure.

"She didn't even say anything, she just sold it!" Lynn rants.

Her hair's a mess, her cheeks are red because she's pissed, and her stormy sky blue eyes are shooting lightning, but she's still the most beautiful woman I've ever seen. I still don't know if I deserve her love, but I sure as fuck mean to keep earning it.

"She told me," I say and get the full force of her thunderous look. It cuts me right to the bone, but not painfully, far from it.

I chuckle and dig in my pocket for a set of keys. "But the good news is, you now own it."

I hold out the keys, but she doesn't take them, her face a frozen mask of confusion now.

"I guess it was a bad idea for a surprise," I tell her, since, yeah, maybe I didn't think this through all the way.

She looks like she's having a silent heart attack, but there's nothing for it now. I have to power through, so I jingle the keys at her again. "Bethany's been talking so much about getting rid of it, and you've been talking so much about keeping it, so I bought it."

She flies at me so fast she's a blur, nearly knocks me right off the chair I'm sitting in.

"Thank you! Thank you so much!" she says, nestled in my lap and holding me so tight her voice is muffled. "I went to the bank about a loan to buy it last week, but they said no way, since I have no work history to speak of."

"I know all that too," I say, wrapping my arms around her even as I lean back so I can look at her face. "And I wanted to give you something you really wanted."

"You've already given me so much," she says breathlessly. "How can I ever repay you?"

I chuckle and squeeze her ass. "Don't sell yourself short, Lynn. You're a real catch. Not many guys out there got a real-life beauty queen at home, but they all wish they did."

She frowns. "I was being serious."

And I know that. All I just said is true, but it's just the tip of the iceberg of all the things she means to me, of all the ways I can't imagine living without her.

"You've already repaid me and then some," I say in a serious voice. "You keep crediting me with giving you your life back, but you did the same for me, and you keep doing it everyday. So we're even."

She kisses me in that spur of the moment impulse she gets sometimes, a sudden need to show me she loves me. I never actively missed being loved by a woman, never spared it much thought, or any at all, but damn did I miss it all these years she wasn't in my life.

"We're not even, not by far," she says. "You're just saying that to make me feel better."

"Nope, am not. When do I ever do that?" I say and chuckle.

"Only all the time," she says and she's not wrong.

"That's just 'cause I want you to feel good and nothing else matters as much as that to me," I say and that's the complete truth, so she better never doubt it. She hugs me tighter, melts even more into me.

"But I'm not just saying it now," I add, since maybe I really don't tell her enough how much she means to me for her to know it. I'm no good at talking, but she needs to know this. "You've shown me there's more to life than just hate and rage and that even a guy like me—someone who's had a lifetime of that and then some— can change. You showed me that I still have a heart. So yeah, you've given me my life back too."

That's about it as far as words go for me, so I'll have to show her the truth of it if she still doesn't believe me. Show her over and over again until she does. Giving her the ranch so she can continue running the shelter is just one of the ways I plan on doing that.

I kiss her and she kisses me back. There's things between us that can't ever be put into words, but need to be expressed, and we both know that. Soon I need more than just kisses and going by how she's writhing in my lap, so does she.

I stand up with her in my arms, startling her. But if she's afraid I'll drop her, she can rest easy that will never happen.

"We got a little time now," I tell her and shift her in my arms so her pussy is up against my hard cock. "But then we gotta go up to the ranch and start fixing it up. That place is as run down as they come."

She gives me the most grateful and the most seductive look I've ever seen all rolled into one.

"We have all the time in the world," she says as she wraps her arms even tighter around my neck.

And she's completely right.

THE END

Want to read on? Visit WatersideDreamsPress.com or scan the QR Code below for more books in this series:

Devil's Nightmare MC
Series

READ TODAY!

Waterside Dreams Press

LENA Bourne
USA TODAY BESTSELLING AUTHOR
Suspenseful. Steamy. Romance.

ALSO BY LENA BOURNE

DEVIL'S NIGHTMARE MC NEXT GENERATION SERIES:

Lily's Eagle, Book 1

Chance Taken, Book 2

Harper's Song, Book 3

Hunter's Girl, Book 4

Summer's Edge, Book 5

Ariel's Ruin, Book 6

Ash, A Novella

DEVIL'S NIGHTMARE MC SERIES:

Cross

Tank

Rook

Scar

Ice

Hawk

Doc

Ink

Ace

Colt

Blaze

Axle

VIPER'S BITE MC SERIES:

Outlaw's Hope, Book 1

Outlaw's Salvation, Book 2

Outlaw's Redemption, Book 3

Rider's Fall: A Viper's Bite MC Novella

HIS FOREVER - An Alpha Billionaire Romance Serial (Completed)

OF THE ARCHERS

Adam (of the Archers, Book 1) — Full-length, standalone BBW Military Romance

NOT LOOKING FOR LOVE - An NA Contemporary Romance Series (Completed)

<u>**MYSTERY/ROMANTIC SUSPENSE BOOKS**</u>

<u>(*Writing as LJ Bourne*)</u>

E&M Investigations Series:

The Fall (Prequel #1)

The Fairytale Killer (Prequel #2)

Pretty Places (E&M Investigations, Book 1)

Bad Roads (E&M Investigations, Book 2)

Lazy Days (E&M Investigations, Book 3)

Ever After (E&M Investigations, Book 4)

Calm Waters (E&M Investigations, Book 5)

ABOUT THE AUTHOR

Lena Bourne is a USA Today Bestselling author of many romantic suspense and mystery novels. When she's not coming up with a new love story or plotting the next perfect crime mystery, you can usually find her drinking coffee and catering to her elderly cat's every whim.

Sign up for Lena's newsletter to receive exclusive sneak peaks at new books, special mailing-list-only offers and other goodies. Copy and paste this link to join: http://www.lenabourne.com/the-list/

Connect with Lena online:

Facebook: https://www.facebook.com/lenabourneauthor
Website: www.lenabourne.com

Made in United States
Troutdale, OR
04/08/2025